WAR
OF
KINGS
AND
MONSTERS

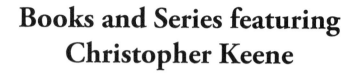

Books and Series featuring Christopher Keene

A Beginner's Guide to Summoning
a Short Story

Super Dungeon Series

The King's Summons
Adam Glendon Sidwell and Zachary James

The Forgotten King
D. W. Vogel

The Glauerdoom Moor
David J. West

The Dungeons of Arcadia
Dan Allen

The Midnight Queen
Christopher Keene

Dream State Saga

Stuck in the Game
Back in the Game
Ghost in the Game
Lost in the Game
First in the Game
a Short Story

WAR
OF
KINGS
AND
MONSTERS

CHRISTOPHER KEENE

War of Kings and Monsters

Future House Publishing

ISBN: 978-1-950020-02-7

Developmental editing by Erin Nightingale and Emma Snow
Substantive editing by Emma Hoggan
Copy editing by Isabelle Tatum
Interior design by Amanda LaFrance

Dedicated to Hayley. Here's my attempt to take something you love—monster battles—and mix it with something I love—medieval fantasy.

CHAPTER 1

THE KAIREN KEY

Nathan sat at his bedroom desk, nosing through a heavy tome. At this stage of his studies, he knew most of what there was to know about first-circle Melkai, but given the wide variety of second-circle Melkai, he had to constantly brush up on them. The bloated tome depicted the stupidly large second-circle Melkai, matching the monsters from the other world with animals that inhabited his own.

Although supposedly above his reading level, at fifteen, Nathan found the book only mildly challenging, mostly because he took the wisdom it contained with a grain of salt. From his experience, men who wrote such large books got out from behind their walls as rarely as he did. The author seemed to be pulling descriptions out of his rear end. Even so, drawn in by the detailed pictures and colorful descriptions, Nathan took pleasure in being a voyeur into the dangers of the world outside the castle walls while still being safe and sound behind them.

Flipping back through the section showing the smaller and weaker first-circle Melkai, he saw that many of them were still much larger than his own, though he doubted any of them would be as loyal as Taiba, his little friend from that other world.

He stretched a hand out toward his bed. "Hey, come out here."

A small blue reptile, no larger than a gecko, rushed out from his sheets, jumped onto his hand, then climbed into the folds of his hood. The Melkai deemed that part of him not only the best vantage point to observe their surroundings, but also the best place to nestle down in if he became too cold. After spending three years with the curious creature, Taiba had become his closest confidant, and he was fond of feeling his cool tail coil loosely around his neck above his chain necklace. He reached up absentmindedly to pat Taiba's head in the place he knew his friend liked best.

There was a loud knock at the door, and they both jumped in surprise.

"Nathan, your presence is needed," Master Morrow called from the other side.

"Don't tell me another apprentice has tried to make a pact with a Melkai in his room again."

"Worse. You have been summoned to the throne room. Best not keep the king waiting."

Nathan squeezed his eyes shut and cursed under his breath. Although he often saw the king on his usual walks through the castle, Nathan had only been in the throne room a few times: once when he had first arrived and several times when he and the prince had gotten caught making trouble together as children, usually for exploring forbidden places in the castle.

His master continued with further knocking. "Nathan, hurry up now!"

"Okay, okay! I'm coming!"

He opened his door to find Morrow, the Master of Pacts, waiting for him in the sunlit hallway, a grave expression on his wizened, bearded face that belied his usual jovial nature.

"Come on." Morrow strode down the hallway, his long robes billowing behind him.

Nathan hurried after him but glanced back at his bedroom door, yearning for his lost comfort. As had been his routine for the last four years, he'd stayed up late last night sitting through one of Morrow's lectures and didn't want to start yawning in front of the king.

"Being called on like this . . . it's a bit unusual." Nathan jogged to keep up with his teacher's long gait. "Does this mean lectures are canceled for today?"

Morrow ignored his question. "Over the last several nights, our court astronomers have noticed a red hue on the moon's horizon. Since then, that sliver of red has become a thin crescent. According to the Kairen texts, this is meant to signal a warning that one of the Kairen's ancient spells is weakening. We have less than one month before it breaks entirely."

I'll take that as a no on today's lectures.

"Which spell?"

Morrow didn't answer him.

"Wait, you're not talking about the barrier to the Melkairen, are you?"

The Melkairen was the world containing the Melkai.

So long as they were trapped within that world, they were limited to their spirit forms until a caller bound them to a pact item. But if the barrier between the worlds were to go down, the Melkai would roam freely, endangering all they came across. If Morrow's lessons were anything to go by, few if any were as friendly as Taiba.

Morrow gave an almost imperceptible nod but only said, "Best leave your questions for the king."

They approached the throne room doors. Frazzled by the prospect, Nathan combed his sandy hair and attempted to remember the etiquette required for an appearance before the king. It had been so long since he'd needed to draw upon such knowledge.

The guards on either side of the entrance opened the doors, and Nathan followed his instructor into the large hall. The throne was on a high dais at the back of the room and faced not forward, but to the left. White ribbons hung in arcs above where the king sat with a thin-lipped expression.

When Morrow and Nathan reached the end of the long red carpet, Nathan shuffled nervously, shifting his weight from leg to leg as Taiba fidgeted in his hood.

Two people stood on either side of the old king. To his left was his Lord Chancellor, a long-faced man with graying hair. He had a strict, almost menacing focus in his cold eyes.

Prince Michael stood to the king's right. Despite the tension in the room, Michael failed to hold down his smile. The smile didn't suit his giant frame or stubbly face, for Michael appeared more intimidating than he actually was. Nathan's first memory in the castle was of Michael, still a young boy himself, saving him from a squad of soldiers who believed him to be an urchin sneaking into the castle.

They had been like brothers ever since. Now the prince was twenty and in command of those soldiers. He had the armor and broadsword to prove it.

"Come forth," the king called.

Both he and Morrow moved closer. The large doors closed with a boom, and as the echo died, Nathan and Morrow knelt before the dais.

"I'm sure you're a little confused right now," the king intoned.

Nathan followed his master's lead and rose to his feet. "I . . . Yes. What gives me the honor of being summoned like this, Your Majesty?"

"I have taken care of you in my kingdom for . . . what is it now, ten years?" he asked.

Nathan nodded. The reason for this had always eluded him. It wasn't like he was anyone special.

"When you arrived from Avatasc, I took you in and protected you. Now, in our most desperate hour, I call you forth to ask you to help us in kind."

Nathan drew in a breath. *Me, help the kingdom?*

"I entreat you to take a journey that may save us all. Do you understand, Nathan?"

Taiba must have sensed his rising fear as Nathan felt him shift within his hood.

He shook his head roughly, all etiquette fleeing his mind. "N-no, how could I? I'm just an apprentice caller, Your Majesty."

The king cleared his throat. "Do you still have the key you were given as a child?"

Nodding, Nathan took the golden chain out from his collar and showed the crystal key to the king. He had possessed it for as long as he could remember, but couldn't recall who had given it to him. It was one of the few objects linked directly to his past, and he never took it off, hoping it might one day be recognized by some visiting diplomat or noble who could tell him what it was. Now, however, that was no longer necessary.

"What you hold in your hand is the Kairen Key, quite literally the key to our survival, young man. However, it is not complete. It's only one half of what is required to reseal the barrier locking away the monstrous Melkai." The king's tone became grave. "The other half is owned by someone of royal blood in the kingdom of . . . Avatasc."

"Isn't Avatasc our enemy? Your Majesty, even I know no one takes the peace treaty between the kingdoms seriously."

The king nodded. "That is so."

"This doesn't make sense, Your Majesty. Why me?" Nathan shook his head. "I—I haven't even called a second-circle Melkai yet. I'm not ready!"

"I agree, Father. He has no experience of the world outside the walls." Michael raised a hand to his chest. "Surely, I—"

"Only a Kairen can use the Kairen Key!" the king shouted.

Michael went to protest stubbornly but stopped when he realized he didn't know how to counter this point. He lowered his hand and stepped back.

"Kairen," Nathan uttered, dumbfounded. "I'm a Kairen?"

He had read that the Kairens were the first race to call forth Melkai. Indeed, the kingdoms had been founded on their power. Yet no one had ever told him he was a descendant of those ancient summoners.

"That's right, Nathan," the king continued. "Long ago

there was a lasting peace between our kingdoms. It was proven by dividing the ownership of the Kairen Key, a half of which you now hold."

"That key is the only thing that can prevent the invasion of Melkai into our world," Master Morrow cut in. "But both halves must be located to reseal the barrier to the Melkairen!"

Over the years, Morrow had given Nathan news of journeymen and adventuring callers who had come across and, on occasion, fought against unbonded Melkai who slipped through the barrier. At first, Morrow had spoken of it as though they were anomalies or tall tales men used to gain fame and notoriety, but such reports had become more frequent of late and more and more journeymen were going missing. Although only a handful of Melkai had escaped the barrier, those few that had were vicious and out for blood.

If I really want to become an Advanced Summoner then it's now or never that I prove it.

He looked down at the key-half.

But even if I find the other half of the Kairen Key, do they think my Kairen blood will just kick in and I'll know what to do with it?

"A-and I am to go alone?" Nathan asked.

"You're joking, right?" Prince Michael called. "I'm going with you. Father thinks it necessary that I prove myself on this journey. It's you and me, big guy."

Relief washed over him. Michael was the most skilled fighter in the kingdom, and his experience on the road would be invaluable. The idea of a prince guarding a novice caller was ridiculous, but then the idea of this whole quest was a little ridiculous.

Taiba's head perked up and his tail began to wag. He

liked Michael.

Despite the prince joining him, Nathan's heart still raced. He knew better than anyone the dangers of the outside world, particularly now that the Melkai were escaping the Melkairen. Indeed, he had just been reading a book on the dangers of the Melkai. He longed to return to his room to continue reading or even see if he could bring it with him, but the tome was so large he doubted he could fit it in a rucksack. He sighed and shook his head, regretting not taking notes when he had the chance.

Nevertheless, he would go. He was indebted to the king for allowing him to live in the castle and take lessons under Master Morrow, the greatest Advanced Summoner in the land.

He looked up at Morrow. "Will you be coming with us, Master?"

Morrow shook his head, eyes red with weariness. "I must remain here to prepare the junior callers in case you fail. It's possible, and as you well know, Melkai are attracted to large groups of people, so, to lower the risk of enticing them, you two will be on your own."

Nathan nodded, jaw clenched in both fear and determination. *I'm a Kairen. This is my fate.*

He looked up at the king. "Okay, I'll go."

"Everything for your journey will be provided for you in packs at the main door. You must collect them and leave immediately," the king said, and the doors creaked open behind them.

Dragon's breath! They sure are eager to send us on our way.

"C-can't I at least take some books with me?" Nathan babbled. "Surely, I—"

"The weakening of the barrier will occur when the moon has turned completely red. Second-circle Melkai will be roaming the land, so you must be careful. You must travel light so you can go quickly. The packs provided are intended for that purpose."

Michael jumped down from the dais and grinned up at the king. "Don't worry, Father. With me accompanying him, he'll have nothing to fear."

The king scoffed. "Your foolhardy words cause me more worry than any Melkai."

Michael waved this off. "Don't lose sleep on my account. I'll be sure not to run into a fight blindly. Besides . . ." He patted Nathan on the shoulder. "I'll have him to watch my back."

The king nodded, a proud gleam in his eyes. "Just be careful, my son."

"You too, old man."

With a wave, Michael strode past Nathan and exited the throne room. Looking back nervously and receiving a curt nod from Master Morrow, Nathan followed.

CHAPTER 2

MELKAI

Nathan winced as the castle doors boomed shut behind him. The majority of Nathan's studies had been focused on a time when Melkai were either free to roam the lands or when people could simply summon them to kill each other. The castle walls had felt like the only thing protecting him from those potential threats.

As he opened his eyes and saw only a flock of birds flying over the empty green fields, his rigid body relaxed.

At his reaction, an amused smile spread over Michael's face. Unlike him, the prince had been out on expeditions into the world before and was far more knowledgeable about how to deal with its trials.

Nathan returned the grin but still looked back at the gates of the Terratheist city, walling them off from all that was familiar.

Michael led them down the hill. Seeing the outside world from the ground was different from seeing it from his window, and the further they walked from the castle, the more overwhelming the vastness of the surrounding grasslands and valleys became. Now, they were trekking down the Menophilly Hills. Once at their base, their next destination on the way to Avatasc would be Terratheist city's water source: the Talis Lake.

"So, why did you *really* decide to come with me?" Nathan asked.

Michael laughed. "Why do you think? Someone had to watch your back on this journey."

Nathan gave him a pointed look.

The prince rolled his eyes. "Alright, alright, you got me. Father wanted me to come to demonstrate my worth. He thinks this journey will prove me to be enough of a man to succeed him someday. But even if that wasn't true, I still would have asked to come to help my little buddy."

"Yeah, yeah," Nathan replied playfully. "Just try not to hit your head on the top of any doorframes when we get to Avatasc. They still have to repair the dent you made in the Summoners' Spire."

"It's not my fault you callers are all so puny," he retorted, "but I promise not to step on you once I've reached my full height."

Nathan grinned. "Don't make promises you can't keep."

Although Michael was protective of him, Nathan suspected his friend had other motives for joining his quest. In his youth, Michael's father had been known to travel far and wide, and for all Nathan knew, Michael wanted to surpass his father's epic tales with an adventure of his own. There was no one Nathan thought more likely to achieve such a feat.

They made their way steadily down the hill toward the rise down which Talis Lake ran. Left of the lake were the hills covered by the Kydian Wood, and for some reason unknown to Nathan, Michael was leading them toward it.

"We're after some royal from Avatasc, right? With most royals living in the Avatasc Castle, heading there is naturally our best shot at finding them—though, how we plan on sneaking in seems to be a 'we'll cross that bridge when we come to it' sort of thing. Even so, wouldn't the quickest direction to Avatasc be straight ahead? It's just across the Solvena Plains, after all."

"That's true, little buddy. But you're the clever one here. Would it really be smart to cross the border of two previously warring countries out in the open? Countries that have barely been able to create a peace treaty as it is?" Michael raised a finger toward the thick forest. "Our best bet is to find this royal with the other key-half either by consorting, or more likely, threatening Avatasc nobles. Then we can combine the two halves to stop the Melkai from escaping and return home without starting a war, right?"

"I never pegged you for a naive optimist."

"Well, if we do it my way, we should accomplish all this before the month is up and without being found out. Therefore, our path is not *through* the war zone but around it, through the Kydian Wood."

Nathan shivered: a vanguard of soldiers had gone missing in the forest only a week back.

"What about the Melkai?" he asked. "Being clever won't help us hide from monsters that can follow our scent . . ." He sniffed Michael and screwed up his face. "Particularly yours."

"I've faced Melkai before," Michael said, raising his palms. "It shouldn't be any problem. Besides, my manly musk will more likely frighten them off."

"Is that what you call it?" Nathan shook his head in amusement. "Those were first-circle, Michael. Most of them would have known from your size alone that they couldn't have beaten you, and the king told us that Melkai of the second circle would slip through the barrier first. Second-circle Melkai vary in size a lot more than first-circle ones. Some of them would tower over you!"

Michael frowned down at him. "You should know by now that size isn't everything."

Nathan crossed his arms, still unconvinced.

"Trust me, we'd much rather take a chance with the Melkai than fight with other soldiers. And if it's true what Morrow and Father said about them not getting here until the moon turns fully red, I think that if we get through fast enough, we won't even have to worry about them."

Although Nathan was still hesitant, Michael had managed to convince him. It *would* be better to go through the forest than to reheat the flame on the border. Besides, if they journeyed straight ahead, a confrontation was a certainty. By cutting through the forest, they had a chance to go around it uninterrupted.

Nathan looked down and confessed, "I—I can't move as fast as you."

Michael smiled and ruffled his hair. "Would you like me to piggyback you like I used to?"

Nathan shoved his hand away. "I'm quite alright, thank you. Fine, I see your point," he grudgingly admitted. "But take a bath in the lake before we enter the forest. If not for my sake, at least so the Melkai won't smell you as easily."

"Out here, the smell of soap stands out more to monsters than body odor." Michael tapped his temple. "I've learned from experience, little buddy. There's a method to my madness."

Nathan winced. "And a stench to it too."

Nathan surveyed the fields as Taiba did likewise from his perch atop Nathan's shoulder. Feeling a little nervous about being out in the open, Nathan found another reason why traversing the forest was the smarter option. It would at least stop them from being spotted by any flying Melkai.

Sensing there was no immediate danger, Taiba basked in the sun's rays on Nathan's shoulder. If Nathan wasn't a caller they could have traveled on horseback, but it was a well-known fact that Melkai of any kind frightened horses. It was for this reason that many callers used Melkai for mounts. Nathan figured Michael expected him to summon something stronger than Taiba on their journey, and that's why they hadn't just left his little friend behind. However, after nearly being killed the last time he had tried, the prospect terrified him.

Instead of entering the Valley of the Two Kings, Michael veered left, leading them uphill toward the tree-covered horizon. Nathan scrambled to keep up with Michael's brisk strides. Each hill they climbed rose higher than the last, leaving Nathan out of breath, but also increasing his view of the forest border in the distance. He kept his eyes glued to the trees as though he could summon them to himself and save them the time walking. It didn't work.

While watching the ever-distant trees, Nathan started measuring distances in his head. If they sighted the Talis

Lake before noon, they would be able to get there by nightfall at this pace. Nathan resisted the urge to watch the sun's progress across the sky. He didn't want Michael to offer him a piggyback ride again.

Less than an hour later, they were stopped by a terrible smell. Nathan didn't recognize it, but Michael seemed immediately on edge. He stepped in front of Nathan, standing sidelong with a hand out to stop him, his wide eyes darting about their surroundings.

"What is that?" Nathan asked.

"Death," Michael said. He moved slowly forward, hand on his sword hilt. When he found what he was looking for, he called Nathan forward. "It's alright. He's been dead a while. We're not in any immediate danger."

Nathan approached the body slowly. The first thing he saw was the blood. It was everywhere. The body looked to have been torn apart. Underneath the blood, Nathan could just make out the armor-plated form of a Terratheist soldier. Taiba retreated back into his hood as Michael studied the corpse.

"No man could have done this. I didn't believe Melkai could get this powerful." Michael wavered for a moment but then stood sharply. "It happened earlier this week. It appears he's one of the soldiers that never made it back from the search party."

"Dragon's breath! So, this is what a Melkai of the second circle can do to a man . . ." Nathan had to reswallow his breakfast. This was his first experience with the horrors of the outside world, and it made his stomach churn. "It's awful, but . . . I bet you've seen worse before, right?"

Michael's gaze met his, and he forced his face into a

nervous smile. "Of course . . ." He nodded unconvincingly. "A lot worse."

Michael was a terrible liar.

"Should we go back and get help?" Nathan asked.

Michael swallowed and frowned. "No. We have to keep going. We can't afford to waste time out in the open like this."

Michael started striding uphill as though he wanted to find the Melkai who had killed the soldier and exact revenge. Nathan shook his head and quickly followed, hoping that Michael knew what he was doing better than the soldier they had found.

They continued up the hill in silence. It took a few minutes to get far enough away from the smell that Nathan could stop focusing all his attention on keeping his breakfast down. As soon as he started to relax, he noticed Taiba was trembling. Taiba was usually full of energy when the sun came fully up, but now he was hiding inside his hood like the sun itself was a predator. From long experience with his little friend, Nathan knew Taiba only trembled when he sensed another Melkai nearby.

Nathan wished he could say to Michael, "Just draw your sword already and put us both at ease!" but to say that was to say that they were in danger, and that was something he didn't want to admit just yet; so he remained silent as Taiba continued to give his unheeded warning.

Michael tried to humor him. "Once we get to the top, it should be all downhill to the lake. I'm sure we can stop there for lunch or . . ."

Nathan followed Michael's gaze up and saw it too: a shadow at the top of the hill. *A bear? No, it couldn't be a bear. What bear has horns and stands upright like that? It must be a . . .* Suddenly it turned and lumbered over to a jagged outcropping on the crest of the rise.

"There it is!" the prince hissed as he finally drew his sword and lowered himself to the ground.

Nathan knelt down next to him. "What do we do?"

"You can't summon anything else yet, anything *powerful,* can you?"

Nathan shook his head and pointed to his hood. "No, only Taiba."

"Then I guess it's up to me." He looked left and then right.

Although only twenty, Michael was a full-grown giant compared to him; yet, Nathan was sure the Melkai was bigger still. Luckily for him, Michael didn't just have a reputation for his size, but also for how he wielded a blade.

He turned to Nathan, his breathing already quickening. "You see that ridge over there?"

"Yeah?"

"I want you to go up and wait there for me. I can't have you getting in my way."

Shows how much my help is worth.

Nathan bit his lower lip, fearing Michael was trying to show off in front of him, covering up his fear with rashness. After what had been done to the soldier, Nathan didn't think rashness was their best option. Overconfidence could easily lead them to become just another bloody mess on the valley floor. Michael wasn't just his best friend, but his protector and navigator also, and without him, he would be lost.

Nevertheless, Michael had more experience fighting Melkai, and Nathan had to trust him. He sprinted up the hill in the direction Michael had mentioned as the prince readied himself to charged up the hill toward the Melkai.

When Nathan came to the ridge, he scanned the summit for threats. He saw none and was just about to continue on when he heard the sound of footsteps on the dirt behind him.

He spun about. The Melkai was large, second-circle by its size. Its front legs were more like human arms than anything else, but it lumbered toward him on all fours. The glowing red eyes in its caprine face were fixed on Nathan, and the drooling mouth opened to reveal pointed teeth.

Nathan couldn't make his feet move.

It raised one of its front legs, reaching out with its palm facing upward like a beggar. From the deep caverns of its lungs, it groaned, "Give it to me."

Nathan had never heard of a Melkai that could talk. He didn't know Melkai could form words at all.

Never mind that! What does it want from me?

It drew closer, still on three legs, still with its front hand up, its long, pointed claws gesturing. "Give it to me!"

Nathan was still frozen.

"Yah!" Michael dropped from the rise above them onto the Melkai's back, stabbing his sword into its shoulder. Blue blood streamed in a river down its back as it wrenched Michael from side to side, flinging him off. He landed disarmed next to Nathan. The Melkai grabbed the sword and roared, pulling it free of its shoulder and throwing it into a nearby bush.

The Melkai began to advance on Nathan.

Michael jumped up from where the Melkai had flung him. "Nathan! I need my sword! I'll distract it. Go!"

Without giving Nathan enough time to respond to him, Michael grabbed some stones and threw them at the Melkai. The stones hit the Melkai in the head, and it snarled and turned toward Michael, who began waving his arms and screaming, "You like that, you stupid overgrown goat? Well, I got a lot more for you than that so come and get it!"

He ran up the rise as the Melkai growled and chased after him. Nathan snapped out of his trance as soon as the Melkai lumbered away and ran toward the bush where the sword had been thrown.

"Come on, come on! Where are you?" he groaned as he rummaged through the branches. "There!"

He grabbed the large weapon and turned back, but both Michael and the Melkai were gone. *Michael is fighting a second-circle alone without a proper weapon!* Nathan rested the flat of the blade on his shoulder and sprinted in the direction Michael had run.

He climbed to the top of the hill where a veil of trees outlined the clay rise. The shadows covered him, and silence pervaded the path. He moved as cautiously as possible between the trees. As he crept under the foliage, the lack of movement or sound from anything but him made his situation even worse, and he jumped at every bird that flew by and every stick that snapped under his boots. He felt Taiba trembling on his shoulder.

His first thought was that if there was something out there, he wished it would just come out and face him. This was proven wrong as a sudden groan behind him made him freeze in terror.

"Give it to me!"

Nathan didn't have enough time to turn before the

points of the Melkai's claws jabbed into the skin on his midsection. The large hand wrapped tightly around his body before lifting him from the ground. He was brought around by the large arm so that he was face to face with the massive Melkai, the red eyes peering into his own. Hands shaking, he dropped the sword, and felt the Melkai's strong grip tightening around his waist.

He struggled desperately, trying to wriggle free. If he wasn't in the belly of the beast yet, he soon would be if he didn't act quickly. He hoped the cold sweat running down his back might make him slippery, but he couldn't budge an inch within the Melkai's grasp.

The Melkai brought him close enough that he could feel the warmth of its breath against his face. "Give it to me now!"

What does it want?

He would have tried to fight or even answer that he didn't know what it was talking about, but once again, he was frozen. The fear constricted him more than the Melkai's claws.

The hand tightened further, and he cried out in pain.

"Now!" it demanded.

Something small dashed out from his hood.

"Taiba, no!" he gasped.

The quick little creature ran onto the Melkai's hand. Taiba sunk its tiny teeth into the large forefinger, but the massive monster didn't even flinch. The Melkai rose up onto its hind legs, bringing Nathan further up into the air, and swatted at the small lizard with its other hand.

Taiba fell to the grass and bared its teeth. This rocked Nathan from his paralysis, and anger flooded him to the point of madness. Pulling one arm free, he frantically searched the small rucksack he had been given before leaving. He drew out a small dagger and stabbed it into the Melkai's eye. Blood squirted and ran down its face as the huge beast roared and threw Nathan to the ground.

He landed and called out, "Michael!" at the top of his lungs.

A moment passed as the Melkai arched upward, screaming in agony. Michael appeared from the shadows and quickly knelt down beside Nathan.

"Nathan, are you okay, little buddy?"

Nathan pointed toward where he had dropped his weapon, his innards feeling like they had been crushed. "The sword," he wheezed.

Michael spotted it and quickly got to his feet, snatching it up as he ran. He closed in on the Melkai and struck down on it, but having gotten over the pain of its wound, the Melkai caught the sword mid-slash. Michael flinched, his sword overpowered by the monster. It raised the blade up slowly in one bloody claw, bringing the prince with it.

"Michael!" Nathan shouted, uncertain whether he should step in to help or not, not seeing how he could help if he did in his injured state.

Michael's struggle appeared fruitless, and Nathan hesitantly rose to assist him.

"No, Nathan! Stay back!" Michael growled through bared teeth as he fought to keep his footing. "I'll handle this!"

Nathan halted, but not because of Michael. The monster was coughing up blood. The thick blue liquid ran from its jaws and suddenly its hind legs gave way under it and it fell back. Michael returned to his feet, and ignoring his stroke of luck, he regained control of his weapon. He planted his feet and thrust it down in a stabbing motion.

"Die, monster!" he screamed.

At first, the beast struggled, but as the blade drew closer to the Melkai's chest, it looked up at the prince and sneered. "You think . . . I'll die that easily?"

The blade suddenly glowed a deep red as Michael stabbed through its chest and into the thing's heart, killing it in an instant.

Silence filled the hilltop. Nathan exhaled the breath he had been holding as he watched the Melkai thump to the ground. Michael stood over it, panting, knuckles white from clenching his sword's hilt. Clutching his side, Nathan staggered over to Taiba who licked his finger to show that he was okay. They rushed to the prince's side. He was looking down on the massive monster he had slain.

Seeing the Melkai's corpse, Nathan's shoulders slumped, and his head lowered as relief washed over him. The adrenaline from his fear eased, making him exhausted and light-headed. He wanted to lie down, to take a nap, but Michael's condition was more important.

"Y-you did it," he uttered in the eerie silence.

Michael's voice was breathless as he whispered, "Not quite."

He collapsed onto the grass, unconscious.

CHAPTER 3

PACT ITEM

The Avatasc guards towered over Laine as they opened up the large doors to the throne room. She straightened her shoulders and entered the massive green hall where King Kissick, dubbed the Snake King by his scornful subjects, sat high on a dais between two golden columns. The top of his face was draped in shadow, and his right hand grasped a long green scepter.

She strode over the padded green throw rug until she reached the platform where two golden serpent statues hung down from the high ceiling. As she halted before the king, she did not bow. She did not need to. She merely suppressed her scowl.

She had been getting better at hiding her facial expressions after a glare had slipped out in front of her mother, the queen, and the king had forbidden Laine from spending time with her, claiming her to be a bad influence.

"Young daughter," King Kissick spoke in his eerie voice,

"a use for you as the court's caller has finally come."

She wasn't his daughter, but the king liked to think of her as such. As his heir, she could be married off to anyone he chose, making her a useful tool in choosing his true successor. After all, he could not conceive a child of his own.

"Do you know why I have summoned you?" King Kissick asked.

Her lips twitched ever so slightly, hiding her disgust of the man. Her hatred didn't just spawn from how he treated her and her mother, nor how his decisions affected the country—although both would have been more than adequate reasons—but because of how politically weak he was.

If he hadn't been such a pushover for the wealthier nobles in the belief that he needed their soldiers, he wouldn't have connived against and usurped the previous king in the first place. If he didn't listen to Lords Ronund and Wilkow, he wouldn't let their men get away with every crime they committed and he wouldn't be taxing the land into an impoverished state.

"Answer me!" he shouted.

Laine raised her head to him, neither frowning nor smiling. "Why?"

"The necklace you have is the key to great power. However, it is only half of what you need to gain. It is known that the other half is owned by someone high up in the kingdom of Terratheist." He fingered his long, crooked nose and smiled. "You are to find him, kill him, and bring both keys back to me before the moon turns red, understand?"

The speech sounded recited, and Laine assumed he'd had one of his chancellors write up the commands for him. With the amount of heated political arguments they had shared and how easily she made him resort to threatening her with violence to shut her up, it made sense for him to not want to drag out their conversation. However, his desire to keep his instructions brief and to the point gave her adequate reason to request clarification.

"And *you* know how to use it?" she asked, exaggerating the skepticism in her voice.

King Kissick waved a hand in front of his face. "Of course I do. Any Kairen can—" His eyes grew wide and he stopped himself, smirking. "Very clever, daughter, but beside the point. So long as both key halves are in our possession, the boon of strength it will give us will be substantial enough to achieve all I have desired since gaining the throne."

No! This would put the lands under the power of an incompetent, sock puppet tyrant.

"What is this power?" Laine pushed further.

"You little . . ." King Kissick spat, but seeing that his reaction to the question had no effect on her, he quickly changed his tone. "When the moon turns completely red, all Melkai without a pact to a caller will be released from their prison, and whosoever wields this key will have the power to control them. With the power of a Melkai army, it will be possible to end this farce of a treaty and finally take hold of Terratheist."

Laine nodded and hid her smile. Ideas blazed to life as she realized that such a power would be in her possession first. Not taking her key first was a major flaw in the king's plan, even for someone as foolish and as arrogant as him. If she gained possession of something that could control Melkai, she had no intention of handing it over to the person she hated. With an army of Melkai loyal to her, she could overthrow him and take charge.

"I understand," she replied.

"You think you do." The king chuckled. "To make sure of your loyalty, these two will be accompanying you."

From the shadows at either side of the dais appeared two of the king's knights, two of the largest she had seen in his army, Kinson and Bronus. They were actually Lord Ronund's men, the worst of the worst. She had heard they burned down peasants' houses for fun and did worse to their daughters. They moved to her side, broad and intimating, towering over her. She didn't look at them but just nodded and turned toward the entrance. She did not leave.

"Anything else?" she asked.

"The other person with the key may be a caller as well, but you must bring it to me at any cost, and these two will make sure of it." King Kissick smiled as she began to stride to the throne room doors. "Bring it to me and I will permanently put an end to this war."

"As you desire, *Your Majesty*," she murmured as she walked from the throne room, the two knights hurrying to keep pace with her.

The doors closed loudly behind her.

Laine kept a snappy pace, forcing the knights to catch up with her, not unveiling her smile until she left the throne room. She wasn't just thankful for the excuse to leave, she was eager; she couldn't have left soon enough. As soon as the clanking suits caught up, she hid it again, wanting to appear disappointed by them tagging along, but she knew ways to deal with them . . . or rid herself of them.

As for now, she had to keep up the act.

"Princess Laine," Bronus bellowed, "you must understand that the king only wishes for peace."

Laine sneered as they walked down a set of stairs to the castle entrance. "Only if it ends up with him on top. All he cares about is power, but then, what man is any different?"

Kinson sniggered. "What they say about the princess hating men is true after all."

Laine shook her head. "Only those who feel that their power makes them superior. But why am I telling you this? Like you would listen to a little girl like me."

Kinson stuck out his bottom lip and shrugged in agreement. He and Bronus opened the main doors that led out into the castle courtyard.

The sky was dull with gray clouds, and sheets of light rain streaked toward the horizon. This made Laine feel justified in wearing her hooded cloak. The three of them made their way through the gardens to the stairs leading down into the outer-settlements.

The city was an incredibly morbid place, even by her standards. The only people who didn't appear to be starving were the soldiers stalking the shops. It had been this way ever since King Kissick had taken the throne from his older brother. He dedicated most of his power to the expansion of his land while not improving the quality of life for those living within it. Every day farmers would come to the king, begging for him to relent in his heavy taxation, and every day they were shown the door.

They walked through the wet hardpan of the city. Wooden cabins and shacks were spread out around them. Laine hated what the city had become. It once thrived, but was now neglected. Its people and animals were wasting away. As they came to the edge of the city, they passed the muddy farmlands that led up the mountains into the Kydian Wood.

It was said that long ago the legendary warrior race of the Senadonians crossed the Jile Mountains. The people believed that one day they would come back to help return the kingdom to its former glory. However, it was only hearsay among the peasants that kept these rumors alive, and Laine for one didn't buy them.

Life isn't that easy.

"Remember, Princess, we're here to guard you so you should try showing us some gratitude." Bronus sneered suggestively. "After all, we know your true relationship with the king. As far as we're concerned, this journey he sent you on is just to get rid of you and now we're your only protection against any who might . . . try to take advantage of you."

He laughed and Kinson leered at her, appearing to agree with Bronus's unspoken suggestion.

"You're not serious," Laine said in disgust.

"Why not? We could make you our slave on this journey. What do you think, Kinson?" Bronus asked. "Am I serious?"

Laine hid another smile, amused that they thought they could. How long would she have to keep up the act of being weak around them? She wasn't sure if they even knew what callers could do. After the new king had taken over, he had executed many of them, suspicious that one of them could claim to be of the Kairen royal bloodline. With no male heir, it wouldn't have been difficult to claim the right of succession.

King Kissick had kept her alive, claiming her as his daughter to marry her off to someone loyal to him. She doubted even he knew that she, being a caller, would have other uses for him until now. With reports of Melkai roaming the land, only callers and well-guarded journeymen were safe beyond the walls. Yet, even if her guards had seen a caller in action before, no one expected someone of her age to be able to summon a Melkai of the second circle.

"I don't know," Kinson teased. "Depends if she beha-ha—" His eyes drifted up, mouth agape.

They were just reaching the borders of the forest, but the knight's reaction caused them to stop. Laine followed his eyes up, and Bronus halted in front of her. High up in the distant blue-gray sky was something big enough that it was clearly visible, even at a distance. It appeared to be a thick red S of muscle and scales with large hind and front legs and two flapping wings.

"I-I don't believe it," Bronus said in awe, gripping the hilt of his sword in horror. "I-It's a dr-dragon!"

The dragon swooped down over the forest trees. In less than three powerful flaps of his mighty wings, it flew toward them. Laine could hear her knights shaking as it landed with a thump before spreading its wings wide and letting loose a shaking roar.

Kinson's eyes bulged, petrified where he stood.

"Oh no! Please don't let it eat me!" Laine cried out in feigned horror.

Bronus drew his sword with shaking fingers. "Dr-dragon . . . stay back, Princess!"

The dragon bared its fangs at them. *"I recognize that magic. Are you Armalon?"*

The knights showed no sign of being surprised that the dragon could talk. Bronus's terror got the best of him, and he charged toward it, screaming with his sword raised to strike. The dragon swiftly swatted him away with one claw, and he flew backward, landing with a heavy splat in the mud.

Not learning from his comrade's mistake, Kinson rushed at the Melkai also, not even drawing his blade. The dragon spun, and Laine found it hard to believe such a massive thing could move so fast. Its heavy tail hit the man hard enough that he skidded ten meters on the grass before finally coming to a stop.

Groaning and amazingly still alive, Bronus rose up onto his hands and knees, but the dragon's hind foot came down upon him, crushing him to death with a short scream.

Laine frowned, but then stuck out her lower lip and nodded, impressed by how easily the dragon had killed the knights. Of course, she had planned to get rid of them herself eventually, but thanks to a fortunate Melkai appearance, now she didn't need to.

The dragon's foot lifted, and Laine's lips drew back from her teeth in disgust as she saw Bronus's mangled body. However, she then smiled at the dragon, realizing she no longer had to keep up her act anymore.

After Kinson had gone silent as well, the dragon finally turned its gaze on her. Laine raised her hands up as the dragon moved toward her and she once again heard the voice in her head: *"Tell me now. Are you Armalon?"*

Laine stepped back and grabbed the collar of her long, hooded cloak. She might have been just another victim of the dragon if not for what she was wearing.

"You don't scare me. Not while I have this. This cloak is my pact item," she said. "Would you like to meet *my* Melkai? Its name is Terachiro."

The dragon took another step forward, but before it could attack, Laine gripped her cloak and pulled, ripping it from around her shoulders and throwing it at the dragon. As it flew, the cloak quickly transformed.

The ragged tail became the wings, the hood became the head, and the space between grew the claws of a giant Melkaiic bat. It toppled headlong into the dragon, claws reaching. As it collided, the two rolled over one another before separating and taking to the air. They circled each other and flew together again. Laine watched as the two Melkai clawed it out in an aerial duel.

On the ground, Laine was summoning her magic power into the blade of her hand as it began to glow a bright blue. It was an Advanced Summoning ability, and she had taught it to herself vigorously when she had seen another caller do it, but even he hadn't perfected it as she had.

The two Melkai continued their fight, equally matched in their struggle. From what she knew of dragons, its ultimate attack would be its flame. For some reason she couldn't comprehend, it hadn't used it yet. The two Melkai drew together once more. The bat's claws raked the dragon's armored scales as the dragon attempted to snap at its head before they both pulled back.

Laine's spell had completed, and she raised the blade of her hand. Then she swung it in the direction of the dragon. As the dragon sailed back, it was caught unaware as the glow from Laine's hand shot up toward it in a line of light, and with a yelp, it hit the dragon's left wing. However, the force of the strike also flung it backward, and with the combined momentum of its movement, it flew over the horizon of the forest. With a dull thump, it vanished into the trees.

As soon as the dragon was gone, the light drizzle became a downpour. She sighed, knowing that tracking it would be impossible in this weather. Her jaw clenched in agitation. Dragons weren't just big lizards. They could have long memories, and she dreaded one holding a grudge against her. A breath of fire could be a devastating surprise attack when caught out in a forest. She had been careless to let it get away alive.

"Terachiro, to me!"

Swiftly, her Melkai changed direction and headed back to her. In a couple of flaps, it flew down and transformed back into her cloak to settle itself around her shoulders. The glow from Laine's hand faded as she returned it behind the cloak tail, using her other hand to replace the hood back over her short brunette hair.

"Did you have fun?" she asked her cloak to no reply. "It was definitely interesting to watch. This journey might be more interesting than I'd first thought."

Heaving out a sigh at finally being on her own again, she entered the deep shadows of the Kydian Wood, trying to ease herself out of the excitement the battle had left her.

She had cared nothing for the two knights. After hearing all the horror stories of what they had done to the peasants, she was glad there were two fewer murderers in the world. Although free to be herself now that they were dead, Laine reminded herself that there were potentially worse things than knights and dragons in the woods.

CHAPTER 4

THE MAN AT THE LAKE

Nathan gagged into his sleeve as he pulled his dagger from the Melkai's eye. Keeping the dripping blade out of eyesight, he wiped it on the long grass until it came back clean, and then he returned it to its holster in his rucksack.

Michael showed no signs of waking. Nathan checked him and found no injury, so he was perplexed that he would fall unconscious like that, even after fighting a Melkai—one which still lay dead on the grass right next to them. Seeing them lying so close together had been unsettling, but Nathan couldn't move Michael in his heavy armor.

After what they had just been through, Nathan wanted to collapse as well, but one of them had to keep watch. What worried him more was how long Michael slept and that he wouldn't come to even after Nathan tried shaking him awake. So Nathan spent the time studying the Melkai they had just killed.

He was getting a closer look at such a monster than he could have ever hoped. The creature was fascinating: its fangs a bloodred, its red hair mane-like, and its skin leather smooth. Taiba watched the monster intently to make sure it didn't move, and Nathan stroked him absentmindedly in an attempt to calm him down.

Nathan had wished to observe Melkai on this journey, but thought he would only get to do so from a distance. Granted, he would have preferred that this prize wasn't at the cost of being in a life-risking situation, but that didn't stop him from making the most of it while Michael was unconscious.

Michael finally awoke in the late afternoon.

As his eyes flung open, Nathan's shoulders relaxed and he rushed over to his friend. The prince followed him to his feet.

"You had me worried."

Michael looked at his hand for a moment, opening and closing it with a baffled expression. Ignoring Nathan, he studied the giant corpse of the Melkai he had killed with a wide, victorious smile.

"Hello? Michael, are you okay?" Nathan asked.

Michael glanced at him, his smile fading. "I feel fine." He strode over to where his sword lay next to the Melkai's body. He slid it into the scabbard on his back.

Nathan frowned.

"Come on," Michael called as he began walking.

Nathan nodded, confused by his friend's sudden change in demeanor. Then he shook his head and ran to catch up. "Wait, Michael . . . ah!" He winced as he pulled at the bruises on his sides, but gritted his teeth and tried to ignore them. "Listen, I fully acknowledge you've fought Melkai before, but please don't tell me you pass out after every encounter."

Taiba leapt onto his boot and climbed up his pant leg so he wasn't left behind.

"What can I say?" Michael called back. "This one took a bit of effort."

"I'd say! Dragon's breath, you managed to defeat a second-circle Melkai in a power struggle!" Nathan exclaimed. "But it doesn't make sense that it started coughing up blood all of a sudden, does it?"

"I guess I should thank your little friend for that," Michael replied. "After all, it was he who saved us in the end."

Nathan's brow furrowed. "What . . . Taiba?"

The little creature climbed silently onto his shoulders.

"That's right. It was not my strength that overpowered the Melkai but that thing's poison."

Nathan remembered then how, when the Melkai had hold of him, Taiba had run out from his hood and had bit its finger.

"I didn't know." He shook his head. "Taiba has bitten me before, and I was never affected by it!"

Michael smirked. "It must only be used when needed then, but it was your little friend's bite that saved the day, not me. It couldn't help but be overpowered when the poison was in its system."

Nathan turned to the small lizard and smiled, putting a finger out to stroke its smooth scales. The little creature nudged into him, but for some reason, he was still trembling.

Michael wasn't there to see the Melkai being bitten.

"How are you so sure it was poison?" he asked.

Michael shrugged. "Trust me, I just know."

Nathan nodded. He was just happy they had gotten out of the situation alive, despite how bruised his sides felt from nearly being squeezed to death. While striding down the hillside, the Talis Lake stretched out below them before the Kydian Woods.

"I can only guess how many more are in the forest," he murmured. "Maybe we *should* go around."

"No," Michael cut in. "I have chosen our path, and now I know how to beat them, so we have nothing to worry about."

Nathan's mouth opened, but he stopped himself, knowing there was nothing he could say to persuade him. Yet after barely surviving their first battle, he couldn't fathom why Michael was so unperturbed with the possibility of encountering another second-circle Melkai. Was it due to their difference in vocation, perhaps?

Undoubtedly, the castle's Master of Arms had beaten into Michael the need to be strong enough to slay Melkai without the need of magic. Master Morrow, on the other hand, had constantly pressed Nathan every lesson with the need to both respect and fear Melkai, particularly those of the third circle. Despite how rare they were, considering their size, there was a higher chance of running into one unaware among the tall trees.

"*They are impossible to control,*" Morrow had warned him during one such lesson. "*Whenever a caller has tried to make a pact with one, a catastrophe follows in its wake.*" Morrow's voice in Nathan's memory was so clear that he felt like he was reliving the lesson all over again. "*Now, you have probably heard fairy tales of someone succeeding, or the legend of a first-circle Melkai transforming into a third-circle. They're all nonsense! You see, Nathan, they are self-aware and have intelligence on par with our own."*

Nathan had been sitting on the edge of his seat at the front of the class while Taiba played with the feather end of his quill.

Morrow held up a book on the subject for Nathan to read more. "It's of the utmost importance that you never call forth one of these Melkai. If you do, it could mean the end of your life and the lives of everyone you know. If you remember nothing else of what I say, I implore you, remember that."

Morrow's lesson had worked. Not only did he remember it, but the fear of the more powerful Melkai stayed with him to this day.

They soon arrived at Talis Lake. Nathan halted in surprise, noticing a figure lying in the mud at the edge of it. It was a man in tattered clothing, and like when he had seen the first soldier, a panic rose up within Nathan.

"Another soldier?" After what they had been through, Nathan's body moved instinctively from his renewed panic, believing the man had been attacked by a Melkai as well. It might have been the one they ran into earlier; it might have been another that was hidden somewhere in the woods. He took off running toward the waterlogged figure.

"No, wait!" Michael called, but Nathan was already at the body.

He glanced around quickly, feeling maybe this was bait for a trap. Nothing appeared, so he leaned forward to check the body.

The man was on his front, half in and half out of the lake, a sheathed sword clutched in his hand. Nathan stood over him and noticed that, unlike the last man they came across, this one had no armor and was in a lot better shape. In fact . . . he was still breathing.

"He's still alive . . . Michael, he's still alive!"

Michael came upon the scene slowly, trudging toward him with a deep frown on his face.

"Michael, help me pull him out!" Nathan pleaded, but the prince merely stood there.

"I don't think that's a good idea," he replied coldly.

Nathan continued to try and heave out the body. "What are you talking about?"

Michael was breathing heavily as he looked down at the man, his eyes wide with some indescribable emotion. "Let him be."

"No!" Nathan had finally dragged him free of the water, seeing now that there was a bloody wound on his left shoulder. "Look, he's bleeding. We have to help him!"

Jaw clenching, Michael ran forward and hauled the wounded man onto his shoulders, carrying him onto the grass and laying him down. He looked up at the sky and cringed. The sun was setting and they had only just made it to the border of the forest.

"Take the gauze from your rucksack and bind his wound!" Michael shouted and walked briskly to the forest.

"Where are you going?" Nathan asked.

"Night's approaching. I'm getting some deadwood to make a fire," he called back and ran into the forest.

Nathan unhooked his pack and pulled out the bandages that had been packed for him. With a bit of difficulty, he turned the man onto his front and used his cloak to dry his skin before pulling up his arm and rolling the gauze around his shoulder. Taiba peered around, searching for something—something he could smell but couldn't see. When he was done, he pushed the man onto his back. The man gasped and cleared his throat, causing Nathan to jump.

"Th-thank you," the man whispered before passing out again.

Nathan smiled and looked at the stranger's face. The man looked to be around the same age as Michael, was tall, and had auburn hair. Other than how they had found him, which Nathan had to admit was a little odd, there seemed to be nothing abnormal about him.

Michael returned with some firewood. In a matter of minutes, the sun had sunk into the horizon, and a fire was blazing through the darkness. The two of them sat on one side of the fire with the stranger lying on the other side, the sheathed longsword they found with him still clutched at his side. Taiba slept in Nathan's lap, warming himself in the firelight.

Michael ground his teeth. "We shouldn't have done that. We don't have the time to take care of him."

"We had to help him," Nathan replied.

"I wanted to be in the forest by nightfall. With the fire, anything could spot us out here!"

Nathan balled his hands in frustration. He was just doing what he thought was right. "What happened to the brave warrior that could take down second-circle Melkai?"

Michael looked away in anger. "Well, about that . . ."

There was silence for a moment before an unfamiliar voice said, "If not him, I reckon I could."

They all jumped at the stranger's gravelly tone and turned toward him, Nathan in shock, the prince in anger, and Taiba trying to relocate the comfortable position he had been sleeping in before being disturbed. Looking over the flames at the man they had just saved, Nathan pondered how he ended up in the lake in the first place.

"You have some explaining to do," Michael said, his voice accusing.

The man coughed out a laugh. "Yes, I suppose I do."

"Why were you in the lake?" Nathan asked, pitching his voice to sound sympathetic.

"I fell from the sky after a battle with two powerful Melkai. They wounded me," he said, hinting at his shoulder.

Nathan and Michael looked at each other in confusion.

Nathan turned back and asked, "What's your name?"

The man smiled warmly. "You can call me Aisic. Your own?"

"I'm Nathan, and this is Michael, Prince of Terratheist."

"Prince?" Aisic sounded amused. "I'm sorry, but I'm a little hazy on who reigns over Terratheist now? What are your family names?"

Michael grimaced and returned, "Nathan and Michael are the only names you need for now. We will not ask for yours and you will not ask for ours."

Aisic shrugged, wincing from his wounded shoulder. "So be it."

Nathan frowned at Michael, trying to figure out why he was being so terse with the man. However, he was also a little thankful that he didn't have to answer his question. He had never known his family name.

"Now, *Aisic*," Michael replied harshly. "We don't deal with strangers. So, as far as we're concerned, as soon as it's dawn, we part ways, got it?"

Aisic shook his head. "No."

Michael's face contorted, scowling like the stranger had slighted him. "What do you mean no?"

"My life belongs to this young man now." He stared at Nathan. "He will decide what will happen to me. But right now, I can only offer my service as a protector." Aisic looked to Michael, his eyes daring him to challenge this statement. "I am now just the dead, a ghost who belongs to him. It's as simple as that."

Nathan looked down, not knowing how to reply to Aisic's declaration.

Michael ground his teeth and lay down. "It's time to sleep. We'll discuss this in the morning."

Nathan nodded and lay down also as Taiba scrambled into his hood. However, with so much to think about now, sleep didn't come so easily. What Aisic had said to him kept coming up in his mind, and he whispered aloud, "Did he just say . . . he fought off *two* Melkai?"

The argument rekindled the next morning, the sun already up in the clear azure sky.

"But I want him to come with us!" Nathan pleaded. "The more the merrier, and besides, he says he can fight off Melkai!"

"No, he's not coming," Michael replied, roughly packing up his gear. "Call it my warrior's instinct or whatever you want, but I don't trust him."

Nathan looked at the stranger who stood next to the lake. He was wearing one of Michael's borrowed shirts and a pair of his extra pants as Aisic's tattered clothing had barely been enough to cover him. The sword found with him was now slung over his shoulder, appearing unaffected by his wound.

Aisic wanted to come with them as a protector. Nathan could understand the feeling of wanting to repay a debt as he did for the king by going on this journey. Taiba must have liked him too, for he had finally stopped trembling.

"This is my journey. I hold the key and I decide who comes with us!"

Grinding his teeth, Michael grabbed the collar of Nathan's shirt, his huge arms lifting him up off the ground in anger like the Melkai had done the day before.

Nathan stared back at him, his eyes determined, unafraid by the threat, despite Michael's size. "If you don't like it, you can leave now," he stated clearly.

Michael's eyes closed, and he forced a smile. He put him down and patted him on the shoulder. Then he walked over to Aisic. Nathan was uncertain, but he swore he saw the man's hand drift down from the hilt of his sword, as though he'd been ready to draw it if Michael became too violent with him.

He frowned at Michael. His friend was usually friendly and open to everyone from the king to the lowest servant boy. Nathan had never seen him instantly dislike someone like this before. He was being ridiculous. Sure, Michael was determined to protect him, to prove himself on this adventure—but Aisic wasn't a threat. Nathan stayed close, ready to break up a fight that might start up between them at any second.

After sharing a few heated words Nathan couldn't make out, Michael shook his head and walked off. Nathan picked up his pack and followed after. There was nothing left to do but move forward in their quest. Aisic grinned and winked at Nathan as the two of them walked side by side. As they circumvented the edge of the lake toward the Kydian Wood, Nathan took it upon himself to let Aisic in on the goal of their journey.

"We are on a mission to Avatasc to find someone who has a certain object. This object, when joined with one we already have, has the power to reseal the weakening barrier to the Melkairen. But we must do this before the moon turns completely red because that's when the barrier will be broken completely and Melkai will walk freely into our world."

Nathan was puzzled to see there wasn't any expression of surprise or even amused skepticism on the man's face, although he did appear to be deep in thought.

"The second-circle Melkai will be able to break free of the barrier before it gives up completely, and you can be sure that they will be trying to stop us from resealing it when they do."

"And that's where I come in, I assume," Aisic replied.

Nathan smiled, despite Michael striding ahead of them. "Well, if you can fight off the Melkai as you say you can, then yeah, I guess so."

"Then we have nothing to worry about," Aisic said, his gravelly voice confident.

"Why are you fighting Melkai?" Nathan asked.

"I've been searching for one, one that I mean to kill with my own hands. Unfortunately, the one I ran into wasn't the one I was looking for. I . . ." He paused and shook his head. "No, never mind."

Nathan's brow furrowed as he stopped talking, longing to know more about him. If Aisic had fought a Melkai, *two*

Melkai, did that make him some kind of Melkai-slayer? Was that his job or was he looking for a particular Melkai to get revenge, maybe one that killed his family or destroyed his village? He had so many questions.

Unlike what Michael had explained to him, he felt drawn to the man. Perhaps he was naive, but just like Michael claimed he was doing, Nathan was trusting his instincts. "What kind of Melkai is it? What does it look like?"

"I don't know, but I will when I find it."

Nathan frowned in confusion, wondering if it was a Melkai that could change its form. He didn't know Melkai like that existed, but he had underestimated Melkai before by assuming they couldn't speak.

Going at a brisk pace, they quickly reached the edge of the trees that made up the Kydian Wood. They moved between the tall trunks, their branches shading them from the sun. For a while, they traveled in silence, but this was soon broken as Michael slowed down for seemingly no reason and began glaring at Aisic.

"Doesn't look like it's going to be raining warriors today, does it?" Michael asked.

Aisic calmly faced him. "Why are you so suspicious of me?"

"You tell me!" Michael shouted. "A stranger we find wounded on the edge of the lake suddenly wants to join us for no reason other than he was given a little help to get on his feet again; why do you think I'm suspicious?"

Because your time surrounded by monsters has made you overly paranoid of strangers?

"Alright, that's enough!" Nathan shouted. "There's no reason to get so angry. We helped him and he wants to return the favor. It's that simple."

Michael grabbed Nathan by the arm and pulled him aside roughly.

"Michael, what's gotten into you?"

"Nothing," Michael hissed and peered around. "I just don't trust him."

"Why?"

"I can't explain it. Something about him just makes my blood boil." He balled his hands into fists. "The way he speaks to you. It just makes me wanted to . . ." He ground his teeth rather than finish his sentence.

Nathan shook his head, baffled by him. "I don't feel anything like that."

"Yeah, well, you don't have as much experience out here as I do. You're too trusting."

Nathan caught his eyes. "Michael, you know we can't face the Melkai in this forest without him. I don't care if you're too proud to admit it, but we need him."

Michael raised his hands in exasperation and stormed off. He walked at such a brisk pace that the two of them couldn't keep up. Nathan fell back to walk with Aisic.

"I don't get it. Why is he so angry?" Nathan asked himself.

Aisic quickened his pace also, but as Nathan looked up through an opening in the trees, he halted mid-stride, mouth agape. The moon sat in the clear sky, its waning horizon shining bloodred.

The promised time was beginning.

CHAPTER 5

THE KYDIAN

Laine had been certain that she would cross paths with another Melkai before she arrived in Kydia, but the barrier wasn't weakening as fast as she had assumed it would. She arrived at the village during lunchtime, the sun almost pinpoint in the middle of the sky. The village was not what she expected.

History talked of the vibrant forest life that surrounded the tall wooden buildings of Kydia, but all the greenery on the borders of the village had been stripped from the branches. She came out of the trees onto the damp mud of the carriage track and looked at the morbid village. The houses were small and stubby, built on the burned ruins of their predecessors. The people were mostly old and dying, and a soot sky hung overhead, reminding her of the grimness of her homeland.

She scrunched her nose at the vile smell of death that filled the air. Carts of the dead were rutted in the roads, and crows were flying in and eating their fill. She watched as a man who owned one such cart exited a house with his masked partner, carrying a dead woman between them before dumping her on top of the others. The crows broke into flight as the two heaved the cart out of the mud and rolled it down the road to the next house.

Looks like this place has been hit by an illness.

She walked at a steady pace down the carriage track, which appeared to be the only road in Kydia. Arriving at one of the larger buildings, she heard a ruckus arising inside. At first, she ignored it. However, as soon as she saw a sign proclaiming the building to be an inn, the door opened and two large men carrying a young woman exited, throwing the woman to the mud.

"You better have Callahan's money next time you show up 'ere or you'll live to regret it!" one of the men bellowed as he slammed the door shut.

The girl rubbed the shoulder she had landed on. "I owe him nothing!"

The girl rose to a sitting position in a pout. She looked up at Laine through the curls of her strawberry blonde hair, seeming to realize only then that Laine had been standing right beside her.

Laine sighed and extended a hand. "Are you okay?"

The girl jumped up freely and knocked once on the side of her head. "I'm fine, made of harder stuff than most."

Laine raised an eyebrow at the closed door. "What was that about?"

The girl sighed. "Rotten brutes think I owe them money, AND I DON'T!" she roared at the closed door.

Laine shook her head. "I'd be willing to help if you tell

me exactly what happened. I can't stand it when men abuse their power to gain a profit."

The girl looked at her in confusion, but then gasped when her eyes fixed on the symbol sewn into Laine's hood. The symbol was an orb with bat wings on either side.

"You're a caller, aren't you?" she asked. She quickly turned to the onlookers in the street and grabbed her by the hand. "Not out here. Too many people to see."

Laine frowned and stared down at where the girl grasped her. She was about to pull her hand free, then hesitated as she noticed the desperate, imploring look in her eyes. Laine let herself be led down a path and behind one of the many wooden houses on the side of the road. Behind the house was a bench under a veranda which kept away the light rain that was starting to fall.

"Okay, I reckon you should know now," the girl started, "I also do magic but of a different kind—old Kydian magic. It's no secret around here that I'm one of the few town healers."

Laine nodded. "Must be hard in a village like this. There looks to be an illness about."

"That's the thing!" she blurted, slamming her hand down on the wooden bench. "I'm exhausted! Look, I understand some people not paying for my services, I really do, but I accept whatever they can give me. You see, with my abilities—well, they make me kind of valuable here and . . ."

Laine nodded, understanding the girl's plight all too keenly. "It puts a lot of responsibility on your shoulders . . . and sometimes you feel like a slave to them."

"It does feel that way sometimes, yeah." The girl shook her head. "But with Callahan it's different. He owns the inn and is the richest man in the village. So, when I got called upon by him, I was promised a big reward, something I could live off for a while, you know? You see, he got infected, too. I mended him the best I could, but afterward, he gave me no recompense and pretended it never happened. Oh, I got so mad!"

"And you decided to take matters into your own hands and took what you thought you were owed?" Laine asked.

The girl nodded.

Good to see she still has some fight left in her.

"Now they want me to give it back. I only took what I was owed!" she growled, balling her hands into fists. "It's so infuriating!"

Laine stood up from the bench swiftly and turned to the girl. "I will help you in this matter. This man, *Callahan*, is abusing his power, and I will not allow it. Not in my kingdom."

"Your kingdom?" asked the girl, the confusion in her tone becoming awe.

The girl's open expression was sincere, a plea to any who might witness it. In any other situation, Laine would have thought this a scam, but her tired face showed her to be someone who was honestly trying to help people. Laine decided to take a risk and trust the girl. It was the only way she might be able to help her. Besides, her strawberry blonde hair reminded her of her mother's.

Laine put her hand out. "I am Princess Laine of Avatasc, court caller of King Kissick."

The girl's eyes grew wide. "I-I'm Kendra," she replied and took her hand.

Laine pulled her up and took off.

"So, what are we going to do?" Kendra asked as she followed on Laine's heels.

They began walking back in the direction of the inn.

"Simple." Laine smirked. "We're going to take his money and leave. With no wealth, a man has no power."

"But there are guards on the borders of the village. Dozens of them!" Kendra cried. "Callahan owns them. We won't make it out alive!"

"Not without his coin he doesn't," Laine replied. "Leave it to me. I'll handle it."

They moved around the house and out into the road. Waiting for a carriage to pass, Laine led the way across the track to the front door of the inn. Laine raised her hand as the blade of it started to glow the same blue with which she had attacked the dragon. She opened the door and rushed in. Kendra quickly followed behind her as Laine ran through the few ragged people in the bar toward the girl working at the counter.

"Callahan's office is behind that counter and up the stairs!" Kendra called.

The girl behind the counter screamed and ducked as Laine vaulted over it. Once she landed, she kicked the door down to a room which led to a set of stairs. Kendra quickly followed her onto the stairwell and then up it.

As they came to the room on the second floor, Laine opened the door and saw three men sitting in the room. The two she had seen already, the large ones who had thrown Kendra outside, were clearly the man's bodyguards. The other, sitting behind a large desk, was just as obviously Callahan. He was dressed more lavishly than anyone else she had seen in the village, wearing a clean white silk shirt, its buttons stretching over his bloated, hairy body.

"What is this?" Callahan asked in outrage. "I told you not to come back here unless you had my money. And who are you?"

Laine advanced on him, but the two guards rose to intercept her. Using the blue blade glowing on her hand, Laine slashed at the wooden floor just in front of her, tearing away at it as chips of wood flew up in front of her. The two guards approaching her lost their balance on the planks and fell through into the room below, landing with a crash on the first floor. Laine jumped over the hole toward the desk as Callahan drew a knife, but Laine once again raised her glowing hand.

"Now, if you don't want your establishment more messed up than it already is, I suggest you give up your stash, old man," Laine sneered.

Quivering, Callahan put his knife on the table, opened the locked drawer on his desk and pulled out a large wad of notes and a brown pouch filled with gold coins: a small fortune. "T-take it, b-but you won't make it out of this village alive. Y-you know that, Kendra!"

In all the excitement, Kendra appeared to awaken from her trance and raised her hand to her mouth.

Laine simply grabbed the paper and pouch of gold, turned, and jumped back over the gap in the floor she had made, pulling Kendra along with her. "Come on!"

As they descended the stairs, Laine noticed that the bodyguards that had fallen through the floor were no longer there. She came to the door to the main hall, pushed it ajar, and peered through. The two guards were in the bar section of the inn explaining the gist of the situation to four more guards.

"Who's out there?" Kendra whispered in panic.

Laine shut the door quietly as she noticed one of the guards turning toward it. "Six of them. I don't think I can handle all of them by myself. We need to get outside."

"But out there is the only exit. What do we do?"

The glow appeared once again on Laine's hand as she calmly answered, "Make our own exit."

Turning to the nearest wall, she slashed twice in an upside down V. Before anyone could come through the door, she kicked down the portion of the wall she had cut out, grabbed Kendra's arm, and ran out into the street. Quickly heading around the corner of a store next to the inn, they stopped in hiding for a rest. Kendra was panting as Laine peered around the corner, seeing two of the guards and Callahan himself come out onto the carriage track.

"It was Kendra and another girl in a robe!" Callahan screamed as they scattered in all directions. "They took my money. Find them now! Make sure they don't leave the village!"

Laine leaned against the wall next to Kendra, who was crouching and trying to calm herself. From her drawn expression, the action had exhausted her.

"Okay, we need to get out of town." Laine glanced down at her. "I'm heading to Terratheist. If you want, you can tag along with me. With the money we stole, living there shouldn't be any problem."

Kendra stood up slowly, her breathing finally steady. "I can't. Not with the way the village is now."

Laine shook her head. "You owe these people nothing."

"Being a princess, surely you understand that—"

"It's because I'm a princess that I'm saying this! Your only responsibility is to live your own life the way you choose. If you keep on going the way you have been, you'll eventually burn out, or worse, become a slave to these people. You have to get out now while you still have a chance."

Despite the obvious flaws in her argument, the rush of their snatch-and-grab was undoubtedly coloring Kendra's decision.

The girl inclined her head and said hesitantly, "Well, I *have* always wanted to visit the Terratheist capital. The city is supposed to be amazing! But you see . . . my grandma still lives here. She's looked after me since I was a baby and taught me everything I know. I can't leave her in this village, not with those men looking for me."

"Hmm . . ." Laine crossed her arms and nodded, considering this. "Well, does she have someone nearby she can trust?"

"There's the neighbor, John. He's a kindly blacksmith, but—"

"All right, well, Callahan's men are after *us*, not your grandmother, right?" A smile played across Laine's face. "So, how about making her and her neighbor, this John, the richest people in the village? We can pay him to help her, you see. Surely, as a blacksmith, he would know some reliable mercenaries that he could hire for protection."

At first, Kendra's brow furrowed, but as Laine's words dawned on her, the girl smiled warmly. "Ah, yes, I see! That might work actually! Okay, this way."

Kendra took off, weaving between buildings and shacks. Laine trudged behind her, her nice boots getting covered in mud.

"How do you deal with this every day?" she complained. "Surely someone in this village thought about putting a road down?"

"Sure, but who's going to pay for it?" Kendra called back. "With the taxes we pay to the king, you'd think he'd be the one to make the roads."

Laine snorted. "Good luck telling him that."

They arrived at a homely cottage that belonged to Kendra's grandmother. It was pouring by the time they arrived, and once the wiry elderly woman saw them, they were ushered inside.

"Nana, this is Laine. She helped me today," Kendra said as the three found chairs in the sitting room. "She has an idea that will hopefully put Callahan and his goons out of business."

"Oh, really?"

Laine stopped studying the old family memorabilia, paintings, and porcelain around the room and nodded. "I was thinking maybe you could convince John to round up some boys for protection after coming into some substantial wealth."

"Substan . . ." She smiled and waved her hand. "Why, those youngins. All they do is waste their time around the inn anyhow. You would need something awfully convincing to get them off their backsides."

Laine leaned forward and showed her the coins. "Will this work?"

Kendra's grandmother smiled and her tune quickly changed. "Oh, yes. John is a good strong lad with lots of friends that could do some good with this money." She rocked herself onto her feet. "I'll go see if he's still up and about."

A minute later, they were talking to the large, handsome blacksmith and making a deal on getting him involved in their scheme. Before the evening came to an end, the matter was settled, having taken less than an hour to go over everything with John before hands were shook and the money was shared between them.

They agreed to go thirds, with them taking their own share for their journey.

"You know, despite his money, I heard rumors that Callahan was actually up to his nose in debt." The old woman gave them a gap-toothed grin. "I don't suppose he would have much objection to selling his inn to an old lady when the loaners come demanding their money, do you think?"

Laine laughed. "Considering how it will be run by a healer, I imagine it will become the most popular inn in the village."

The two of them stayed the night in her grandmother's guest room, Laine accepting the shelter away from the rain. As she watched it drip down outside her window, she wondered if she was doing the right thing. Kendra was one of the only village healers. Even so, she hated to think of her as being a prisoner here because of her ability.

No, she's a young woman and can make up her own mind.

She also couldn't help but draw parallels between what was happening to Kendra with Callahan and what was happening to her mother with King Kissick and wondered if she was doing this for the catharsis she couldn't have gotten back home.

Either way, I'm sure this is the right thing.

Kendra came to her as the dawn sun rose. Laine awoke slowly, it being her first night in a soft bed since she had departed Avatasc.

"About leaving . . . I wasn't sure about leaving Nana at first, but I've made up my mind." Kendra smiled doggedly. "I mean, I might as well see the world while I'm still young and beautiful, am I right?"

Laine agreed, although she couldn't help but think that the last part had come directly from her grandmother's mouth. They packed their things, said their goodbyes to Kendra's grandma and John the blacksmith, and strode from the small cottage, walking between the houses and alleys toward the main road.

The sun was out and warming them, but the rain from the previous night had made the sodden path difficult to traverse without getting it on the tail of their cloaks or sticking to the bottom of their shoes.

"They'll catch us out here!" Kendra murmured, but then noticed Laine's smile.

"Now that we're out in the open, it doesn't really matter," Laine replied, her tone confident. "Even if they don't know that their boss just became broke and can't pay them, his guards still won't try to attack us once they see what I can do."

"But he owns over twenty men in all: a small army!" Kendra cried.

"Don't worry, just trust me. As I said yesterday, I'll handle it."

They walked through the village, doing a loop to try and throw off Callahan's men, but they didn't run into any of them. In the meantime, they used much of Callahan's money to buy supplies from the local stores. When Laine was ready to continue her journey to Terratheist, she led them in a beeline toward the edge of town.

As Kendra had expected, there were men waiting for them at the borders of the village, though unlike what Laine had expected, the boss himself had shown up with his bodyguards. There were a good twenty men there, just as Kendra had warned. The fat Callahan and his mercenaries sneered as they approached; Laine and Kendra appeared to be nothing but two young women. Like the knights she had left Avatasc with, they had no idea what she could do or what the cloak around her shoulders really was.

As they halted before them, Callahan swaggered in front of his men and said, "Give me back my money and there will be no bloodshed. Just . . ." He exhaled heavily. "Just give it back."

"We don't have it anymore!" Kendra called, but then murmured, "Well, not all of it anyway."

Callahan ground his teeth and shouted, "Then tell me where you put it, you little witch!"

Laine put a hand out, warning Kendra to stay back. "Alright, that's enough. You're blocking our path and we need to get through."

Both the guards and Callahan looked suddenly to Laine and laughed, Callahan gesturing back at his mercenaries. "Is that so? You're even shorter than the pest behind you. Do you really think that pathetic little hand ability of yours can make us move? If so, you're mad."

"Not that technique, you're right." Laine pulled her cloak from her shoulders and threw it high into the air. "But with this one, it will be as easy as scraping you off the soles of my shoes."

The smiling faces suddenly darkened as the shadow of the Melkaiic bat, Terachiro, transformed and landed with a mighty thump before them. Behind her, Kendra gasped and squelched backward.

Laine doubted many of them had seen a caller summon a Melkai before, let alone one from the second circle. One of them screamed, "It can't be real! It's just an illusion!" and charged in to strike it with his ax, which looked like it was intended more for chopping wood than for combat.

Terachiro shot into the air, causing the ax-wielder to stagger. The eyes of Callahan's men followed it up, the blustering wind blowing their hair back. With another devastating thump, it landed on top of the guard, long talons pinning him to the ground. Terrified cries from the others, including Callahan himself, were drowned out by Terachiro letting loose a high-pitched shriek. The guards ran screaming, dropping their weapons as the Melkai advanced on them, loyalties breaking as quickly as falling glass.

Callahan whirled about helplessly as they left his side. He turned back to come face to face with the giant bat, and in horror, he fell onto his backside in the mud.

"Terachiro!" Laine called.

As though deciding that the fat man wasn't even worth killing, Terachiro snarled and returned to Laine. It morphed back into her brown cloak and wrapped itself sleekly around her shoulders.

Callahan was alone now, his eyes wide in horror and his jaw slack in shock. Laine smiled back at Kendra who was as speechless as Callahan. They walked around the once richest man in the Kydian village, now nothing but the indebted owner of a wrecked inn.

As they passed him and moved to the borders of the forest behind the village, the fat man snapped back to life, spinning on the dirt and yelling, "You'll pay for this! Remember the name Callahan Ludious the Sixth, for it will be the last name you'll—"

"I've already forgotten it!" Kendra yelled back, laughing freely as they left the dying village and disappeared into the forest.

CHAPTER 6

RAMANNON

Michael's brisk steps took him further up into the hills than he intended. In his anger, he had walked a good half-mile ahead of the others. It didn't make sense that he wasn't back with them. It was his responsibility to take care of Nathan, yet he had left him there with a stranger that he not only mistrusted but felt an irrational hatred for.

But why? Why do I feel so agitated around him?

"What are you doing?" a rumbling voice whispered.

He stopped and looked around to see if anyone was following him. He saw no one. Shaking his head, he continued on, but just as he went to brush a branch from his face, he heard it again. It was barely audible but sounded so near to him, like a lover's whisper.

"Where are you going?" it asked, and Michael stopped again, looking around in panic. There was no one there, and yet he heard the murmur so close to his ear that the whisperer could have been right beside him. He thought it

was someone else, yet he was completely alone.

"He's not that way!"

Panic struck Michael, and his breathing sped up. "Where are you?" he asked, eyes darting about, feeling suddenly delirious. "What do you want from me?"

"Stop. Yes. Wait here. He will come to you."

"Who?" Michael asked, but cringed as a dull pain began to fill his head. "Who . . . are you?"

"The dragon will come!"

The pain increased, and he winced, clutching his head as it began to spread to his muscles. "Stop it! What are you doing?"

"I want you to kill him."

"Argh!"

The ache flared anew. It was so bright and painful that it blinded him. He crouched low, his vision going dark. As he screamed in pain, the reddening moon appeared to shine brighter above him.

The evening was approaching, and Nathan and Aisic had yet to catch up with Michael. They had been walking uphill for most of the day, and Nathan's legs were beginning to feel like jelly. From his steady gait, Aisic had no trouble keeping pace, but it seemed like he knew how Nathan felt, and he began telling Nathan stories of the old times to keep Nathan's mind off his sore feet.

Nathan swore the man must have memorized a history book, considering his extensive knowledge of past wars. For some reason, Aisic made many references to the Akai uprising. Despite it being a war fought without Melkai, occurring long before callers knew how to create pacts with them, Nathan still found himself being drawn into the tale.

"Of course, the Akai uprising took place nearly five hundred years ago," Aisic said with a shrug.

Nathan frowned in thought. "But why? Was there something wrong with the monarchy at the time?"

Aisic shook his head. "The land was an empire back then, not a kingdom. The rulers were the Armalons of the Kairen bloodline, the ones who locked the Melkai up in the Melkairen." He smiled as Nathan looked up in interest. "You see, the Kairens weren't a powerful race individually. The magic of their bloodline was very subtle; only when combining it with another Kairen could it become greater. Some even say that it was their entire race's united power which created the Melkairen itself and ended the War of the Melkai, but conjuring up an entire world sounds pretty unbelievable, don't you think?"

He raised his eyebrows and grinned at Nathan, who nodded for him to continue.

"The first Armalon reign was under Armalon the First."

"Seems convenient for historians," Nathan remarked.

Aisic inclined his head at Nathan's bad joke. "He decreed that any wife betrothed to the emperor should also be of Kairen blood in order to keep the magic of their bloodline strong within the royal family. But then he fell in love with a woman from the bloodline of the Arion."

Nathan scoffed. "Wow, hypocrisy right from the beginning?"

"Not only that . . ." Aisic raised an eyebrow, as though the worst was yet to come. "Individual Arion were more powerful than the Kairens, but unlike the Kairens, Arions couldn't control their powers, most only releasing them during near-death experiences. It was the copulation of Armalon the First and his Arion lover which resulted in the birth of the genocidal tyrant, Ramannon."

"Genocidal?" Nathan frowned, trying to recall what the word meant. "Did he wipe out a whole race?"

"Several races." Aisic breathed slowly in and out, sounding personally affected by the tale. "Born of immense power like individual Arion, but also with the ability to control it at will, Ramannon was the empire's ultimate weapon. Yet, because of the emperor's decree, he was born out of wedlock and couldn't become emperor; he was destined to be nothing more than the guiding uncle to the many heirs that followed."

Nathan's brow furrowed.

"You see, the combined powers he inherited through his parents' bloodlines made him immortal. Although his body succumbed to aging, he somehow continued to remain as a presence to guide the future emperors' decisions. For all intents and purposes, he was the emperor, but it wasn't until the fourth generation of Armalon's reign that he decided to take the throne. As evil as he was, the four generations he waited before doing this attests to his patience." Aisic's voice became bitter. "But I guess patience comes easy for those who live forever."

"I wonder what caused him to do it then." Nathan shrugged and suggested, "I guess I could understand how living forever would be enough to make anyone go a little mad."

Aisic shook his head. "No, Ramannon's malevolence was much deeper than that—one that could only be inspired by an unshakable desire to kill and a hatred so strong that only the eradication of an entire race could satisfy it: A true evil."

"But even then, he did it multiple times, didn't you say?" Nathan asked. "Surely such malice couldn't have come out of nowhere, could it?"

"Who knows?" Aisic's eyes shifted, as though uncertain of his next words. "I *assume* that he found out something about his Arion mother, for his first act in power was to have the Arions eradicated. His campaign of fear created an order in the empire unlike any that had been known, and he chose a new race to be demonized every few decades, many of them being wiped out as a result."

Aisic looked into Nathan's eyes in the dimming light and smiled, his eyebrows rising when he saw Nathan was still paying attention to his story. "Ramannon was eventually defeated by Cullen Armalon, but only after much sacrifice and the disappearance of their hero . . . the Scion of Akai."

Nathan had read of the Scion of Akai, although his heroic deeds sounded more like something out of a fairy tale than actual historical events. He supposed five hundred years of people adding embellishment could do that to a story.

"A hundred years later," Aisic continued, "callers were born and the land was split into two kingdoms fighting for dominance with their pact magic, a magic descended from the Kairens—but you should already know that."

Aisic said this as though stating something completely obvious, but Nathan just shook his head.

Aisic looked taken aback. "But you must know, you're a caller after all, aren't you? You haven't been told where your powers come from, your relationship to the royal Kairen bloodline?"

Nathan shook his head again. "I mean, I know I descended from the Kairens, but does that really mean I might have royal blood in my veins? Could I be royalty?"

Aisic grinned in amusement and inclined his head. "Maybe. Not all Kairens were kings and queens, you know. But the ability to call does come from their bloodline. They were the ones that locked away the Melkai so that they could bring them forth into our world with pact items, just like your little friend, ah . . ."

Taiba suddenly came out of Nathan's hood into the shadow of the trees, seeming to know he was being talked about. Nathan looked at his small lizard friend in confusion, still not quite understanding everything Aisic had told him. "But Taiba has no pact item—he never has. He's always been like this for as long as we've been together."

"Interesting." Aisic looked at the creature in curiosity. "Yes, even being of the first circle, it is a very bizarre little Melkai."

They continued walking through the darkening woods. The scenery was calming even considering the time of night. As they walked, Nathan studied the sword hanging from Aisic's shoulders. It was in its sheath and looked normal enough, but the cross guard was different from most swords. It looked like it was made of two bat-like wings.

His mind drifted, wondering how someone could defeat an immortal when he heard a loud scream of agony up through the trees ahead of them.

"It's Michael!" Nathan yelled and began to run up the hill to where the noise was coming from.

Aisic called, "Wait, Nathan!" but Nathan's concern for his friend drove him on.

Even before he found Michael, Taiba had begun trembling again, an unvoiced warning left unheeded in Nathan's panic to reach Michael. When he found him, Michael was crouching on the ground and screaming in pain. Nathan had never seen Michael make a fuss over a wound before. It sounded like Michael was dying.

"Michael, are you okay?" Nathan asked and looked around, but there was no obvious reason for why he was screaming. "What's going on?"

"Something's attacking me!" Michael cried through clenched teeth.

"Where, I can't see it!" Nathan ran in front of him to fend off the invisible enemy.

"It's inside my head!" Michael yelled, and his armor began to glow a bright white. "Argh! I can't fight it!"

Nathan whirled about, helpless. Michael was the tough one. He handled things while Nathan panicked. Nathan didn't know what to do with the roles reversed. It felt like a pillar of his reality had been pulled out from underneath him.

Then Michael fell silent. He rose slowly to his feet, a low rumble coming from deep inside his throat.

The prince looked up with glowing white eyes and extended a hand as the rumble formed the words, "Give it to me."

Nathan gasped. It was the exact same thing the Melkai had said to him.

"Nathan, get away from him now!" Aisic came out from between the trees.

Nathan shook his head. "He wouldn't hurt me. He's my friend!"

66

There was a sudden movement behind him, but Aisic quickly ran forward and pushed him out of the way. Nathan fell onto the leaves and soft dirt, turning to see that Michael's sword was drawn, its position low like it had been slashed in the direction where he had just been standing. Michael had attacked him. He was speechless, unable to comprehend it.

Aisic faced Michael in the dark woods.

"Get out of here!" Aisic shouted, his eyes only flicking to Nathan's for a moment before returning to glare at Michael.

D-did Michael just attack me? But . . . why?

Nathan looked around, frozen in trepidation, watching Michael run in to strike down on Aisic. Aisic drew out his own sword, parried the first blow, and countered by slashing out.

"Michael, what are you doing?" Nathan called, feeling utterly helpless.

"Reveal your true form," Michael growled at Aisic as they disengaged and drew back.

Aisic's eyes widened. "Wait . . . how did you—"

Michael aligned his blade with Aisic's face and charged.

The two warriors went head to head before coming to a stand down as Aisic kept yelling, "Run, Nathan! Get out of here!"

Nathan winced at the sharpness of his protector's voice. He returned to his feet and ran through the trees, whimpering at being forced to leave his friends behind.

He ran until his chest burned, stopping when he heard a rumble behind him. Panting, he squinted up as a glowing form and a massive Melkai shot into the sky.

"Michael!" he called to no reply.

In the panic of everything, he'd lost the path and couldn't

make out any footprints in the darkness. "Dragon's breath!" he panted.

The dark forest appeared all the same no matter which direction he turned, and the further he climbed, the thicker and more confusing the brush became. Heading back down to find a safe place to wait out the night was his best option.

Sighing in exhaustion, he started down. "I need to find the river at the base . . . then I can get my bearings."

Perched on his shoulder, Taiba licked his ear reassuringly, no longer trembling.

Their fortune changed when he found a small cave in the side of the hill, overhung with trees. If he slept there, he would be well hidden. He went about setting his things down for the night, but found it difficult to doze off after what had happened to Michael.

"He just attacked me out of the blue like that . . . and Aisic saved me. But why was he repeating what that monster we first fought said? I don't even know what they wanted me to give to them . . . wait . . ."

He gasped as the memory of both encounters came together. He'd been frozen as the talking Melkai approached him, its glowing red eyes directed as his chest, one grasping hand raised toward him, just as Michael's had been. Nathan pulled down the collar of his coat and brought out the key, amazed that it still glistened in the near pitch-black darkness of the cave.

"Is . . . is this what the Melkai was looking for?"

Taiba shuddered, spun in a circle three times, and curled up to sleep.

CHAPTER 7

THE DRAGON

"Now that he's gone there will be no more distractions," Michael said in a low, rumbling voice.

Aisic bared his teeth. *Alright, time to reveal my true fangs then.*

He growled under his breath and let the Melkai trapped inside him take over. He slid his blade back into the scabbard on his back. The sword and scabbard straightened and began to transform: the wings of the cross guard grew, stretching out, and the blade of the sword inside the scabbard emerged as a giant scaly tail. Plates of hard skin came out from either side of him, covering his body. His head stretched up, and the handle of the sword expanded and engulfed it, forming the head of a dragon.

Michael's glowing eyes widened for a moment, but he raised his weapon and charged. He struck down, but Aisic's long dragon neck shot out and caught the sword in his maw, snarling as his eyes met with Michael's glowing gaze.

"Ah! So, this is your true form!" Michael laughed and tried to pull free, but his sword was wedged between Aisic's teeth.

Aisic's eyes narrowed, and with a flap of his massive wings, they both took off, hurtling through the trees and up into the night sky. Michael flew back in the wind, barely holding onto the hilt of his sword, the blade still caught in Aisic's mouth. Aisic continued to rise. From his upward path through the dark clouds, he swooped downward, and at full speed, he tucked his wings and plummeted back through the fog toward the hilltop. He set a course for the peak of the hills they had been climbing.

Michael's body came up as he continued to hold tightly to his sword's hilt, his armor still glowing a bright white. Aisic suddenly spread his wings in mid-drop, opening his mouth. The sword shot from it and Michael fell quickly to the ground along with it. As Aisic saw Michael fall through the trees of the hill's summit, he quickly called forth his flame.

Taking a big breath in, Aisic breathed a column of flame down on the hilltop. The fire spread through the trees, destroying everything in its path, the entire top of the hill becoming nothing but a ball of heat.

He stopped his attack and stared down as the flames devoured the trees and everything below him burned away.

Nothing could have survived that blast.

The light of the flames faded and slowly went out with a blowing wind. He stared down at the barren wasteland of dead trees and earth blackened with ash. At first, he couldn't see anything, but his keen eyes then widened in shock. The prince rose to his feet in the middle of the clearing, shrugging

off an ash-blackened tree trunk as though it weighed nothing.
No . . . How?

Michael stood tall in his still-glowing armor, appearing completely unharmed by Aisic's attack. He looked up at him with a satisfied grin. Aisic ground his teeth, furious that his fire hadn't even fazed this possessed human.

Swooping down again, he spread his wings and landed on the scorched earth with a loud thump. His head lowered as he roared at Michael, who was walking slowly around him toward his weapon. With a quick roll, Michael came to the place where his sword had landed after he had dropped it. He snatched it up and rose to his feet, clutching it tightly in one hand as Aisic lunged at him, fangs gnashing.

Using his other hand, Michael grabbed hold of Aisic's snout. With unimaginable strength from the Melkai that possessed him, he flipped Aisic onto his back and raised his sword to stab him in the throat. Aisic's long tail flew up and whipped at him, knocking Michael off balance just long enough for Aisic to roll back up onto his feet.

He spun, lashing out again with his tail. Michael quickly dropped his sword and caught his tail in mid-swing to hold him at bay. Aisic's eyes narrowed in anger. It was the first time he had seen this kind of strength in a human. He growled, pulling harder. Even when he had fought the man in person, he never demonstrated such might.

Screaming, Michael hauled his tail to one side and spun as Aisic was thrown skyward. He sailed back and spread his wings again to balance himself. Glaring down from the sky, Aisic watched as the prince picked up his sword from the dirt, and with a flourish, readied it to fight.

Aisic soared down again into an attack, his mouth

reaching. As he landed, Michael jumped onto his back, his sword driving into the thick scales on the back of his neck. Aisic roared in pain, but before the cut could get too deep, he swatted the prince to the dirt with the talon of one wing.

That was too close! I must retreat.

He swiftly turned back to meet Michael, exhausted and bleeding.

Michael came to his feet, laughing. Such a low rumbling voice emerging from such a small creature made it sound more Melkaiic than if it had come from any monster.

"Well, you're stronger than most of the Melkai I've fought before."

The prince's head cocked up. *"But you know I'm no ordinary Melkai, dear Scion."*

"Then what are you?"

Smirking, the Melkai possessing Michael said, *"You know what I am. After all, I've returned for the same reason you have!"*

He charged, sword raised to strike.

Aisic roared and let loose his flames once again, but the prince ran through them and stabbed forward. The sword scraped across the scales on Aisic's face, but Aisic quickly shot out one claw and caught it, lifting the weapon high as the prince came up with it.

I'm getting too wounded. I have to finish this now!

He lashed out with his tail, but the prince quickly pulled his sword free from Aisic's grip, and with a thrust, impaled the blade through the attacking appendage. Aisic yelped as pain shot right up his spine, but he ground his teeth and tried to ignore it. This wound wasn't fatal, and he now knew what he had to do.

Aisic raised his wings and flapped them down as hard as he could. Ash blew everywhere. He shot up, and with the sword still in his tail, the prince ascended with him. Aisic's wounds made it harder to fly, but he had to get rid of the Melkai before he killed him.

He flew higher as the prince again held tightly to the hilt of his sword, his body trailing behind Aisic's tail. Before the prince could try to climb up Aisic's massive body, Aisic stopped and spun, flicking out his tail in the same angle from which he had been stabbed. The sword dislodged, and like a shooting star, the prince's glowing, armored form flew across the sky, down toward the earth.

Aisic sighed in relief now that there was some distance between them, but he knew from his first attack that this tactic would not have killed the prince. He began to doubt that it would've even wounded him. If the Melkai could move from body to body, the only way to defeat him would be to help Nathan reseal the barrier to the Melkairen. If Nathan failed, nothing would be able to get in that monster's way.

At least he was safe for now.

Feeling suddenly faint, he flapped weakly and descended into the forest, his wings barely having the energy to support him. As he came to the trees, he slowly began transforming back into his human form. His tail shrunk back to become the blade, his wings reforming to become the cross guard, and as he dropped to the ground, the plates of his armored scales retracted back to become the scabbard.

He collapsed onto the dirt of the forest track next to his sword, exhausted and wounded from the fight and only able to guess at who or what would come across him next.

CHAPTER 8

THE MAN IN THE WOODS

Kendra's boot heel slid on the wet mud. Her leg kicked out, and she waved her arms to regain her balance. Instinctively, Laine reached out and caught hold of the girl's shoulder to steady her.

"Thanks," Kendra said as Laine let her go.

"The path is treacherous," Laine muttered and continued along the track. "Be more careful."

Having packed up their campsite early in the morning, Kendra sluggishly followed her through the upper parts of the forest. They circumvented the thick Kydian trees and made their way up a narrow ridge of dirt and thick roots.

They had been hiking for most of the morning now, and Laine could tell by Kendra's slowing pace that she was becoming exhausted, but Laine was determined to walk throughout the day. She was held up a full day in Kydia and needed to regain the ground she had lost.

From the ridge, they could see right down over the sharp banks of the forest, but the trees blocked everything in the far distance from view. Kendra dawdled slightly, appearing to be scanning their surroundings for a place to sit down while Laine's focus was straight ahead. Laine strode onward, and Kendra skipped to catch up with her.

"What you did back in Kydia was amazing!" Kendra said. "I mean, you had all of those huge men running for their lives and you didn't even need to attack them. It was incredible!"

Laine shrugged. "It was nothing."

"Nothing?" Kendra cried. "You had them tripping up over themselves trying to get away. Only moments before they were thinking that we weren't even a threat, and then bam! It was pretty amazing, Laine."

Laine smiled and nodded. "Yeah, I guess it was."

"The greatest thing about it is that you didn't even have to hurt anyone!" Kendra replied, turning back to the road.

Laine's smile became a frown. "What do you mean? Don't you think they deserved it?"

Kendra sighed. "Even so, if you had hurt them, I would have had to stay around and heal them."

Laine's eyes widened. "Why? They were going to attack us!"

"I know, I know." Kendra bit her lip to quash a remark, but then shook her head and said it anyway. "It's the healer's code."

"Healer's code?" Laine scrutinized the term. It left a bad taste in her mouth.

Kendra nodded. "It's a code that was created from the

old Kydian Tree Keeper philosophy. You see, all full-blooded Kydians love life, especially of the trees as Kydia itself used to be covered in them. But after the war, Kydians became the minority and these new people came to live here: foreign races that had no love for life as we did. That's why Kydia changed so much after the war."

Laine listened, not interrupting. All her history lessons had been made up of stories about the monarchy and past wars, but this sounded like actual, modern-day, cultural politics.

"Anyway, the Kydians who believed in this philosophy turned it into the healer's code to protect life. For instance, if you had to hurt those people, I would have had to make sure you didn't kill them, and if we were walking along and there was a wounded stranger in our path, I would have to help him. Does that make sense?"

Laine bit her fingernail, trying to decide whether or not to add her own views on the subject. It would be a long trip, and she didn't want to have an ongoing argument with the girl. Of course, the idea of helping people made sense, but it was naive to think that all people would be worthy of help. As Callahan had demonstrated, not all those in need of help deserved it.

"Helping a friend is one thing, but helping an enemy or even a stranger is another thing entirely."

"But that's the idea behind the code. Don't you see? We believe *all* life is equal, enemy or ally, it makes no difference." Kendra smiled and looked down. "It's dumb, I know."

"Different yes, but not dumb. Of course, it would depend on the circumstances," Laine said, trying not to sound too dismissive. "Now that I've heard that from you, I don't think

I would know what to do if I ran into a wounded stranger. I guess it would depend on the circumstances."

Laine turned her attention back to the road, noticing how narrow the ridge they were walking on was becoming. They had to walk single file just to get through. The path was not only narrow but slippery, the rain from the night before dampening the already muddy track.

"Be careful," Laine warned again, voice rising. "As I said before, the path is not to be trusted."

Kendra's eyes suddenly widened, and she cried out, "A bridge!" and ran past Laine, despite Laine's clear warning.

Arriving next to the bridge, she leaned against its outer railing and sighed in relief. As soon as Kendra's hand touched the wood, Laine noticed the muddy bank around it begin to shift.

"Don't stand there!" she shouted.

Kendra responded with a perplexed, raised-eyebrow expression. A single dirt clod fell from the side of the bank. Then with a lurch, the entire outer corner gave way underneath her. Kendra screamed and waved her arms to balance herself on the failing ground. Laine ran up to the bridge, reaching out her hand to catch her. She missed by an inch.

"Help!" Kendra screamed.

Laine's shocked eyes caught Kendra's for just a moment before the ground below Kendra separated from the hill in a mudslide. She hit the dirt on her butt and began rolling down the bank, behind the bushes and out of sight. Her screams faded as the falling earth from the slip vanished with her.

Laine ground her teeth, hand still outstretched. "Damn

it!" she hissed. She stood there, staring pensively down the bank's steep drop, still holding her breath. Then she whirled about and screamed in frustration, "Argh, you idiot!"

This was not part of her plan to find the key, in fact, this went completely against her plan; indeed, it tied her plan in a veritable knot.

"Going down to get her will waste even more of my time, and the hill doesn't go down for a while still!"

The stupid girl! I warned her twice to be careful!

Laine growled and looked at the links of the bridge's structure, now visible after the erosion. It still looked stable enough to cross. Throwing caution to the wind, she strode across the bridge. It led to a slope going up to the summit before going down again. She would have to go in an entire loop just to get back on the track again. Her feet pounded along the bridge in anger as she contemplated what she should do, whether it would matter to Kendra if she went back for her or not.

"Melkairen!" she cursed.

We've only known each other for a couple of days. I mean, what is she to me really?

She sighed. The girl was naive and clumsy and . . . well-meaning. Laine shook her head and blew out her cheeks, trying to revive the cold, hardened side of her that hadn't flinched when the knights had died. However, as she thought of Kendra's smile, her strawberry blonde hair that reminded her of her mother, she couldn't muster it.

No, she was a nice girl, and you promised to help her. You can't abandon her like this!

Although angry at the prospect of having to go find her, she still hoped that Kendra was alright after her fall. Laine had told Kendra when they left Kydia that if they ever got separated, she should head downhill where there was a river passing through the forest at its base. She'd assumed the separation would be because of a Melkai attack or Callahan, but she'd hoped they wouldn't have to use the rendezvous point.

If only there was a quicker way to find her, some way to get a bird's eye . . .

An idea dawned on her, and she removed her cloak to summon Terachiro. She flicked her arm, and her cloak flew up. Her giant bat glided down in its place, perching on the bridge railing, long talons gripping the wood, ready to do her bidding.

"Terachiro, go find the girl," she commanded, pointing in the direction Kendra had fallen.

Spreading its wings, Terachiro flew off, swooping between the large trees and out of sight.

Laine's shoulders lowered, and she continued walking. The bridge was a long dark old thing that looked like it had been there for a long time, and by the solidness with which it held her footfalls, she assumed that its wooden supports went deep into the damp soil. She strode across it, looking over the side to see if she could see anything through the trees, but the brush was too thick and blocked her view. A bird flew through the branches which averted her attention for just a moment as she arrived at the end of the bridge.

She turned back at a groaning sound ahead of her. The wooden railing blocked her view, but she heard it again: a low, husky moan of pain coming from deep within a man's throat. Apprehensive, she picked up her pace to a jog and saw there was a wounded man lying on the track.

You're kidding. What are the odds?

"Please . . . help me . . ." the man whispered as Laine came upon him.

Laine looked down at the man, analyzing his state. He had several nasty wounds up his body. If she was to find Kendra as quickly as possible, she couldn't waste time on this stranger. However, Kendra had been a stranger in need of her help when they had first met as well.

Is it because he's a man that I'm hesitating to help him?

Her jaw clenched in trepidation. Who knew how he got here? He could have been on the wrong end of a robbery, or maybe he was a robber who was incompetent or even turned on by his own crew. He could have done any number of crimes in his past—likely, or he could have been a hero who was on bad times—unlikely. Still, how much worse would she be if she just left him here to die? He was hurt and probably dying so there was no way he would have superiority over her in this situation, but . . . would he later?

Can I judge this person just because he's of the opposite sex? Am I that shallow?

The man stared up at her. He was about six-foot-four, and had auburn hair and golden brown eyes. He wore a torn white shirt that was covered in blood from his wounds and loose-fitting pants that were also soaked in blood. From the stains, she could see where the blows had been dealt: one was on his back, another on his neck, and there was a cut on his face, all of which looked shallow enough not to be fatal. Then she spotted a deeper gash on his lower leg, blood still seeping from it.

"How did you get like this?" Laine asked.

"I was set upon . . ." the stranger replied, "by a Melkai."

"And you survived?" She crossed her arms. "Highly unlikely."

"I managed to escape, fortunately."

"With those wounds, I doubt you could have gotten far."

His worst wound was on his left calf muscle which looked to have been run through. He couldn't have run away with it. Such an injury would have crippled him. The pool of blood was deeper than the others, and if the leg wasn't bound, he could possibly die of blood loss.

The man shrugged. "It must not have liked the taste of me. It didn't search for me for very long after I managed to get away."

Laine smirked at this and looked around for any sign of evidence that disproved his claim. "Well, there aren't any other tracks besides your own . . . which seem to have come out of nowhere."

"It dropped me from the trees. Do you see the sticks that fell around me?"

Laine nodded at the twigs and leaves scattered around him. "Checks out, I guess."

She knew from her first glance that it wouldn't take much to stop the bleeding and save his life, but she still hesitated. Something about him put her on edge, but she couldn't put her finger on what it was.

Kendra's words *All life is equal* sprang up in her head, and she winced.

Stupid girl with her stupid idealism.

"Alright, fine."

She quickly went to work, pulling a roll of gauze from inside her cloak, and knelt down to study his wound. She pulled up his pant leg, the material thickly caked with his dark blood. Tearing away the cuff, she went about cleaning and binding his wound. It wouldn't have been enough to allow it to heal completely, but it would stop him from bleeding to death.

The man's body twitched with laughter. "I was starting to think you weren't going to help me for a moment . . . but thank you."

"Well, if I hadn't lost my friend just before I came by you . . ." Her eyebrows knitted in frustration. "She's a healer, you see, and could have fixed you up like it had never happened."

And now you've held me up from getting to her.

"You have lost your friend, too? Well, that is unfortunate," he said in his gravelly voice, sounding amused. "I have also lost my retainer, the one I am to protect. We have a shared situation, you and I. Maybe we should help each other."

Laine smiled, amused. "I don't think so. I bet you can barely walk with that leg as it is."

"All the more reason," the man said. "Don't worry. With a tree branch, I'll be faster than you might think. Don't suppose you could find one around here?" he asked, looking at the thick branches on the trees all around them with a playful smile.

Laine couldn't help but find herself smiling also, but then shook her head. "How do I know you won't just slow me down?"

"We'll make up time by searching together," the man insisted. "You're helping me. Is it so strange that I'd want to return the favor?"

Laine's decision was beginning to sway even as she stood up to start walking again. "Even if you can walk, how would you even be able to recognize my friend?"

"How many people do you think travel this forest? I doubt two people would be too hard to find."

She turned back to the path hesitantly but still did not leave him.

"Please, let me return the favor," he insisted, his voice soft this time.

She ground her teeth but turned back to one of the large trees around them. She cast her blue-blade spell, using the glowing blade of her hand to snap off a thick branch. She tossed it toward the man.

"Fine. If you say you can walk, then walk!" Laine shouted.

Faster than she had expected, the man staggered to his feet, leaning on the branch.

"Ugh, all right, but once we find my friend, I'm leaving you. Got it?"

"I guess that's fair," the man said, walking to her side with the stick as a crutch and a smile on his face. "I'm Aisic by the way."

Laine took in his smile and returned it with a frown. "You better have good eyesight." She narrowed her eyes at him. "And if we find your friend before we find mine and then you leave me, I'm going to kill you for reneging on our deal. Got it?"

He nodded. "Got it."

"Laine," she replied grudgingly and strode ahead.

Aisic shrugged and started hobbling along after her. Laine didn't know why, but she felt safer traveling with him. Yet, with her abilities and his injury, she could only put it down to his size being useful as a deterrent to anyone they happened to cross paths with. Either that or it was the prospect of being alone again that he was truly saving her from.

She shook her head to rid the thought from her mind and continued, gradually slowing to a pace Aisic could more easily keep up with.

CHAPTER 9

REUNION

In his dream, everyone towered over him. He was being pulled along a tiled walkway by a tall man in a dark cloak. Finally, the man let him go and gestured for him to explore the Terratheist Castle. He knew the place well, but strangely it felt like it was his first time visiting. He found a beautiful courtyard filled with gardens that were clustered with the colors of different flowers.

The man was no longer with him. Instead, there stood a young man of about ten years.

"Who are you?" Nathan asked.

The older boy didn't reply. He followed him wherever he went in the garden, not opening his mouth once. However, there was something about his gait that wasn't threatening but careful. Nathan walked from the garden down the path to the lower courtyard. He still didn't know exactly where he was supposed to go, but the boy followed him like a shadow all the while.

The sound of his ragged cloak filled the air as he moved. He stopped and stared down at his bare feet until he heard the clatter of armor descending a staircase. He looked up. Standing in front of him was a group of large armored men. They looked to be soldiers, but in their broad plate armor, Nathan had never seen anyone so intimidating in all his life. He froze.

"What's this?" the man in front asked. "A homeless kid creeping into the castle is a punishable offense. What say you?"

Another man at his side murmured, "And now he won't move from our path, little delinquent."

Nathan couldn't move. Fear held him like a vice. He was only five years old and the soldiers' words landed as if on deaf ears. Suddenly, he was shoved by one of them. He fell to the stone path below him, skinning his elbow and making him cry out.

"Get out of here, kid!"

"Leave him be!"

He looked up then, his eyes widening upon seeing that the boy who had been following him was between him and the soldiers. It was the soldiers' turn to freeze. The boy didn't look frightened at all.

Why are they afraid of him?

"B-but your grace!"

"This is my father's guest and my new friend. You shall treat him with respect!" the boy yelled.

The soldiers knelt before him in a bow. "Please accept our apologies!"

The prince shooed them off with a wave of his hand, and the soldiers scurried off as quickly as they could. The older boy turned to him, and Nathan watched as he reached a hand out to help him up. "Nathan, right? You and I are friends from now on, okay?"

Nathan nodded at the prince, and he grinned wide. He took his hand, and the prince helped him up. "My name is Michael."

Nathan awoke when the morning sun shone brightly through his clenched eyelids. For a moment, he wondered where he was; the memory of his first meeting with Michael was so accurate in his dream that he thought he was still in the castle. But he was in a cave. He'd gone from having his oldest friend and a stranger who he had trusted with his life by his side to having no one at all.

Then Taiba climbed up his arm, reminding him that he wasn't ever completely alone.

The lizard glanced out the opening then back at Nathan, appearing to say: "Get up. It's morning!"

They tramped around the base of the forest hill. Nathan knew he would eventually arrive at the river bank where he could refill his waterskin. That he was now alone and basically lost in this place was absurd to him. The memory of what Michael had done, running from him and getting lost, made him grab his hair in frustration.

"Argh, this is all Michael's fault! I mean, what was he thinking?"

Taiba appeared to nod along with his lamentations as he walked.

He patted his friend resting on his shoulder and said, "It's okay, Taiba. We'll find them and then we can get out of

87

this place," more to console himself than Taiba.

He balled his other hand into a fist, refusing to let despair drown him, and looked up at the sun that shone through the trees. The land leveled out onto a mud track, and he was glad he now had a path to follow.

"At least it's a good day for walking." He shook his head. "I can't even lie to myself, can I? I mean, Melkairen, I don't even know the direction to Avatasc!" He put his arms out in an exaggerated plea. "Dragon's breath, what am I supposed to do?"

He suddenly heard screaming. A piece of dirt fell beside him, and before he knew what was happening, a girl fell from the trees above him and into his outstretched arms. He caught her, but the force sent him to his knees, the still-healing bruises on his ribs pulling under her weight. He opened his eyes to see the girl clutching him, her eyes wide with shock, as wide as Taiba's.

Speechless, Nathan looked up at the sky, wondering if more girls would come raining down from the heavens. The skies were clear so he returned his startled gaze to the girl he had caught. She had long strawberry blonde hair and a slim frame.

"Ow, wow!" she cursed. "Wait, where did you come from?"

Taiba cocked his head in confusion, looking like the girl had taken a thought from Taiba's head and given it words.

Nathan shook his head. "But I . . . but you . . . how?"

She laughed, and her smile was beautiful, her strawberry blonde hair reminding him of someone he once knew, though he couldn't quite put his finger on who.

He let her down and rose to his feet, helping her up onto

her own. "Um . . . are you okay?"

"Yeah," she replied uneasily, but then jumped to her feet and knocked herself on the head. "I'm fine." She leaned in his direction, looking surprised but happy, then exclaimed, "You saved me!"

Nathan scratched the back of his head and smiled. "Yeah, I guess I did, b-but where did you come from?"

The girl looked up through the trees that she had fallen from and pointed. "There was a bridge way up there that I was about to cross with my companion on our way to Terratheist. The ground I was standing on slipped away and I fell. I must have fallen from pretty high up. I'm amazed we can't even see it from down here!"

"I see, hah! So you came from above." He shook his head. "Yeah, I've lost my companions in this Melkairen-cursed forest as well."

"Do you know what direction they would be heading now?" the girl asked as Nathan turned and noticed that she had pretty amber eyes.

"No," he replied unsteadily. "I mean, yes, well, all I know is that I should head to the river and then, if I'm not mistaken, we can follow it back to the path to Avatasc."

He didn't know this but didn't want to look completely incompetent in front of her.

"That's great!" the girl cried, clasping her hands together.

"What do you mean?"

"We can go to the river together. That's where I said I would meet up with my partner before we got separated!" the girl said excitedly, but then calmed herself. "If that's okay with you?"

Nathan shrugged. "Sure. I mean, I've been told it's

dangerous in this forest. The red moon brings out creatures you wouldn't want to face alone." He smiled, thinking that he wouldn't be of any use even if the Melkai did come.

"Right, let's go!" the girl said, facing the direction Nathan had just come from.

"No, no, I'm pretty sure the river is at the base of the valley," he replied and gently turned her. "Besides, I just came from that way."

"Okay then, this way. Let's go!" she called again and began walking down the path.

Nathan let out a short, nervous laugh and ran to catch up with her. "By the way, my name is Nathan and this is Taiba."

"You have a lizard as a pet?" She stopped to stare at Taiba, brow rising as though just remembering something. "Oh, I forgot to tell you my name. I'm Kendra."

"Nice to meet you. It'll, ah, be a lot better traveling through the woods with some company." Nathan shook his head. "Ah, with you, I mean."

And even more so considering the company is not fighting amongst each other.

Kendra gave an enthusiastic nod. "Agreed. When we meet up with my friend, we can all travel together."

Nathan looked down. "That would have been nice, but didn't you say you were heading to Terratheist? As I said, me, my friend, and my protector are heading to Avatasc."

Kendra screwed up her nose. "Why would you want to go there?"

"We are on a mission to find something there." Nathan frowned in thought, face going red. "Or someone . . . I'm sorry."

Kendra shook her head, curls whipping from side to side. "But surely we can still travel together if you want."

"What do you mean?"

"Well, from what my new friend told me, this path leads in a loop up the hill which cuts off and goes back in the direction me and my partner were heading." She balled her hand into a fist in front of her. "I'm sure she'll come and get me, then we can travel together until we get back to the cutoff. How about it?"

Nathan smiled. "Sounds good, your partner, ah . . . ?"

"Her name is Laine." Kendra put her finger to her chin in thought. "Honestly, I don't know that much about her. She has pretty green eyes, like you . . . I mean . . ." She shook her head and blushed. "Anyway, I was talking for most of the time we were traveling together. What I do know about her is that she's a caller from Avatasc."

Nathan's eyes narrowed for a moment. "Oh, a caller you say?"

Would it be a smart idea if I say that I'm a caller also? We are from enemy countries, after all.

"Yeah, you don't have a problem with that, do you?" she asked.

Nathan shook his head. "No, I don't mind. May I ask where you are from? You don't take me as someone from Avatasc."

"No, I'm from Kydia," Kendra replied with what sounded like a smidgen of pride in her voice.

Nathan sighed. A mixed party would be easier to deal with, and as long as he didn't tell the truth about what he was or where he was from, they should get along easily enough. The two of them moved through the wilderness toward the river. While they talked, Nathan attempted to bend the truth when answering her questions so he wouldn't give away too much about his quest. It was easy to do, especially with how much Kendra talked.

"So, anyway," she said, concluding the story of how she wound up falling into his arms. "One thing you know, I'm being kicked out of an inn for stealing Callahan's money, the next I'm falling from a bridge and landing on you."

Nathan grinned. The afternoon had turned to evening by the time she had finished the whole tale. The girl loved to talk, but that was okay. He liked to listen.

"Well, that sounds like an exciting story."

"How did you end up breaking away from your friends?" she asked.

Now that she had told him her whole story, she seemed to think it was only common courtesy to ask for his. He had hoped she would just keep talking.

Nathan thought back, trying to find the vaguest way possible of telling her. "There was some danger . . . and my companion told me to flee. I, ah, just didn't think to look where I was going."

"A danger?" she asked, face filled with curiosity.

"Yeah . . ." Nathan looked down, trying to come up with something. If they were going to be traveling together, it would be easier if she knew the truth. And he wasn't sure he could bear lying to her for much longer. "Well . . . okay. Here's what happened."

However, he didn't have time to say anything before he heard her scream in delight.

"The river!"

Kendra ran out of an opening in the trees toward it.

Nathan rushed through the brush after her and halted, gazing about in wonder. It was evening, and the bright stars were out in the night sky. The lights in the sky reflected on the clear flowing water as Kendra stopped to take it in also. She looked beautiful standing there in the moonlight.

"Pretty," she said and turned to him.

He nodded in agreement, still staring at her. Taiba suddenly started shaking in his hood and Nathan frowned back at his interruption. Then, as though feeling what his companion felt, fear rose within him and his eyes returned to the river. Behind Kendra, something shifted under the surface of the water.

"Kendra, get away from the water!"

Quickly, he looked up at the sky. Now that they were no longer under the trees, he finally had a chance to look up without the trees blocking his vision. The moon was bright pink, a crescent of it glowing bloodred.

Taiba appeared from out of his hood, his small body trembling. The water moved. Kendra screamed as something black arose.

Two sharp horns connected to a slimy black surface that shone in the night. As it emerged onto the bank, it gave off the appearance of some kind of underwater bull. Its first half looked bovine and slick with water, where the second half had the long, finned, tail of a giant serpent, which was still sloshing about in the water. The creature was massive, and despite having no legs, moved swiftly on land.

He wished he had brought his speciation book for he wanted to see if this Melkai was recorded in it. He had never seen a water-based Melkai before, let alone one that could fight both in the water and on land.

Can this one speak, too?

Nathan knew there was no way he could defeat such a thing with just him and Taiba, even with his Melkai's poison. In order to survive, he was going to have to call something more powerful. After all his training with Morrow, he was sure he could pull off a pact with a second-circle Melkai, but he had been afraid to open a seam to the Melkairen ever since he had called forth Taiba.

"You have to focus," Morrow's old voice said in his memory. *"Feel the Melkairen and then pull it apart with your mind, just enough for a Melkai's spirit form to get out. After that, you have to create a pact with that Melkai, the only way you can do that is—"*

"Nathan, what are you doing? Get out of the way!" Kendra called, breaking his line of thought.

Nathan opened his eyes to see that the massive monster was now standing right in front of him. He jumped to the side as the Melkai's head came down, meaning to skewer him on one of its horns. As he leapt back, the horn instead stabbed into the earth. This allowed him just enough time to flee before it pulled itself free again.

Nathan ran toward Kendra and grabbed her by the hand, pulling her along the riverbank as fast as he could.

"What is . . . that thing?" she asked, breathing heavily as they ran.

Nathan tugged at her hand to keep up with him. "Melkai, second circle!"

"Whatever it is," Kendra called as she looked back over her shoulder, "it's catching up!"

Nathan turned back to see that it was on their tail. He pushed Kendra to one side and jumped to the other, falling to the sharp pebbles of the bank as the bull slid between them before skidding to a stop. Wincing from the impact of the fall, Nathan pushed himself up onto his feet.

He had to summon something now or they were both dead.

The Melkai slid about to face them, readying itself to charge again. Nathan staggered on the hard stones and placed his hand out in front of him, trying to feel the barrier to the Melkairen with his fingers. "Come on!" he pleaded, searching the air for a seam.

The bull Melkai charged at him. Then he felt it, what he had been looking for, a seam in the barrier. It felt like the air had become pages in a book. All he had to do was pull them apart.

"There!" he yelled, but then froze as the Melkai bowed its head. "Now I just have to . . ."

Nathan gasped. A sudden shame rose up in him as he realized his last thought was going to be that, after all of his lessons, he had forgotten the one crucial part of making a pact item: the item itself.

I don't have anything to create a pact item with!

Just as the Melkai was about to hit him, there was a deafening shriek. A giant shadow with huge black wings fell from the sky, its giant talons stabbing into the monster's wet back. The bull Melkai collapsed to the stones under the creature's weight, dead in seconds.

Nathan swallowed the lump in his throat, once again unable to move. The bat Melkai had killed the bull Melkai so quickly, despite its size and the speed that it had been charging. The giant bat's long talons must have pierced an organ; it was the only way it could have won so quickly. Of course, it was the talons that made him freeze up, imagining them slicing through his own body.

The bull breathed out its last breath. The bat raised its massive head, baring its fangs. Nathan's eyes widened in panic at the giant winged monster looming before him. If he couldn't defeat the first Melkai, he had no idea how he was supposed to fend off this thing.

Kendra then called, "Laine!" and ran over to the monster.

Nathan put his hand out to stop her, but then another girl skidded down the bank behind the giant bat. Recognition of the girl's name from Kendra's story came over him, and he just about collapsed in his relief. The girl was her friend, the caller from Avatasc, and the bat was her Melkai.

CHAPTER 10

ANOTHER CALLER

"Looks like we made it just in time," a husky voice said beside him.

Nathan turned with a start to see a familiar face. "Aisic!"

"How's it going?" Aisic asked, smiling down at him.

Nathan looked him up and down. He was using a branch as a crutch and had a scabbing cut on his neck.

Then he noticed someone was missing. "Hey, where's Michael?"

Aisic's smile faded, and he didn't reply. Instead, he turned back, and Nathan followed his gaze to see Kendra with the shorter girl. The bat morphed into a dark cloak, which settled around the girl's shoulders.

"That was perfect timing, Laine!" Kendra called.

"You're lucky I sent out Terachiro to search the surrounding area," the girl murmured, shoving her arms through the cloak's sleeves. "There's a good chance you two would have died if I hadn't."

Seeing this girl, someone who looked his age if not younger, transform a second-circle Melkai into a pact item made him feel ashamed that he hadn't yet made a pact with one. He frowned down in frustration.

He'd thought that summoning his first Melkai at such a young age had proved his talent, but in less than a minute, this girl had revealed him for the novice he was.

Her face was filled with an emotion that he couldn't quite read, confused and wary, but also like she recognized him from somewhere.

"You . . ." she said, her voice serious but soft as she gazed his way. "So, you're a caller too, aren't you?"

She must have seen me trying to breach a seam in the barrier.

Nathan froze, not because he was afraid, but for another reason that he couldn't quite pin down. Something about her voice perhaps, or maybe it was her hair, reminded him of something for a moment, but then the memory was gone.

"Who're you?"

Nathan swallowed loudly in the eerie silence. Kendra turned from Laine to Nathan and back again.

"Where's your pact item?" Laine demanded, as though seeing it would help her assess what threat he might pose.

Nathan stepped back. "I . . . I don't."

"You're a caller too?" Kendra asked.

He suddenly felt like he had lied to her by omission. Despite the intense stares coming his way, Nathan's gaze didn't leave Laine's.

Seeming to see the situation for the potential danger it presented, Aisic raised his hands and said, "Everyone, it's night. We should set up a campfire. You two find a good place, and Nathan and I will grab some more firewood. We will discuss this later."

Nathan studied Laine, wondering if she had any other pact items on her, until Aisic put a hand on his shoulder, breaking his concentration. Nathan turned with a start, but went with Aisic as he moved off to gather wood.

They moved under the shadow of the trees as Nathan's questions began to flow. "Aisic, what's going on? Who is this girl?"

"As you just saw, she's a caller," Aisic stated as he stood up, hooking a collection of broken branches under one arm. "But I think you can tell there's more to her than that, can't you? I suggest you don't tell her about your quest."

"Yeah, I figured that," Nathan replied, recalling her suspicious glare.

"What about her companion?" Aisic asked.

"She's nice." *And beautiful.* Nathan hurriedly ducked his head and picked up his own pile of dried sticks, which Taiba had crawled over to investigate.

As they walked back to the river bank, he noticed that Aisic was either limping or leaning his weight on the branch he was using as a crutch.

The fight! Michael!

"Wait, what happened to you . . . and where's Michael?"

Aisic's eyes remained on his wood. "I can't say."

"Please tell me. He's my best friend!" Nathan shouted.

Aisic just continued looking for firewood.

"Why can't you tell me?"

"It's complicated. Please, Nathan, listen to—"

"Just tell me if he's okay."

"I don't know, Nathan! I'm sorry, just hear me out." Aisic looked down. "We ran into a bit of trouble . . . a Melkai."

His grave tone told Nathan more than his words might have suggested.

"We got separated during the battle," Aisic continued. "I don't know where he is now. But at the moment, we need to focus on where we are. Judging by the Melkai you just ran into, we'll need to get out of this forest as soon as we can. It's too dangerous here."

Is he avoiding the subject or does he really not know what happened to him?

They made their way back to where the two girls had set up camp with a fire already blazing. They walked toward it, threw down their wood, then sat next to it, across from the two girls. Kendra smiled at him happily now that they were in a larger group, but her face twisted in concern as Aisic grunted uncomfortably as he lowered himself. Nathan's eyes shifted to Laine, who was staring daggers at him.

"This is Nathan," Kendra said, gesturing to him. "Nathan, this is Laine, my friend."

Nathan nodded. He would have been impressed that she had the courage to speak first if he hadn't spent most of the day listening to her talk. "This is Aisic, my protector."

"Your friend, ah . . . Aisic looks to be in bad shape," Kendra replied. "Is he okay?"

"He got attacked by a Melkai," Nathan replied.

"A Melkai? Like the one we saw here?" Kendra asked.

"Kendra." Laine's voice sounded demanding again. "Go over there and heal him."

"All right." Kendra nodded as she got up and went around the fire.

"And you, boy," Laine continued. "Come over here. Give her room to work."

Nathan rose to his feet, frowning at the way she called him *boy*. "My name's Nathan."

Laine said nothing in reply to this, and he walked around the fire to where Kendra had been sitting, trading places with her.

As he passed Kendra, their eyes met. "I didn't know you could summon," she whispered.

"Yeah . . . well, you didn't really give me the chance to tell you."

He sat down next to Laine, whose hunched shoulders showed she was still ready for a fight at any moment. Instead of paying her any mind, he watched as Kendra went to work mending Aisic. Her hands moved to his leg and began to glow green in the darkness.

"You did it wrong," Laine said, the light of the fire dancing along her intense features.

Nathan swiveled. "What do you mean?"

Laine rolled her eyes. "When creating your pact, you did it in the wrong order. That's why it took you too long." She snatched up a stick to give him an example. "The pact item must be used as a conduit through the Melkairen barrier to make the connection. It looked like you were trying to do it the other way around."

Nathan smiled and face-palmed. It was a novice mistake. "I know . . . you're right." He turned to look into the warm firelight. "Thank you for saving us."

"Just be careful," Laine replied and screwed up her face. "Otherwise, there'll be one less caller in the world."

Nathan nodded, pleased that the two of them had found common ground for a conversation. "I'll remember. It's just strange; I never had to use a pact item when I called forth

Taiba. I guess I forgot about it."

"Taiba?" Laine asked, suddenly on edge again.

"Oh, yeah!" he said as he raised a hand to his hood. "Come here, boy."

The quick little lizard crawled onto his hand and down his arm as its eyes searched the darkness for the girl in front of them.

Laine's shoulders lowered. "Oh, I see . . . a first-circle Melkai. That's a relief." She sighed, reaching up to stroke her cloak collar.

This action reminded Nathan of how he patted Taiba through his hood. The similarity between them made him smile. "You do that too, huh?"

Laine quickly lowered her hand. "What?"

Nathan stroked Taiba. "You know, reassure your Melkai like that. I personally find it's more for my sake than for his sometimes."

Laine's frown softened. "Oh . . . I suppose so."

In that alone, we are kindred spirits.

Laine peered closer at Taiba. "I could have easily mistaken him for a regular lizard, but I definitely sensed the presence of another Melkai somewhere. I just didn't think it would be one so weak."

Taiba was looking around in curiosity, mouth hanging open and tail wagging.

"I already know he's of the weakest circle." Nathan smiled. "I keep him around me for the company more than anything."

"You keep a Melkai as a pet?" Laine asked incredulously.

"Pet?" Nathan shook his head. "No, he's my friend. He's more useful than you might think."

Laine shook her head, smiling. "Well, now I can sleep tonight."

"Of course, why wouldn't—"

"Now that I know you aren't any kind of threat."

Nathan winced at her retort. "Wow."

Laine's brow furrowed. "What?"

"I mean, I've never been great at making friends. I never fit in with the noble-born dandies that made up my classmates or their cutthroat world. But I have a feeling you have the same problem for the complete opposite reason. How can you hope to get along with people if you treat strangers so coldly?"

Laine's lips pulled inward, and Nathan hoped she didn't take what he said as an insult.

Instead, she lowered her gaze to the flame guiltily. "You're not the first person to make that observation."

"Don't worry; you're better than most people I've met. There are a lot of vile people in the world."

"I hear you. I hope they don't bury you in Avatasc. I've heard that's where you're heading." She smiled back at him when he nodded. "But I've never thought of myself as one of them before. Kind of sheds new light on my world back home, I suppose."

Laying on the stones, Aisic looked over the flames of the campfire, seeing that the girl who had been acting so cold to him before looked to be talking more openly with Nathan. The boy had that talent about him: a friendliness that made people wish to let their walls down and open up to him.

"She's a noble, is she not?" Aisic asked as he looked back

at Kendra.

Kendra continued to focus on his leg. "Why do you think that?"

"The way she acts. The way she carries herself." Aisic noticed this about her even as she talked freely to his companion. "She must have wealthy parents."

"That's strange . . ."

"That I can tell her parents are rich?"

"No, not that." Kendra intoned, her head drawing back slightly from his leg. "I'm doing my best but there's not much of a wound here to heal."

Aisic laughed. "Well, Laine did bind it beforehand, and I've always been known to heal quickly."

"Yeah, but that's the thing. No one I've met has regenerated this fast during the mending process before." Kendra stopped her spell and the glow faded.

Aisic sat back up. He looked at his leg and moved it about to see if there was any pain. "Maybe you underestimate your own ability," he said.

Kendra still gave him a strange look, but then just shrugged off the subject. "Well, all I know about you is that you know Nathan somehow."

"I'm his protector," Aisic cut in.

"Right . . . but my real question is how you came across Laine."

Aisic sighed. "It's more like she came across me and decided to help me out. She seemed quite hesitant though, helping a stranger." His eyes shifted with a smirk.

Kendra tittered, deriving some meaning from this that he failed to discern. "If you think that's funny, Nathan literally caught me mid-fall, and, after we finally got to the river, a rogue Melkai showed up. It's been a very exciting day."

She continued to talk about her experiences and how they contrasted with her boring life in Kydia. All the while Aisic watched as the conversation between Nathan and Laine played out.

Although Nathan had tried to brush it off, the dismissive tone in Laine's voice when she said he wasn't a threat made a sudden anger rise in him. But then, with how he had frozen against the charging Melkai, he thought he shouldn't be surprised by her reaction.

He tried to recall exactly what Aisic had told him about callers. "I heard that the power to summon came from the bloodline of the Kairens."

Laine stared into the flame. "The Kairens were nearly wiped out during Ramannon's reign. That's why there are so few of us."

"The Kairens were nearly wiped out as well?" He frowned in thought. "Well, it was the bloodlines of both the Arions and Kairens which made him immortal, so it makes sense that he would try to wipe them both out so another like him couldn't be born."

"He tried to wipe out the Senadonians as well because only they had the foresight to see how his orders would affect everything. That's why they joined the fight against him in the end," Laine added, eyes going distant. "They knew only the Kairens could lock away the Melkai when the time of the barrier weakening came. Maybe that's why they left. After all, they were only trying to save the land from the Melkai invasion, and yet the Ramannon Empire ended up trying to eradicate them as well."

Morrow had taught him about the Senadonians. However, unlike when listening to the old man's lectures, Nathan was drawn in by her words. Even her speculations on the past were engaging. "I don't understand everything, Laine, but I can't help but feel that this is all connected."

Laine's gaze dropped to the ground but then rose to meet his. "Yeah . . . I have to say you do look familiar somehow. By chance, have you ever lived in Avatasc?"

Nathan nodded. "Yes, actually. Well, from what I've been told, I was born in Avatasc."

"But I assume you left?"

Nathan nodded, though he could barely remember it.

"When?"

Nathan frowned. "I honestly don't know. I was too young to remember, but the kin—" He stopped talking and corrected himself. "But everyone I know tells me that's where I originally came from."

Laine cupped her chin. "You don't say . . . Then I guess you were lucky. You must have left Avatasc just before the throne was usurped. You weren't around long enough to see it fall into squalor."

Nathan's eyebrows pulled inward at Laine's bitterness. "Why do you ask?"

Laine shrugged. "When I was younger, much younger, I knew a boy who you remind me of." She smiled. "We were friends, I think. I didn't have many friends back then. Still don't, really. But this boy used to always be by my side. We went everywhere together. Then one day he was gone. I always wondered what happened to him."

"And you say I look a lot like him?" Nathan smiled. "This

friend of yours?"

Laine nodded. "Of course, he was much younger than you are now."

"But so were you, from what you're saying." Nathan inclined his head. "Well, whether or not I am this boy you remember, I hope we can be good friends, too."

Laine waggled her head and flashed her own grin. "Perhaps. With how you handle your Melkai, I admit you're interesting for a caller, but we'll see."

Nathan's eyes locked with hers, but before he could say anything more, Aisic called, "Alright, you two, you'll need to get some sleep or you'll just be a burden for us tomorrow."

Nathan nodded and stood, noticing the troubled frown on Laine's face. *Was she enjoying our conversation that much?*

"I'll give you some pointers, boy," she called as he walked around the fire. "At least, enough to make sure you don't kill yourself or us before we part ways."

"As I said, my name's Nathan," he replied.

He caught Kendra's eyes as they traded placed and he averted his gaze before looking back. For once, Kendra didn't say anything, only giving him a wry smile.

He sat down next to Aisic. "What did you tell her?"

Aisic lay down and said, "Don't worry, you'll find out soon enough."

No more words were shared between them. He noticed that Aisic and Kendra were also unpacking their gear and preparing to go to sleep. He did the same. However, he tossed and turned under his blanket.

I really am a pretty pathetic caller. I should be more like Laine. In fact, when it comes to fighting in general, I need to get better!

Laine had broken the illusion that he was ahead of everyone else. Now *he* had to catch up.

CHAPTER 11

PARTING WAYS

There was something in the air the next day that put Laine in high spirits. Aisic had risen first and was at the water's edge before she had even opened her eyes. That he hadn't taken their stuff and fled was a good sign. The boy's lizard Melkai was sunbathing on a rock next to the river bank. She was still getting it through her head that the creature was a Melkai, let alone one loyal to a caller and not confined to a pact item.

The black remains of the fire had been kicked out, likely by Aisic, so they would avoid detection. She looked at Nathan. His green eyes and sandy blond hair reminded her of King Kissick, yet his friendly nature was the polar opposite of the cruel tyrant. He yawned, stretching with his arms in the air before getting up and walking over to Aisic.

She grunted, disgusted that she would allow herself to have her mind changed so easily by the boy, if even for a moment. Nathan was naive to be so kind without power.

Anyone could take advantage of him or betray him. Of course, when she achieved her goal of gaining the key to the Melkairen, maybe then she would have enough power to let down her guard. These two had seen her Melkai and Nathan's reaction to it showed she would have an upper hand in a fight. Now she just needed to be careful with what she said about the keys.

Laine woke Kendra, and they spoke of what they needed to do next. "We'll have to follow the track up so we can go back the way we came."

Kendra nodded. "I promise I won't fall off this time."

"Be sure you don't." She smiled in the direction of the two by the river. "What about them?"

"Well, we are heading in the same direction." Kendra bobbed her head from side to side. "I thought we could travel together for a while. I mean, we'll be separating at the cutoff anyway, right?"

Laine sighed. "I suppose so. I also want more time to talk to this young caller. I did promise to teach him, after all."

Kendra continued talking, but Laine phased her out, focusing on Nathan and Aisic's lips to make out what they were saying.

"Laine said she would tutor me," Nathan said.

Aisic looked over his shoulder at her. "She's a dangerous girl so be careful with what you say around her."

At least the big one knows not to mess with me.

He was cut off as Kendra called out, "You two! We're leaving, and you're coming with us!"

They muttered something that Laine couldn't see, shrugged, and walked toward them. Together, the four of them set off. Kendra began filling the silence with her amazing ability to talk about nothing for long periods of time before Laine finally decided to interrupt her, eager to converse with Nathan on their shared vocation.

"Alright, Nathan, show me what you already know."

Laine remembered how hard it was for her to learn to summon. The pressure put upon her by her teacher had driven her to tears more than once. If she wasn't so determined to gain a semblance of the power Kissick had, she never would have pulled through. Rushing had done her more harm mentally than good, and she knew she would have to be patient with Nathan so he didn't turn out the same.

"Okay." Nathan nodded and stretched out his arm. "I put forth a pact item and try to find the barrier to the Melkairen. Then I find the seam and . . ." He looked at his hand.

He had a scabbing wound on his palm. Laine assumed he must have cut himself when diving onto the rocks to avoid the bull Melkai. It must not have hurt too badly since he hadn't noticed it until the sun had come up, but she winced seeing it.

"Hmm, how did that happen?" he murmured.

"Would you like me to heal that?" Kendra asked, sounding concerned.

Nathan shook his head, feeling heat creep up his face. "No—uh—it's only a scratch. It's healing easily enough by itself."

"Are you sure?" Kendra's tone grew concerned. "Even a cut like that can get infected."

He waved her off. "I'm fine."

Laine took one of her leather gloves off and handed it to him. "Here. It won't heal it like Kendra can, but if you're going to be stubborn about it, it will at least take your mind off it while we talk."

"Thanks," Nathan said, sliding it on.

Laine picked up from where Nathan stopped. "Once you find a seam to the Melkairen, you should be able to breach it. Make a hole only big enough to stick your pact item in. From that point on it's all a matter of will. A Melkai with desires similar to your own should unite their spirit with your pact item. Afterward, you pull it out and then the seam will close."

Not that there's no risk to this whole process.

She clutched her cloak, Terachiro's pact item. If the monster hadn't had the same desire for power as her, its spirit form wouldn't have been drawn to her, but once it had gained its true form and saw she was just a small girl, it must have been unimpressed. It had lashed out at her with its claws. While one had raked at her, she had used her blue-blade to cut the talons from the other, revealing to Terachiro that she was much more than she appeared. It had then wrapped itself around her. At first, Laine cried out in fear, thinking it was going to finish her off, but it instead bonded with her cloak, becoming her pact item. She still had the scars on her back from where it had slashed her. Now it was her most trusted companion.

"The pact item acts as a conduit from the Melkairen to your mind, that's why the Melkai only transforms at your demand. In the end, your will determines what circle the Melkai is from. Obviously, you would want the most powerful second-circle Melkai you could possibly get considering third-circle Mel—"

"Yeah, I know about third-circle Melkai." Nathan rolled

his eyes. "You can't control them because they are self-aware, right? It must be hard knowing you can't control a third-circle Melkai, even someone with your skill."

Laine grinned. "Not yet anyway."

Taiba suddenly came out of Nathan's hood and rested its head on his shoulder, facing Laine. Nathan didn't so much as flinch at the creature's close proximity. Laine shivered seeing it run wild while not in its pact item. Nathan treated his Melkai so familiarly. A human being on friendly terms with a Melkai was ridiculous, but something about them had rattled her walls. She had been taught that even first-circle Melkai were dangerous and couldn't be treated like pets, yet the defenseless way Nathan played with his Melkai, the childish smile on his face, even though he looked to be the same age as her, was in complete contradiction to her lessons. She didn't trust it.

The lizard seemed to whisper in Nathan's ear and Nathan frowned. "Sorry, what do you mean by that?" he asked.

Laine looked down and shook her head. "Oh, nothing."

She hoped she hadn't said too much about her own mission to these strangers. It needed to stay a secret, particularly from other callers like Nathan.

She bit her lower lip. "But, of course, you would want the most powerful Melkai possible. Melkai are *only* weapons to gain power, *nothing* else."

Nathan frowned at this and looked to Taiba, who closed its mouth and appeared to try and frown also, causing Nathan to smile again.

Laine rolled her eyes at this display of familiarity. "When people abuse that power, they create wars. That's obvious in the fact that calling created this conflict between the kingdoms in the first place."

Nathan patted Taiba, and it returned to his hood. "There's the treaty to consider."

She shook her head. He was naive to take such an agreement seriously. Kissick was hoping to take the land and everything with it and was willing to allow Melkai out of the Melkairen to achieve this. "The treaty will only last until one of them gains the upper hand. It's only a matter of time."

"Then I hope no one does."

She balled her hands into a fist, remembering that the very purpose of her mission was to gain such an advantage herself by finding the other half of the Kairen Key. "It's not that simple. There *needs* to be a power shift. My only hope is that the leadership shifts into more capable hands."

"And who would you say those more capable hands belong to?" Nathan asked. "You?"

"I don't know. I guess anyone who wouldn't abuse their power."

Preferably a woman.

Nathan stuck out his bottom lip and looked up at Aisic. "What do you think?"

"The old order needs to return," Aisic said like it was the simplest thing in the world: a problem that had been solved centuries ago. "The monarchy was bred for leadership. That's why such positions should always go to someone of royal blood. So long as that system is in place, war will always be minimalized."

Laine smirked. "More inbred leadership then."

Aisic raised an eyebrow at her. "What was that?"

"If blood was all that mattered, royal marriages would always be between blood relatives. We tried that and look where it got us: a divided land. The true flaw in that system lies in who is chosen to be the heir. It's always the firstborn male, no matter how unworthy he might be."

Aisic nodded. "Indeed, it is a roll of the dice as it were. Yet where the failures can be catastrophic, the successes can lead to a thriving country and prosperity for all. You must admit that the sacrifice is worth it."

"Not if a more worthy heir is available!" Laine retorted.

All three of them looked at her, shocked by her serious though obvious answer. Laine waited for a response, but Aisic just smiled and raised his palms in a shrug.

Kendra shook her head. "Just make me queen! I'll sort 'em out, stop the war, set people to work, share the wealth, just like that!"

After the intense conversation they had been having, what she said sounded so logical in theory that they all just laughed at her.

They walked on through the warm day with Kendra talking about what she would do if she was queen. When Kendra ran out of steam, however, Laine returned to giving Nathan pointers until Kendra got bored.

"You're going to Avatasc, right?" she asked.

Nathan nodded. "That's right."

Laine pursed her lips. "Well, if you're heading there, don't expect to be treated like a welcomed guest. King Kissick will do anything he can from taxing to thievery to extract whatever wealth you have on you. Being a visitor, you'll be lucky to leave with a single coin left on you."

Laine paused, realizing that she was warning him despite not knowing why they were heading there.

Do I really want to know?

She wasn't going to share her goal of saving her mother by disempowering her stepfather, and she *definitely* wasn't going to tell them that her plan to achieve this was by acquiring the key to the realm of monsters to overtake his kingdom. There was a good chance a fellow caller like Nathan would disapprove of such plans.

Aisic spoke up from the silence she left. "Thanks for the warning, but we're not expecting a warm welcome."

"Why are you going there?" Kendra asked. "Didn't you say you were looking for something?"

"No, uh, yes. That item, that . . ." Nathan stuttered and quickly corrected himself. "A pact item, to be particular. One that would be the best for a caller like me, you see."

Kendra stuck out her lower lip. "Why go to Avatasc for that?"

"Leave him alone, Kendra," Laine cut in. "They have their own reasons to keep their journey a secret, just as we do."

"We do?" She turned to her in puzzlement. "Well, I just thought that if we knew, we might be able to help them."

"You don't have to worry about that!" Nathan blurted out. "Ah, we're from Garland after all!"

There was silence for a while after this outburst, but Kendra then started to let out short breaths through her teeth, trying to hold in her laughter. Everyone knew Garland was the town that created and enforced the peace treaty and did everything they could to remain neutral.

"A caller . . . from Garland?" Kendra shook her head. "That doesn't seem very likely, but it does make sense considering you don't know much about how it works."

Nathan shrugged, trying not to look put out. "I guess."

"But what about you?" she asked Aisic. "He doesn't seem to be from Garland. His skin is too tanned."

Laine shook her head. "Kendra, what is it that you want to hear? That one of them is from Terratheist, and then what, we discover that we could be enemies?"

Kendra crossed her arms in a sulk. "Alright, I guess I see what you mean."

Nathan laughed nervously. "You don't have to worry. We're harmless."

"With you heading to Avatasc, that's actually what I'm afraid of." Laine smiled at them, feeling like she had smiled more today than any other. "In any case, I don't think you are our enemies."

"Especially if you're from *Garland*," Kendra laughed.

Before they knew it, the cutoff in the path stood before them, and upon seeing it, the laughter subsided. Kendra looked absolutely devastated to say goodbye, and Laine found herself locking a neutral face into place, as though she were before the king. It was silly. These people weren't going to punish her just for being sad to see them go.

"Well, I guess this is it," Nathan said, sounding dismayed.

"Yeah. Maybe . . . if it is meant to be . . . we might travel together again someday." Taking a steadying breath, Laine forced out, "I really hope so."

Nathan smiled and nodded. "Until then."

"Maybe on the way back," Kendra said excitedly. "Until then!"

"Until then," Laine and Aisic echoed.

She turned off in the other direction, and Kendra followed her. The two of them were silent for a while.

"That Nathan was kind of cute, don't you think?" Kendra

finally spoke up.

Laine shrugged. "I thought you would be more into the older ones like Aisic."

"I don't know. Aisic was really strange." Kendra's voice rose in pitch, sounding like something had just sprung to mind. "When I was healing him last night, he healed faster than any other person I've helped before. It was like he didn't even have a wound when I first started."

Laine frowned. "What do you mean? His leg looked to have been run through when I came across him."

"That's what I mean!" Kendra said. "It looked to have been badly impaled, sure, but like it had also been stitched up over a month or two ago. It didn't make any sense."

Laine's brow furrowed and she stopped.

Maybe he's got a magic propensity for healing himself. It doesn't mean anything, does it?

"What's wrong?" Kendra asked, looking concerned.

Laine stared back, a sudden suspicion dawning on her. She had heard of Melkai with accelerated healing abilities, but not humans. Before her theories could go down that rabbit hole, she shook her head and forced them from her mind. Even if her suspicions were correct, she doubted they would ever see them again.

"No, it's nothing," she said, shaking her head as they continued through the woods.

"It shouldn't be too long now," Nathan said, smiling as they continued along the path.

"We're just about there," Aisic agreed. "Avatasc . . ."

"That's when the real trouble will begin." Nathan sighed.

"Have you ever been there before?"

Aisic nodded. "I lived there for a while."

"Is it a good place?"

Aisic smirked. "Let's just say I didn't get a very good send-off."

"What happened?" he asked.

Aisic shook his head. "It's a story for another time." He took in a heavy breath, shouldered his sword, and shook his head. "We should be ready."

"I hope we see those two again . . ." Nathan looked down, trying to change the subject once again. ". . . and I hope Michael is alright."

"I'm sure he'll be fine." Aisic frowned. "He's . . . a strong man."

Nathan nodded, feeling somber now that it was just the two of them. He looked down at his hands, and with a start, realized he was still wearing Laine's glove. He had forgotten all about it. It was too late to run back and return it to her now.

Who knows? As Kendra said, we might see each other on the way back.

He gazed up at the moon, a constant omen of the encroaching threat. A quarter of it was now completely red. Although the threat of unleashed Melkai was terrifying, after what Laine had told him about Avatasc, Nathan was more concerned about acquiring the Kairen Key. He had run into two Melkai, both of which had nearly killed him, and yet he was more anxious about trying to haggle, squeeze, or threaten the information out of the Avatasc nobles than about dealing with any monster. Heck, without Michael as their envoy, they would have more of a chance trying to infiltrate the castle than talking their way in. He supposed that if he was confronted by a Melkai rather than a gang, he would at least get to see another interesting creature.

Dragon's breath, I must be the only one in the world who can find a silver lining to being murdered.

"Aisic, could you teach me how to fight?"

Aisic eyed him over his shoulder. "With your body structure, I'm afraid you'll never be a great warrior, Nathan."

Nathan looked down, nodding solemnly.

Aisic grinned and spun about. "But I suppose I could show you a few moves that would work for you. After all, I taught Amberley how to fight."

"Who's Amberley?"

Aisic sighed and shook his head again. "Story for another time, Nathan. First, I'll teach you how to disarm your opponent. No point in learning anything to do with hand-to-hand combat if your opponent's just going to bring a knife to a fistfight."

Nathan stopped in his tracks. "Go on. Show me."

"Alright then." Aisic faced him and put his hands up. "Pretend you've got a knife. Okay, now, try to stab me with it."

Nathan put his hand up and charged, thrusting the imaginary knife at him. The next second he was on his back, staring up at the ominously red reminder of his mission once again.

"How did you do that?" he wheezed.

Aisic helped him to his feet. "Simple. I watched your feet. Look."

Aisic showed him how his body moved when he attacked and how he could read the movement to counter effectively.

He proceeded to instruct Nathan on several other common attacks and suggested ways someone his size could defend himself. Nathan listened intently for over an hour before they continued on their path. Even then, he continued asking questions, forcing Aisic to stop and give him another demonstration.

They eventually decided to leave it until nightfall to practice so as not to slow their journey any further. Nathan went about learning from Aisic the basics of the basics of self-defense. As Aisic had said, he would never be the greatest warrior, but Nathan was determined that, should the need arise, he wouldn't be completely useless in violent situations either.

Although he knew the one thing which could make him more useful in those situations was the rare ability to call a Melkai, the danger forced that option to the back of his mind. After all, the last time he had tried summoning a second-circle he had nearly been skewered to his bed by the monster's massive horn. Learning self-defense with Aisic may have gained him little, but it was still far better than risking everything for only a potential reward.

CHAPTER 12

SUCCESSION

The ceremonial bells of the Terratheist cathedral rang out as soon as the great city gates began to open, as was the custom when welcoming home returning royalty. The massive doors parted slowly, and when they revealed enough of a gap for him to enter, the prince strode between them into the long city street.

This would be the last time he would see the entire city while under this king's reign, and he wanted to keep the memory so he could make a comparison later on.

It was not in the perfect state he would have wanted: not orderly enough to either defend or attack as a force. The people instead were separated in different buildings, not acting for the good of the kingdom, but for their own selfish desires.

The setting sun romantically portrayed the shift in power he was here to enact, and in turn, the next morning it would symbolize it even further—especially when his plans for an ideal kingdom were made real. It was, after all, originally his own.

His teeth ground together in his mouth, not used to that of a human body after years upon years of having to spiritually jump to creatures with great fangs, not these tiny pathetic pebbles. His gloved hands, however, were remarkable: giant things yet so responsive.

"What's he doing here?" he heard in a murmur from one of the open windows.

He knew this would be a moment in history: the first time the king's throne would be taken in force by a blood heir. Of course, the prince knew the implications of his actions—the power shift and the wars that were to come. It would lead to broken loyalties, and those disloyal to him would all die.

The wide strides of his brisk steps were sure as he made his way down the road, dozens of eyes following him as he went. The large buildings that towered over either side of him were full of murmuring people now. The word 'prince' seemed to be every second word. The autumn colored tiles under his feet echoed every time his clinking boots met with the cobblestones, climbing the long stairs into the inner streets of the city.

The people that crowded this section of the township parted as he walked through the middle of them, turning to him in their wonder and confusion at his return.

"Sire, you've returned," one said. There was a pause as though he was expecting a response. He frowned. "Did you succeed in your quest?"

The prince screwed up his face in disgust and continued on to his destination: the castle.

It came into view before him as he made his way toward the keep. The nobles avoided his path like sparrows around a hawk, yet more people parting as he walked past the wooden and brick houses.

He passed under the archway of the inner wall and stalked through the courtyard as the crowd detached from him. The clustered gardens came into view, the obnoxiously bright colors of the flowers agitating his mind. He would not let them distract him.

Finally, he came to the large black-doored entrance to the corridor which led to the castle tower. With little effort, the doors swung open before him, and he powered on through, his steps dulling on the carpet, guards silent and turning to one another in puzzlement as he passed them down the corridor without a word. More doors opened, and he came into the heavy draped throne room. He moved to the middle of it and knelt on the throw rug, as per tradition, hungrily anticipating what was to come next.

"Michael, why have you returned? I told you to protect Nathan."

The old king's question was heard on deaf ears and went without reply.

"Michael . . . ?"

"Father, I have found another way," his low voice now rumbled.

The prince stood from his bow and quickly made his way up the stairs onto the dais. In three swift steps, he drew out the sword from his scabbard and raised it.

The old king pulled back in his large chair. "Son, what? No!"

Guards moved from their stations at the doors, but they

would not make it in time, not until he would be king and their loyalties would turn like a change in the winds. They would either follow or die.

The prince's smile widened in glee. "This is my kingdom once again!"

He slashed down on the old king, the blade cutting through the king's collarbone. Blood ran from the old man's body, and as the prince drew back his blade, a piece of the throne broke off also.

The king choked on his blood and went silent as the prince wiped the blood from his sword on the man's silk robes. He grabbed the old corpse by the back of its head and then threw it down the dais stairs. It rolled down onto the bloodred carpet.

The prince breathed in heavily, the guards halting quickly behind him. He turned and sat down on the throne, his eyes opening to see the two quivering men at either side of the room who didn't appear to know what to do.

He gestured to the body before him. "Remove this from my sight. Your king demands it."

His first command as king was swiftly carried out.

CHAPTER 13

AVATASC

Over the last three days of their journey, Nathan had practiced what Aisic called "the most versatile self-defense and disarming moves," figuring that he might need them if they were confronted on their way to the castle. Going over the hand movements step-by-step, Aisic taught him several attacks and counters, but, although the theory of others made sense to him, Nathan felt that only two of them would work with his lighter-than-average body weight. He still hoped he wouldn't have to use them. Even so, it was reassuring that he'd know what to do if the situation arose.

At some point on the fourth day, they came to the outskirts of Avatasc. It was difficult to tell the exact time of the day as the sun was blocked by the thick overcast clouds, dimming the vast farmland. The pastures rolled out along the hills which led toward the Avatasc Castle.

There had once been a glorious kingdom here, but it looked like someone had taken an oil painting of it and thrown a bucket of water on the canvas, leaving it a dreary and damp mess.

Nathan and Aisic walked down the dry carriage track between the wooden cottages belonging to the worn-out farming peasants of the impoverished outer kingdom. Aisic's gaze scanned the ragged community. His eyes met with Nathan's, whose idea of this kingdom and warm expression had changed since leaving the shadows of the trees. Kendra's reaction when told where they were heading now made sense, and Nathan was worried that this state of desolation had been going on for a while.

The place was a mess. There was not enough life or crops to sustain the people. Soldiers for a war that wasn't even happening patrolled the fields, sucking away at the city's resources, becoming stronger for a *potential* war while everyone else was withering away. The thin cows and pigs were tended by thinner farmers. Even just with their packs, the two of them looked like foreign dignitaries.

"We're too visible," Aisic said. "We need robes."

Nathan pointed to a wooden stand on the side of the road. "Maybe we can get some information there."

As they walked over, the slumped man behind the stand looked at them warily, his draped hair hanging over the sides of his face. "What do you want?" he asked.

"Robes, we need robes," Nathan said as he dug into the pack Morrow had given him and brought out half a dozen gold coins that had been stuffed inside the pouch.

The man looked at the coins in shock. It seemed he hadn't seen so much money on a traveler in years. "Ah . . . here. I don't have anything fancy, only a spare of mine and—" He took out a brown ragged material.

"Don't worry," Aisic said. "We just need to fit in."

They took the garments and put them on, Nathan giving the man the money. The man handled the coins in amazement before his eyes shifted to the nearest soldiers and they vanished from sight.

So that's how it is here. Wealth attracts notice from soldiers.

"Thank you . . . do . . . do you need anything else?" the merchant asked.

Aisic smiled, putting his hood up before grabbing two of the apples from the stand and throwing one to Nathan. "No, but thank you."

As Nathan pulled up his own hood, Taiba went to his usual place inside it, and Nathan gave him the command to remain hidden. Even though he looked like a normal lizard, he was still conspicuous. Now that they were under the disguise of robes similar to that which the other peasants in the market wore, they fit in a lot better. The robes were of the same rough sack-like material but worked well for their intended purpose.

Nathan nodded to Aisic, and they made their way toward the densely populated area of the outer walls. Once they reached the inner market, Nathan surveyed the surrounding structures.

The outer walls of the city were made of cracked boulders and mortar. It circled the vast area around the castle perimeter. However, one couldn't walk a dozen meters without finding crumbling gaps and gaping holes in it. Despite the attention given to the men, the outer wall of the city was crumbling. King Kissick clearly had an offensive strategy in mind for the next war.

Nathan and Aisic looked out from under their hoods at

the soldiers they passed. Two were abusing people wherever they went. As one of them began to trash the food stand of a peasant merchant, Nathan noticed Aisic's eyes narrowing in on the situation.

Two of the fatter soldiers Nathan had seen were stealing food from a stall, and upon hearing complaints, began beating and destroying everything the man owned. Although Aisic would have been big enough to take out these soldiers, Nathan knew he had to stay inconspicuous as they searched for the key-half.

Finding the item to save the lands was much more important than blowing their cover to protect some stranger, as hard as it was for Nathan to admit.

"Stay calm," Nathan pleaded, grabbing Aisic by the cuff of his robe. "Hold all your anger in until we get into the castle. Then you can beat up as many guards as you want. I'll need you to take them out so I can approach the royal family. If this thing will help strengthen the barrier which the Kairens created, and the Kairens are linked to the royalty of both kingdoms as you said, it's only natural that they would leave such a talisman to a descendant of their own bloodline. If we managed to break in, get the king alone, and ask him where it is, he might give it up willingly, and if not, well, I'm sure you could persuade him."

The idea of torturing the information of the key's location out of such a tyrant appeared to appease Aisic.

As they left the market and entered into the wealthier districts, their peasant robes no longer conformed with the finer wear of those who were now walking around them. "We'll have to take the back streets and take these off before we enter the castle. We can't have anyone recognize us in what we're wearing now."

They both turned into a dark alley between two of the stalls and another wooden villa and briskly made their way down the backs of the houses to the inner walls.

The castle loomed over them, dark and oppressive. Nathan shivered at its contrast with the splendor of the Terratheist Castle, exacerbated by the overcast clouds that its highest towers parted like a wave of soot.

The clouds started to spit with rain. The muddy cobbles led up a slight incline as they approached the back of the city where the castle resided. As the higher ground led from concrete steps up onto the courtyard, they were forced to climb.

They traveled carefully up the slippery boulders to the top of the highland, scaling the wall to the outer gardens of the courtyard. When they got close enough to the top to see the overgrowing vines hanging over the stone fence, they could also see an armored guard doing his rounds across the pathway. There were no sudden movements in his actions, so they could tell he hadn't spotted them yet. As they saw him, Aisic stopped Nathan and put a finger to his lips, signaling for Nathan to keep silent.

Nathan nodded, and Aisic climbed on ahead until he was hidden behind the stone wall. Then, just as the guard turned his back to continue on his watch, Aisic vaulted the barricade, and with quick precision, snuck up behind him and slammed his forearm into the man's neck. The guard crumpled to the tiled floor with little more than a grunt.

Aisic waved for Nathan to catch up. Nathan climbed up the rest of the boulders to the wall and jumped over the vines, landing in the overgrown garden path.

Nathan looked down at the knocked-out soldier. "Nice work. He's . . . ah, not dead, is he?"

"No, he is just unconscious." Aisic smiled, bottom lip protruding in his lucky victory. "Managed to get him right under the jaw. A perfect knockout hit if I do say so myself. Quick, before his partner comes back."

They hauled the guard over to the thick vines of the barricade so no one would find him. It was clear that Aisic was some kind of warrior. However, only now did Nathan realize that his first assumption that he only hunted Melkai did not give him his fair due. Seeing how he had acted in the town, what he had taught him in the forest, and how quickly he had taken out the warrior, Nathan was beginning to see him more as a jack-of-all-trades fighting mercenary.

Nathan brushed himself down of the dust he had collected from the climb.

"Well then, let's keep going." Aisic clapped his hands, and they moved through the courtyard pathway toward the castle entry.

"There will be more guards behind those doors, won't there?"

Aisic inclined his head slowly. They passed the gardens and came to the large black doors that led into the castle corridors.

"If my assumption about this place is correct, no one should notice us inside because they wouldn't expect anyone to get past the sentry. Just try to act casual." Aisic touched the hilt of his sword. "And if I'm wrong, I'll handle it."

Nathan grinned.

Aisic pushed open the heavy wooden doors. They entered a green-carpeted corridor without either guard at the walls asking for their information. Aisic had been right; no one came after them.

Nathan marveled at the huge interior of the Avatasc Castle. The giant pillars led to a high ceiling, the green and gold carpet padded their boots underneath, and the more they explored the maze of hallways, the more corridors continued to branch off in different directions. However, there was always the same pattern of gold snakes on the walls, even on the frame of every painting. He could see clearly that this was the symbol of King Kissick.

Nathan had grown up in a castle and so was used to lavish adornments and elaborate tapestries along the halls, but even he didn't feel like he belonged here. It was probably because they were *acting* like intruders, peeking around corners and creeping down halls. If the king knew they were there, no doubt they would be hunted down and beheaded for his entertainment.

Armored guards appeared more frequently as they moved further in. Despite trying to act casual, Nathan must have looked nervous for one of them turned toward them.

"Hey you!" the guard called as they came to another corridor.

Suddenly Aisic was no longer by his side, and the guard was striding toward him. From his confused expression, Nathan thought he must be wondering why some dirty stranger in traveler's garbs was inside the castle. However, while focusing on him, a flaming torch on the side of the wall went out, leaving the hallway in darkness. Rushing up behind the guard in the shadows, Aisic put the guard into a tight headlock to stop his screams. Realizing he was stuck and couldn't call for help, the guard drew a dagger. Nathan ran forward and swiftly disarmed the guard, using a level of finesse he hadn't realized he possessed until now.

Aisic's training has really paid off.

Slowly, his frantic waving and kicking stopped as the lack of oxygen knocked him out cold. Aisic let him go, and the guard sunk to the floor. He caught Nathan's eyes and nodded to him. This time, instead of going straight ahead, they decided to walk through the darkened hallway.

"We're not getting anywhere sneaking around like this," Aisic hissed.

Nathan jogged to catch up with his swift pace as they reached the end of another corridor. "Don't worry. I think I know where I'm going."

A girl ran into him at a corner where two passages met. There was a short squeal from her, and they both tumbled to the ground. Nathan rubbed his forehead as he felt himself being quickly pulled to his feet by Aisic.

The person he had run into was some kind of handmaiden. She looked up at him, looking ready to apologize, but then froze when she saw his face. "Why, you're the one from her majesty's pictures!"

"Pardon?" Before he could even get his balance back, he heard a curse of a distantly familiar voice.

"How dare you run into the queen's handmaid and not apologize!" a woman's low voice said, sounding like she was at the end of her patience. Then she gasped.

As he looked up at the woman who had yelled at him, he took in her great white and red gown and tumbling strawberry blonde hair. She was beautiful for her age, but she also looked drawn. The woman covered her mouth as their eyes met for the first time.

"It can't be . . . can it really be you, Nathaniel?" she asked, stepping back a few paces and looking like she was about to faint.

Nathaniel? No one has ever called me Nathaniel . . . have they?

"Queen Medea." The handmaid got to her own feet now and rushed over to the queen.

Aisic grabbed him harshly. "We must go!"

"No, wait!" the queen called. She steadied herself, walked over to one of the rooms at the side of the hallway, and opened the two large doors. "Please, this way. Hurry!"

Aisic looked at her in confusion. Nathan still felt dazed, but not only from his crash. The tone of the woman's voice was familiar to him, as well as her appearance.

"Who are you?" Aisic asked.

"I know you have no reason to trust me, but there's no time to explain here."

Aisic's gaze shifted to Nathan. "It's your call."

Nathan hesitated a moment, weighing their odds of following this unarmed woman and her handmaid against being found by a dozen armed men, then nodded. "We have little choice."

"Please, this way." She beckoned them into the room. "Hurry!"

They both rushed into the room. She briskly followed after, closing the doors behind her. They entered a nicely furnished lounge full of plush chairs with white frills and even a fireplace in one of the white-walled corners.

The queen moved past them and went to one of the back walls toward a candle holder on the fire's banister. She grabbed hold of it, pulled, and twisted. It came loose with a clink, and there was a sudden rumble. The fireplace then came free at one edge. She walked over to the edge of its mantle and pushed it open. It slid into the wall like a door.

A secret passage!

"Follow me if you want answers!" the queen said and entered into the shadows, disappearing from sight.

Nathan and Aisic nodded to each other. Nathan entered into the space behind the fireplace. There was a rock staircase leading down, deep into the castle's foundation. The secret passage was well lit, and, as they made their way down the narrow flight of stairs, their footfalls left echoes in the stagnant air. A short way down the stairs, they came to a dungeon-like room with a heavy bolted door.

The handmaiden unlocked and opened the door before rushing past them and back up the stairs to guard the entrance. They shuffled into the room, not lit by candle nor torch, but sunlight which shone down from a basement window. The queen gestured to the table, and they all sat down on the wall seats. She then turned to the shelves on the stone walls.

"This is where the hidden documents of the Armalon and Avatasc history lie," she said and pulled out a crested scroll. "The king had all of the copies of this scroll burned when he usurped the throne, but I managed to save this one copy."

"If you're the queen of Avatasc . . . why are you helping us?" Nathan asked in suspicion, puzzled as he studied the focus in the queen's beautiful eyes.

She didn't reply, only unrolled the scroll on top of the desk and placed a loose brick from the wall on each corner so it wouldn't roll back up again. The writing on the scroll was small and faded, but the light from the basement window shone down on it so it could be read.

Aisic looked at the writing on the scroll in confusion. "A family tree, huh?"

"The Armalon family tree," she clarified.

Aisic's eyes widened as he quickly leaned over the table to study it also. "Melkairen, it is! Look up the top, Armalon the First and his two sons, Ramannon and Armalon the Second." He ran his finger down the parchment. "And there's Cullen Armalon, Armalon the Fourth!"

Nathan continued to stare as Aisic announced each Armalon's title, connecting the two houses of Armalon and Kimberling as the queen continued to gaze at Nathan.

"Armalon the Eighth, Ninth, and his brother Kissick, second to the throne." Aisic hesitated, looking up at the queen. "You're sure you want him to know?"

The queen nodded gravely. "Please, read on."

Nathan turned back to the scroll and pointed. "But here, it says that the last in line was Owen Armalon."

"And below him . . . it's not very clear, but it states that he had two offspring before the throne was usurped," the queen continued desperately. "Look!"

Her finger came to the end of the scroll, pointing to the faded scripture at the bottom which led from Owen Armalon's courtship line. There, at the base of the family tree were two names. Nathan gasped, and his hands began to shake.

It read: Nathaniel Armalon—Laine Armalon.

He gasped and stared more closely at the script. *Wait . . . what? Laine!*

"Long ago there was a lasting peace between our

kingdoms," the queen said. "It was proven by dividing the ownership of the Kairen Key, one half of which you now hold."

Aisic's eyes grew wide like he'd just had some kind of internal epiphany.

That's why I have one half of the Kairen Key, which means . . . Laine has the other.

"No, no, it can't be. I'm Nathan, not Nathaniel!" Nathan exclaimed, stepping back in shock. "I'm not anyone important . . ."

The queen advanced on him and hooked her finger under his chain necklace, pulling it out from under his collar. "This proves you are."

"But . . . if I'm the son of Owen Armalon and Laine is his daughter then . . . we're siblings . . . my sister! And if you're the queen . . . then you must be . . ."

The queen nodded, tears building in her eyes. "I'm your mother, Nathaniel. I'm so sorry . . . I had to marry him to protect your sister. He would have killed her!"

He took a deep breath and looked at the woman again. Back when he was a child, the King of Terratheist had once shown him a portrait of his mother as she had looked as a young woman. The king had kept it in his secret gallery and finally brought him there to show him after he and Michael had climbed through a window in order to get in. Although much had changed, the strawberry blonde hair was the same as it was in the painting.

Nathan looked to Aisic for confirmation. The man's face had grown solemn again, sympathetic almost. He recalled his loyalty, his dedication to protecting him on his way here and began to wonder.

"Did you know?" Nathan asked him.

Aisic inclined his head. "I sensed in you magic similar to one I've wielded in the past. The object which possessed it was also forged and passed down by the Kairens, so I felt sure that you descended from that lineage. Now I know that it was the key I was sensing."

His shoulders slumped. He was the rightful king of Avatasc.

"My father?" he asked.

"Kissick had him poisoned before he usurped the throne." Her happy tears became sad. "He began his reign just after you were sent to live in Terratheist."

The king . . . took everything from me.

"Does Laine know . . . about me?"

His mother covered her mouth. "I intended to tell Laine all this when she was older, but as time passed . . . Eventually, the king forbade me from talking to her." She wiped a tear from her cheek. "After every conversation she had with the king, she became so cold and distant, even when the maid snuck us out to talk in secret. And . . . and now . . . he's sent her away to . . ."

Kissick had killed his father, had manipulated his mother and his sister, and now was using her to get the Kairen Key.

And I've brought the other half right to him . . . I have to end this before he gets his hands on them!

"Laine must have arrived in Terratheist by now and learned what you have about the key." His mother closed her eyes in contemplation. "But at the same time, using them to seal the barrier would be almost pointless so long as someone as powerful as Kissick is still planning to use them to begin his war."

Nathan stood. "The moon hasn't turned completely red yet, which means we still have time. Therefore, my immediate priority should be to deal with Kissick first and then return to Terratheist to find Laine when things are set right here."

"No, Kissick is far too dangerous to face alone. With his Melkai, you'll simply be walking to your deaths. Listen, many knights still remain loyal to me," the queen said. "They will help you regain the throne if need be. They will fight for you."

"A rebellion?" Nathan ground his teeth. "No, that will lead to too many casualties. I will do this on my own."

"I won't allow that." Aisic stood. "I'm your protector, after all. I'm sworn to fight for you."

Nathan's brow furrowed. "Alright then . . . but after what he did to my father, I want to hear his confession from his own lips. I must confront him."

CHAPTER 14

THE SNAKE KING

Nathan had been freezing in tough situations all his life. From when he had first met the prince, to being confronted by bullies, to being attacked by the second-circle Melkai, it was all the same. He would become paralyzed and detach himself from reality, leaving his body behind to deal with the threat.

Not this time. He had the blood of kings in him and knew he had to kill this part of himself if he was ever to become who he was meant to be.

"I'll be back soon," he said to his mother.

Aisic followed him as he made his way out of the hidden room. He strode through the secret passage and out of the cavity left by the fireplace. Focused on the task at hand, he walked through the doorway of the furnished room and down the corridor toward the throne room. Nothing was going to stop him from taking back his father's throne.

"Nathan, I must warn you now," Aisic said as they moved

briskly down the green throw rug. "If the situation comes to it, if the circumstances become too dire during this fight, I may have to change."

"What do you mean *change?*" Nathan asked.

"I can't explain it to you," Aisic replied. "But if I happen to change at any time during this fight, you must not panic. Be sure to remember that it's still me and that my vow to protect you still holds true. Accept what I am, and I will continue to be your protector, no matter what form I take."

Nathan didn't know what to make of what he was saying, but nodded in agreement. He trusted Aisic.

Guards appeared in the hallway ahead of them, pointing and drawing weapons. "It's them, the intruders!"

"Crap," Aisic muttered. "Stay close!"

He drew his sword from the scabbard on his back and raised it in a fighting stance. Nathan looked at the glove on his left hand that he now knew belonged to his sister. He was going to clear the path for her, too.

Aisic ran toward the first guard and struck down at him. The armored man fell, and Aisic parried an oncoming blow, forcing his next opponent's blade down and back-fisting him in the nose. The man fell to the green throw rug; spots of red sprinkled across it. Nathan strode ahead, not having enough physical bulk to take care of the lackeys, and so, just left them to Aisic.

As soon as any of the guards came across his path, Aisic swooped in to take them out. Nathan wondered if he could take out any of the soldiers himself with the moves Aisic had taught him. He wanted to help, to show Aisic that his lessons hadn't gone to waste. However, as he moved to assist him, Aisic growled at him and waved him toward the doors.

He then spun and slashed at another striking sword before countering and moving to the next one. Nathan didn't pause, and Aisic continued to remove guards from his path until they finally reached the throne room.

Aisic took out one final guard with an elbow before kicking him to the floor. Nathan rushed to the ironwood doors and heaved them open. They both walked inside the incredibly and immensely massive hall. On his throne atop a high dais, Kissick glared down at them.

Nathan studied the man. He was slim with a hooked nose and a thin smile. It was strange to see that the man who had been the most destructive keystone in his entire life also shared his green eyes. It also sickened Nathan that he shared the same lineage as this man, showing clearly that blood wasn't everything.

"Warriors from afar, welcome." Kissick laughed. He was holding a green scepter at his side.

Nathan knew it was no ordinary scepter because as soon as Taiba spotted it and sniffed the air, he began to tremble.

"It appears my chancellor is absent," Kissick continued, "so if you would be so kind, please introduce yourselves."

Nathan halted on the green throw rug, noticing the large statues of golden snakes that hung above his dais. "My name is Nathaniel Armalon! I have come to take back my father's throne, my birthright!"

Kissick's eyes widened. "A son? I could have sworn I ordered my brother's only son killed. Where have you been hiding all this time?"

"I have not been hiding!" Nathan bristled at the accusation. "I was handed over to the King of Terratheist as a child. My father was the one who created the treaty with

Terratheist, and now you're the one undermining it!"

Kissick smiled. "Your father didn't have enough ambition to be a true king. With the help of the other lords, it wasn't hard to claim his throne."

"At what cost? Have you not stepped outside and smelled the corruption?" Nathan's jaw clenched. "If I have to take your place to fix things, so be—"

Kissick raised a hand. "I can't see why you're so certain, nephew. Your allies are so few. Whereas mine . . ."

A dozen personal knights revealed themselves from the shadows of the hall, coming from behind pillars and doors and even the very dais Kissick sat upon. These ones were different from the guards outside, larger and wearing high quality plate.

Aisic moved to Nathan's side in a low fighting stance. "I can't fight all of them without changing," he whispered. "I'm sorry you have to see this. Just remember what I told you."

Nathan nodded. "Do what you have to do."

Aisic grinned and rose from his fighting stance, sliding his sword back into the scabbard on his back. Nathan was about to ask what he was doing, when suddenly the scabbard began to move on its own. It straightened on his back and then broke apart.

The guards hesitated, watching as the scabbard pieces covered his skin like giant scales. The blade stretched out like a long tail, extending from his growing body. The hilt, which was shaped like a pair of wings, stretched out on Aisic's back. They spread and grew, wrapping around him.

The hilt of the sword appeared to open up and swallow his head, revealing its growing shape as the wings spread out. Aisic and his sword had somehow combined to become a massive dragon.

"A dragon?" Kissick's voice sounded like he didn't believe what he was seeing.

Aisic roared.

Kissick's soldiers either began to flee or run screaming at Aisic with their swords drawn. Aisic made quick work of the knights that advanced on him, slashing them with claws, biting at them, his tail swatting at those behind as they slammed into to the walls and doors, some hitting the very dais the king sat atop.

When he was finished and the rest of the knights had fled, Aisic, the dragon, opened his wings and roared before peering around to see if there were any more challengers. Besides the king, Nathan, and the ones left unconscious around him, there were no more people in the room.

Nathan's whole body shook. Aisic had told him that he and Michael had run into a Melkai in the forest after they had separated. Was he the Melkai? Did he just want to separate him from Michael? Had Michael known this and that's why he tried to attack him?

If Aisic had wanted to, he could have transformed and killed him at any time, yet he had remained to protect him. Even now, he was revealing himself for what he really was in order to help him fight Kissick. Did they somehow make a pact without realizing it, or was it something deeper still?

Nathan calmed himself. He couldn't let this distract him—not now. Aisic had asked if he trusted him, and he did. That's all that mattered. It was as his protector had said: the dragon was still Aisic.

Kissick arose from his throne, still clutching his scepter. "I see."

Nathan and Aisic both turned to glare at the king as he stood above them, his face no longer under the shadow of the parapets. He was Nathan's dark uncle, just like Ramannon had been to the Armalons of the past.

"I admit it, you have a powerful ally. Well . . . that's good." He still sounded amused, or more likely, in denial of his defeat. He raised his green scepter horizontally up in front of him, his eyes peering over the length of it. "Let your hope of victory rise so that I may crush it!"

"Give up!" Nathan yelled.

The scepter in the king's hand began to transform.

"They call me the Snake King, but let me introduce you to the true King of Snakes!"

The scepter grew in both length and size, and Nathan now saw what he hadn't noticed before: the snake head at the end of it. He could feel a sudden presence, like a weight on his shoulders. Just as Taiba had warned him, the staff wasn't just the king's walking stick; it was his pact item.

"Come out and play, Serraba," the king hissed.

With a sudden wave, the scepter grew exponentially, swelling and changing in texture, until its final form was revealed: a giant viper.

CHAPTER 15

THE KING'S FOLLY

Nathan now knew why King Kissick was called the Snake King. His serpent Melkai was large enough to make that clear, taking up nearly a quarter of the hall.

Nathan watched in horror as the thing continued to grow in size, its head rising toward the high ceiling, its forked tongue hissing out of its mouth. Nathan shook his head, trying to control his fear. It made sense to him that Kissick would have the blood of the Kairens in him, but he had never seen or even heard of a Melkai being this big in his entire life.

However, after studying its shape, Nathan nearly rolled his eyes at it. Despite being extremely large and horrible, Serraba wasn't impressive at all, at least by Nathan's standards. He had run into bears with ram's horns, aquatic bulls, and a giant, cloak-like bat with talons the size of swords, yet Kissick's second-circle Melkai was just a snake. Terrifying as it may be, it was so boring in comparison to a dragon, and strangely, this thought alone conquered his fear of it.

Aisic ground his teeth, raised his wings and flapped them down twice, lifting himself into the air. Thanks to the absurdly high ceiling of the wide throne room, he flew about the massive hall with ease.

The king smiled and raised an arm to one side. The snake, Serraba, drew back and struck toward the dragon, easily able to cover the distance in one strike. Aisic swooped to the side, evading the strike, and released his flame upon the mighty beast. His fire streaked the scales black, however, without warning, he was struck by the snake's thick tail and flew back.

As his protector fought the giant Melkai, Nathan advanced on Kissick, digging around in his rucksack for his knife, the same one he used to stab the first Melkai. He bit the inside of his cheek, hard and tasted blood, determined not to freeze again. While Kissick and Serraba were focusing on Aisic, Taiba crawled out from under his hood. His lizard friend flashed onto his forearm, and Nathan brought him around to face him.

"You want to fight, too?" Nathan asked.

The lizard, dog-like, let his tongue fall from his mouth with a tiny sound. Nathan set the fast little Melkai on the floor, and Taiba crawled from him and up one of the walls, making his way to the ceiling. Nathan then pulled free his blade from its sheath and ran at the king.

A loud thump his only warning, one of Aisic's massive claws snatched him up and threw him to the side as Serraba's giant head launched itself, jaws wide, past where he had just been. Nathan landed on his side but quickly rolled onto his feet. Aisic flew overhead, spreading flame over the massive thing's scaly skin. It was no more than a light scorching to the viper.

Nathan dodged to the side with another dive roll as the snake's tail struck at him. The king laughed from above them while he watched the fight. Nathan grabbed the dagger, which had fallen from his grip, jumped over the giant tail of the snake, and ran toward the dais, meaning to kill Kissick where he stood.

"Nathan, watch out!"

He turned to see the snake was right on his tail, its sole intention appearing to be to kill him before he reached its master. The great head of the viper shot forward and Nathan winced as the giant fanged mouth rushed at him. There was a loud crash, but nothing touched him. Nathan opened his eyes and saw that Aisic was holding back the massive Melkai. The viper's giant fang had pierced the thick scales on the dragon's leg.

"Aisic!" Nathan screamed.

Aisic looked back at him. He appeared to be in pain, but Nathan swore he saw the dragon wink at him. Aisic's head snapped back to the snake's head, and with a sudden intensity, his flames gushed out of his mouth, burning away half of the snake's face, blinding it on one side. The massive monster pulled back, flailing around and hissing furiously in pain, though now a very distorted hiss.

The dragon's body collapsed to the floor. Nathan ran toward him. The massive dragon lay unmoving.

"That's the same poison that killed your father," Kissick said as he walked down the dais toward him, his own gem-encrusted knife already drawn at his side. "It's slow-acting, but it paralyzes quickly so you can't do anything more to save yourself from it."

Nathan whirled on the king. The half-blinded snake rose up behind him. He was surrounded on both sides by monsters that wanted to kill him. Despite being paralyzed, he could still hear Aisic's voice in his head, telling him: *"Run away, now!"*

Although the large doors to the throne room were wide open behind him, he hadn't considered trying to escape. He wasn't going to run again.

"No," he said as the king drew nearer and the snake reared up behind. "Not this time!"

They both attacked at once. At the same time, Taiba dropped from the ceiling onto Serraba's face, causing its head to whip around, and Nathan grabbed the king's wrist just as he tried to stab him.

As the small lizard latched onto the giant snake, Nathan used the move he had seen Aisic use against the guards in the hall, one he had taught him on the road. He drew back the king's knife hand and elbowed him in the face just as Taiba jabbed his fangs into the snake's scales.

The king fell back, nose bleeding. Nathan rushed over and used one of the disarming moves Aisic had taught him. He grabbed Kissick's wrist with one hand and slammed the pommel of his knife into the king's knuckles, the strike forcing his wrist back and his hand open. The knife spun to the floor, and Nathan stabbed down on him. Kissick raised his hand to defend himself and Nathan's knife impaled his palm. The king cried out, hand dripping blood. Nathan wasn't finished. He swept down to pick up the gem-encrusted dagger, then stood over his uncle, ready to administer a killing blow. Before he could, however, his hands began to shake.

No! Not now!

He heard a screech and turned back to see Taiba flicked into the air and, with a quick snap of the snake's jaws, impaled on Serraba's top fang.

Nathan gasped as his Melkai, his friend since his childhood, writhed around for a moment before going limp on the viper's tooth. The giant snake swung its head around, and the small lizard flew off its fang, as though not even good enough to be eaten. Taiba landed, rolling to a stop on the green throw rug.

Forgetting about the cowering king beneath him, Nathan ran over to where the small creature lay, his red blood trailing in a line from the gaping wound in his chest. Nathan felt tears well up in his eyes and he sank to his knees before Taiba. He could barely remember a time when Taiba wasn't hiding away in his hood or crawling playfully along his body during sunny days.

"I . . . it can't . . ." He breathed heavily in despair, not wanting to touch him, afraid he wouldn't nudge him back like he always did. "Hey . . . Taiba . . . come on." He bit his lip at the tears that ran down his cheeks.

Ever since he had first summoned the Melkai when he was twelve years old, Taiba had acted like a second sense for him. His trembling warned him of danger, his reactions to his own emotions reminded him to calm down, and most of all, he made him feel like he was never completely alone. It wasn't until now that Taiba was gone that he realized just how much he had depended on his friend for that security, for his company.

Behind him, Kissick returned to his feet, cradling his wounded hand as his giant snake circled him. Serraba's one remaining eye following him. The king smiled at Nathan. As far as he was concerned, the fight was over. Nathan sniffed as the tears flowed freely, his friend was dead and it was his fault, he hadn't been strong enough. He still heard Aisic in his head, pleading with the last of his strength to run.

"Please, run!"

"No!" he screamed. "I've been running away all my life! I always freeze and escape reality, but not this time!"

Each time Nathan had been in trouble against something bigger than him, Taiba had stood before him, ready to pounce, despite the disparity in size. Now it was his turn to stand and face something bigger than himself. "I will not run!"

"Your Melkai are dead, boy. There's nothing you can do." King Kissick sneered as the snake now began to approach him to finish him off. "You should probably be trying to run away right now."

"I'm not going to run!" he screamed, getting to his feet. He held the king's knife out in front of him. "Not this time! You killed my father and now my best friend. I'm not going to let you get away with that, no matter what!"

The giant snake slithered toward him, but he had decided that he would not be killed today—particularly not by such a boring-looking Melkai or such a vile man. He clenched the dagger he'd stolen from Kissick, ready to take Serraba's remaining eye when, out of the corner of his eye, Nathan saw something glowing. He turned and stepped back in shock.

The hole where Taiba had been impaled was now shining like the light of the sun was coming from his wound. Nathan's mouth gaped as the glow spread over Taiba's small body.

What in the Melkairen is going on?

The light covered the entire shape of the lizard's form until he was nothing but light. Then the light began to grow, slowly morphing into a new shape. The form had four legs, a head with a long muzzle like a wolf, and a wild long mane like that of a male lion. His body stretched out on his hind legs as a tail uncoiled down behind him.

As the glow faded, the new form of his Melkai was revealed: a massive, maned canine.

Nathan suddenly remembered what Laine told him when they had traveled together. *"The pact item acts as a conduit from the Melkairen to your mind, that's why the Melkai only transforms at your demand. In the end, your will determines what circle the Melkai is from."*

"I didn't give up," Nathan uttered. "Unlike every other time when I froze, when I didn't give up, you came!"

Long snout, silver and red fur, large hind legs, and a long tail—he was beautiful and Nathan now finally understood why Taiba had acted more like a dog than an actual lizard.

"This is the real you?" Nathan asked.

Taiba lowered his head in confirmation.

The king's surprised expression slowly turned to a look of horror as he began to misunderstand what had just happened. "How? It's not possible! You're a child! This isn't a legend. This is real life. *That* can't be a third-circle Melkai!"

Nathan wiped the tears from his face and pulled back his shoulders. It wasn't over yet. He looked to Aisic who still lay there on the throne room rug. There was still time to save him.

"Go, Taiba!"

Taiba bolted forward. Kissick snapped out of his terror and ran back to his throne. Nathan chased after the king but halted as Taiba overtook him. Serraba may have been injured, but being much larger, it still had the advantage.

"Serraba!" Kissick called. "Defend me!"

The two Melkai closed the gap between each other.

As they met, the giant viper raised its head and launched itself toward Taiba. Taiba's canine form was about the same size as a full-grown man, but several times faster. He jumped as the snake slid underneath him. Taiba then ran along the scales of the snake's back as the large Melkai quickly coiled up again and turned to attack. Taiba swooped down under the coil he had created, moving quicker than he had as a lizard, his new body allowing for much greater speed.

The snake followed him, its head chasing as Taiba quickly changed his course, jumping onto its tail. Using nothing but gravity, the canine skidded down the thing's scales, running at full pace as the burned head of the snake continued to keep up, rushing at the smaller Melkai.

Taiba jumped off the snake's tail and landed on the dais, growling in challenge. As if in answer, Serraba whirled about and shot forward. Not being able to see right below itself because of its missing eye, it could also not see its master.

Serraba's mouth gaped open, but Taiba swiftly caught the king by the back of his furred collar and leapt down the stairs with him, depositing him below the dais.

"No, wait! Serrab—"

He was silenced as the jaws of the giant snake snapped close. There was a loud crash as the snake's head hit hard into the dais with the king still in its mouth, the giant podium crumbling down on top of it as the heavy throne fell from on high, landing on the snake's head and crushing it.

Serraba stopped moving. With that one heavy crash, the

snake's head had caved in and taken King Kissick with it. It was over.

CHAPTER 16

TAIBA

Taiba jumped down from the huge knot he had made of Serraba, padding over to where Nathan was still staring in amazement. The giant dog nuzzled into his hand as Nathan stroked his head.

This was the creature he had summoned when he was a child. Kissick was right. After all, there was no way that he, a mere child, could summon a third-circle Melkai.

Taiba *wasn't* a third-circle Melkai, nor was he a first-circle that transformed into a third-circle—even Nathan knew that much. His advantage, however, was that the king hadn't. Taiba was a second-circle Melkai. The only reason he looked like he had transformed was that the lizard wasn't actually his physical form.

A hazy memory returned to Nathan: how, when he had formed the pact while half asleep, he had grabbed hold of something crawling over him. The lizard had not been what he had gotten out of the Melkairen; the lizard was the pact item.

Using a living creature as a pact item gave a Melkai two chances in battle; one as its pact form and one as its Melkaiic form.

"That's right! Aisic!"

He spun to the crippled dragon. Although not as massive as the snake, his body took up a large area of the throw rug. Nathan searched for the wound, his hands finding the scaled skin as hard as an armored shell. He saw the wound on the dragon's hind leg and studied it closely. It was deep and there was blood running from it.

Aisic slowly began to shrink in size, the armored scales retreating over his skin, the wings and tail retracting. The sword and scabbard on his back went slack when the transformation ended. Nathan was left staring at the unconscious man in amazement.

He couldn't tell if his wound was fatal and wished that Kendra had been with them to heal it. However, now looking at him in his human form, the wound didn't look too deep. In fact, even as he looked at it, the wound appeared to be healing over.

Aisic let out a gasp, and his eyes flung open, his body arched up on the floor. Nathan jumped in fright, but then paused.

Aisic was laughing hard, his shoulders shaking. "I got you good."

Nathan gave him a worried smile. "But the poison . . ."

Aisic sat up on the back of his arms. "You saw yourself; I *am* a dragon. Phoenixes aren't the only Melkai with healing abilities."

This whole time Aisic hadn't been telling him the whole

truth about himself. Indeed, he had been lying by omission. "Why didn't you tell me you were a Melkai?"

Aisic nodded gravely. "I guess I have some explaining to do, but for now there are more important matters at hand . . . Your Majesty."

Nathan's eyes narrowed, mind struggling to comprehend what Aisic was saying in the post-battle exhaustion.

He took a step back as it dawned on him, turning to see that the throne now sat atop the massive viper's head. There couldn't have been a more fitting symbol for the beginning of his reign. If someone had told Nathan at the start of the day that he was to end it as a king, he would have laughed right in their face.

Now he was no longer just *Nathan*. He was King Nathaniel Armalon, the rightful ruler of Avatasc.

Taiba nuzzled his hand. Standing in the silent throne room, he heard Master Morrow's voice as though he was living his lessons for a second time.

"Most Melkai need a pact item. They need it as a physical attachment to this world. If a Melkai does not have one, it will soon become too weak and will be drawn back into the Melkairen."

Not wanting to lose Taiba now, he had to create another pact with him as soon as he could. He needed something to be used for the connection. Looking at the glove Laine had given him, he remembered how she had tutored him on how to use the pact item for his calling.

The glove itself was the perfect object for such a pact item.

Following his memories of her guidance, he placed the glove on Taiba's fur and willed his spirit into it. Aisic's gaze grew intense as the Melkai became his spirit form and then vanished into Nathan's glove. Nathan sighed in relief and beamed as he felt the connection with his second-circle Melkai through the material.

The pact had been successful.

No sooner had he tied off the last end of one conflict than did he hear the sound of running footfalls rushing down the corridor toward them. At first, both he and Aisic were seized with fear that they would have to fight in their state. However, as the soldiers entered the room, surrounding them in a circle, the one commanding them revealed herself.

His mother, Queen Medea, advanced and bent the knee before him. "The king is dead?"

Nathan nodded.

She bowed her head. "Long live the king."

The other soldiers followed her, bowing to him.

Nathan sighed, uncertain of how to feel about people bowing to him, but too exhausted to protest. "I still have to find my sister. Laine has the other key-half we need to seal the Melkairen."

His mother rose. "By now, Laine would have reached Terratheist, and knowing the Terratheist king, he will surely send her back here. We will send a messenger to make sure of this. It was a coincidence that you two ran into each other on your journeys, and we can't risk you two missing each other on the returning trip. What's more important is making sure Avatasc is stable for when she returns. For that, you will need to succeed Kissick and claim your right to the throne. With the many nobles lusting after the throne, it will be no easy task." She raised an eyebrow at him. "Luckily you have me to help you."

Nathan's jaw clenched as a new weight of responsibility fell upon him. "If you are sure that is the correct course, that is what I'll do. Have a messenger sent at once."

His mother smiled. "I already have."

Nathan gazed at her in surprise. "You were so sure I was going to win against Kissick?"

The once-queen put a hand on his shoulder. "Of course. You're your father's son, after all."

CHAPTER 17

TERRATHEIST

Terratheist was well known to be a vibrant city full of people searching the market for the best wares. It was for this reason that, when Laine and Kendra arrived, they were both so surprised. Where Laine was expecting a city alive with beauty and abundance, there was no one in the streets, there were no stands or stalls, and everything was in the shadow of overcast clouds. Instead of the laughter of children and the murmur of crowds, all she heard was the silent moan of the wind.

The reputation of the Terratheist capital had been one reason for Kendra joining her. The girl's disappointment now acted like a weight anchoring her to the tiles. Despite being separated and all of Kenda's slipups and sore feet, sharing her excitement of reaching the capital had kept them in high spirits. Laine was just glad most of the Melkai they had come across had been easily taken out by Terachiro, as putting her life on the line to get here would have only been further salt in the wound. As they plodded through the vacant streets, she frowned and peered down every alley they passed, looking like she was ready to chase down anyone they found.

It wasn't until they came to the cobblestone side streets that they saw a few women clad in hoods moving quickly away from them.

"What in the Melkairen is going on?" Kendra asked. "This place looks like a ghost town!"

Laine shook her head. There was only one reason she could think that the place would be so empty . . . but she didn't want to consider it a possibility.

They can't have all gone to war, could they?

It would have made sense of why she saw no men in the street and why the city, which was usually so lively, was so dim and depressing.

"I don't get it," she murmured. "If anyone was going to break the treaty, I was sure it would have been Kissick . . . but this—I never even considered it."

A shift of power: isn't this what I wanted?

"Are you sure it couldn't have been Melkai?" Kendra asked. "Maybe the barrier has already—"

"No," Laine interrupted her. "There's no destruction to the buildings, no bloodstains, just an eerie absence of people. They have been sent to the border of the Solvena Plains to fight."

Kendra's tone grew sad. "So . . . war then?"

Laine nodded, only now noticing there were shadows lurking around every corner, watching them. She knew what she had to do. She spotted an inn a little way down the road and pointed to it.

"This is where we part ways, Kendra. With what I will do next, I cannot have you involved."

"With what you'll do next?"

"Yes. We have come to a dangerous place. There's an inn down the street. Do you see it?"

Kendra frowned but nodded. "Please tell me why though." From her tone of voice, she knew it was futile to even ask.

"The money we kept should be enough to buy you food and lodging for at least a month." Laine turned to the shadows, which appeared to form from the alleys between houses. "I will come to see you again before the week is up. Just do as I say, okay?"

Kendra stuck out a bottom lip. "Okay, fine."

She walked into the inn with a wave. Laine sighed. Although somber at Kendra's departure, she was relieved that the girl wouldn't have to be involved with the dangers that were to come.

The dark soldiers came out from hiding. She gripped the collar of her hood, readying herself to summon Terachiro if the need arose. Yet the men were not drawing their swords.

"What do you want?" she asked.

"Summoner?" they asked, and although she could not see their lips move under their helmets, she got the impression that they had all said this at the exact same time.

She nodded.

"You must come with us to the castle," the soldiers again said in unison. "The king has requested your company."

It was strange to hear them all talk at once, like their speech and replies all came from one mouth.

"And if I refuse?" It didn't seem like even light could

escape the tight circle they had created around her.

Suddenly the tightly knit circle opened, the only opening pointing straight to the castle. "Your choice is yours to make."

She breathed out with a smile, seeing she had no choice in the matter, but decided it was of little concern. She would've had to go to the castle to find the key anyhow.

"To go to the castle is my own choice then," she said.

In unison, they said, "Indeed."

She started toward the castle, and they followed her up the path on either side of her to make sure she did not turn from their intended destination. They walked through the city streets in the overcast day, the castle looming over them. Laine raised her hood to keep her anonymity. She moved with the soldiers under the stone archway into the courtyard, suddenly feeling like she was being drafted into the war that was being reinitiated.

She gazed around in wonder as they climbed the stairs to the giant doorways of the castle entrance. The men on either side of her opened them up to reveal the red drapes that hung up around the torch-lit hallway. She lowered her head, feeling that the kingdoms could never be rejoined; they were like red and green: so far apart from each other in the spectrum that they could never go together. There was too much power for those in control, too much corruption, and that's why she knew Kissick's plan was unachievable.

They continued through the castle, her eyes shifting to all the gaps in the soldiers around her. She was sure that what she was looking for was here, or at least had been here before.

The hall was long and branched off down many different corridors, with stairs leading higher up into the castle tower. At the very center of the castle's base, which all of the corridors circled, was an opening: a second courtyard which led into the throne room. They made their way past the breathtaking gardens comprised of roses and other flowers of various colors.

Passing through another set of doors, they came into the throne room: a large hall full of red load-bearing beams. The sunlight appeared to invade the shadowed room, and the throne itself was empty. Strangely, it also looked like it had recently had a section of it carved away.

A young but large man with long blond hair stood alone high up on a platform next to the sun-streaked window. They came to a stop before the throne on the red throw rug, and the young king turned to them.

"Has my guest arrived?" his deep voice inquired.

"Yes, Your Majesty," the soldiers replied in sync. "As you said, the girl was a summoner."

Laine was confused by why they kept using that term. *Summoner* was such an old word used back in the times of the War of the Two Kings. Unless of the highest rank, the word used now was *caller*, but maybe Terratheist stuck to the old titles.

"I am Princess Laine Armalon of Avatasc, and yes, I am a summoner, as you put it. Why have you called me to your presence?"

She was determined not to be patronized as she had been by King Kissick. Pursing her lips, she studied the new king skeptically. He was a handsome young man and clearly new to the position, and Laine couldn't help but draw a connection between his appearance and the current state of the city. However, that also meant he might be persuadable.

"You look weary, Princess. Can I offer you something

to wash the road dust from your throat?" the young king enquired graciously.

"Cider, if you have it, and water if you don't." Laine was hesitant to accept anything stronger that would cloud her mind.

"Bring us water."

One of the guards moved off to get the drinks.

The handsome young king, who was fully armored for some prophetic reason, turned slowly and walked down from the platform when the drinks arrived. The guard handed them both goblets and silently returned to the shadowed recess.

"What brings you to Terratheist, Your Highness?" the king asked in a conversational tone. "Searching for something, or perhaps someone?"

Laine's brow furrowed. Not being the king's trueborn daughter, she was not used to the title, and it put her off guard. "H-how did you know that?" she asked more brusquely than she had intended.

"A guess. As the king, there's a good chance I know the person you are looking for." The king's eyes fell to the floor. "But I'm afraid you may have arrived too late to catch him."

"What do you mean?" Laine demanded. "Where have they gone?"

The young king took a sip from his goblet. "Avatasc, Your Highness."

Laine paused and shook her head. "That can't be . . . Why? Will he be returning soon?"

"I believe the Snake King has taken him prisoner, either that or he has turned him against us." The king walked toward her, his abnormally red eyes staring into hers. "You may not be so surprised when learning that this person was sent to Avatasc on the exact same quest as you."

Laine remembered the boy and the man they had run into in the forest, but shook her head again. "No, it couldn't be . . . but then, you think that the Snake King has taken him in? This doesn't make any . . ." She sighed in frustration, her drink forgotten.

"If your quest in coming here was to see him, I'm sorry to say, Your Highness, that your journey may have been in vain from the very beginning." The king shook his head sorrowfully.

She bit the inside of her cheek. Her instincts had told her that something had been off about those two, and the younger one had been a caller. It only made sense that the person who had the other key-half would be a caller like herself. Yet his naive friendliness had gotten the best of her, all while tricking her to let them pass.

She whirled to face the open window.

I'm such a fool!

"No, my mission was to get here, and as long as I'm here, my quest is still achievable."

"Your Highness?" The king turned. "What is your true reason for coming here?"

Laine breathed out heavily. "A power shift. My stepfather must be overthrown or Avatasc . . . the land in general . . . will never get better as long as someone like him is in power. I must defeat him!"

"Power shift, overthrow, conquest . . ." The young man's smile widened. "We have the same goals, you and I. If you fight for me, Your Highness, I will put my entire army behind you and give you this power shift you desire. I do not wish to control the lands. Far from it. But you are a princess. You deserve, by right, to take his kingdom." His red eyes appeared to glow slightly.

Laine met his gaze. "And you can promise this to me?"

The king bowed. "I can promise you this, Your Highness. But you must fight for me against all who oppose me. You must make that one vow in return. If you keep that vow, you will end up destroying what you hate, and in turn, fixing what you love."

What this young king doesn't realize is that if he picks a fight with Avatasc, he will surely lose.

"How do I know you can keep this promise?" She raised an eyebrow. "From what I have seen of this city, you don't have the numbers to come out as the victor."

The king nodded as she said this, waiting for her to finish. "First, Your Highness, show me what *you* can do."

Laine took off her hood and threw it up, summoning Terachiro from it in an instant. The large bat Melkai landed and stepped forward, grunting on the red throw rug.

From the king's grin, he appeared impressed by the size of her second-circle Melkai.

Laine then raised the edge of her hand, which began to glow bright blue from her blade spell.

He clapped. "Very good, very good."

"How impressed you are means little to me," she snapped. "I could command Terachiro to rip your head off right now if I wanted to. Any reason I shouldn't?"

The king walked around her, his smile respectful. "Our Master of Pacts has grown old and senile of late. I need fresh blood to invigorate those under him. How would you like to take his place and command the callers who remain here during the war? Surely, someone of Your Highness's experience could make good use of such power."

Laine took a sip of her water to give herself time to mull the idea over. After all, if the barrier did fall, the callers would be the most powerful force in the land to oppose the oncoming threat. "Why would they follow me? A stranger from an enemy kingdom."

"They will do as I command, and beyond that, you are one of rare talent here." He spread his hands. "I'm sure they would jump at the chance."

Laine smiled at the prospect of having others under her influence, but tried to hide it behind her goblet. Unlike his predecessor, this king seemed to have similar goals to her own. He was planning to go to war with her uncle and wanted her help in the battles to come. However, Kissick was more than ready to defend himself against and destroy any opposition. He had lavished his army with every resource they could need in preparation for such an event.

None of this will matter if we can't defeat him.

"Alright then, what are your plans for striking Avatasc? I need to know your army's strength and the strength of your court callers if I am to be of any assistance. I want to see your power and that of your own Melkai," Laine asked. She wondered what Melkai the king could control, if it was as grand as Kissick's Melkai, Serraba.

The young king began to walk back up onto the platform. "I don't have a Melkai to be summoned for proof. I do, however, have something else which may topple the power of any Melkai you bring before me. If you would be so kind as to join me at the window?"

Laine quickly followed the king up onto the platform,

Terachiro flying up the red stairs.

"As you can see, *my* army is ready to march as we speak. You may ask any questions you have of their numbers or their strength of me, and as for my callers, you may ask them yourself."

Sprawled out across the fields of the Solvena Plains were at least ten to twenty thousand men, all in the same black armor.

How did I not see them upon my arrival? Were they hiding behind the walls? And how did they organize themselves there so quickly?

Not just men, but somehow Melkai also. Dozens of beasts and flying monsters protruded from the rows of their ranks, each one either standing by their caller or carrying them, both on the field and in the air.

The darkness of them swallowed the green of the fields, and with the shock of the sight, Laine turned to the king who had inclined his head in anticipation of her answer.

"I believe your silence tells me you have no further questions. Very well then, good to have you with us," the king murmured.

Although she wished to reply, she could not. For the first time in years, a man had silenced her.

I . . . I think this could work. With my knowledge of calling and his army, we could be unstoppable. I can finally stand on even footing with King Kissick.

With an unheard order, the army turned. Sounding a war horn, they began to march, making their way over the Solvena Plains. When only the tail of the army could be seen, the king descended the stairs.

"Come. Let me show you something else."

Laine followed the king down a long corridor to his war room where maps were laid out over long wooden tables. "Garland and Kydia . . ." he said, waving to the northern borders. "They'll need to be cowed or subdued before Avatasc can be taken successfully. However, once we make our preemptive strike on Avatasc, we will be vulnerable to a rear attack by the Senadonians." He jabbed his finger at a marked fortress over the Jile Mountains. "We cannot afford a war on two fronts; therefore, our first target will be New Senadon."

"Wait, that's where you're sending your soldiers first?" Laine slammed down her goblet, spilling water onto the oak. "Not Avatasc?"

The king nodded. "New Senadon will fall quickly, you have my word. And Avatasc will soon follow."

Laine scanned the area between New Senadon and Avatasc. "Needless to say, the success or failure of this expedition will determine the length of my stay here."

"Then I foresee I will be enjoying your company for some time." He gestured to two guards who had followed them in. "Follow them and they will lead you to your room in Summoners' Spire."

Laine went to follow them, but turned back. "We are both powerful and ambitious people, Your Majesty. Be mindful of that should your ambitions ever begin to hinder my own."

With that said, she left the war room.

CHAPTER 18

WAR COUNCIL

Nathan leaned on the railing of the castle balcony, looking out over Avatasc. The bright sunlight shone down on the surrounding fields. It had been a few weeks since he had become king, and Nathan had found that the reordering of the city had been an invigorating task for him, especially when seeing the look on people's faces when justice had finally been returned to them.

He had the soldiers actually work for their keep now, creating irrigation systems around the kingdom to make the land more arable, while distributing the resources more fairly between them and the common folk.

To his amazement, Kendra's ideas about the simplicity of keeping a kingdom prosperous were actually closer to the mark than the other methods they had discussed . . . in the short term at least.

When the messenger they sent requesting Laine to come back never returned, he knew something was clearly wrong.

Warning of Terratheist's advance arrived not long after. He couldn't fathom why Michael's father, someone he had known since his childhood, was acting so rashly. He sent him letter after desperate letter explaining that he was now the king and the fighting could stop, but the letters were never responded to.

The king may have lost his sanity not hearing a word about his son.

He had to make peace, but if peace was impossible, he had to make sure Avatasc's defenses were solid before he made his return journey. That meant repairing the walls: the only thing that would protect the people from the Melkai should they fail to reclaim the key.

Aisic's huge dragon form swooped into view after taking a better view of the structure from above. He lifted another boulder from the pile of rubble into place for it to be melted along with the others he had since hauled in from the mountains to fill in the gaps. Soon the wall would be complete, ahead of schedule thanks to the might and flame of Aisic's Melkaiic form.

He had assisted with most of the improvements. His fire had burned away the brush to expand the farms alongside the crumbling castle, his claws had cleared away ditches for the new aqueducts for irrigation, and even his large neck could lift stonemasons into place without the use of pulleys.

The last few boulders were mortared in place and set by the heat of Aisic's blackening fire. Then Aisic flapped his wings and took to the sky. He flew toward the castle, changing into his human form as he landed next to Nathan.

"That should be all for the defenses, Your Majesty." He turned and raised an eyebrow at him. "So, what's next?"

Nathan clasped his hands behind his back. "Go get dressed in the armor I've had the smithy provide you with. I've summoned a war council and need you to look as intimidating as possible."

Aisic bowed and strode away to don his new armor. After changing, Nathan waited a few minutes to head to the council room. He didn't want to arrive before Aisic. When he heard Aisic leaving his adjacent room, he stepped into the hallway, running his strategy over in his mind. Like him, Aisic had been geared up in full battle regalia, and Nathan had never seen his protector look more like a warrior than he did now.

Nathan's king's armor and garments had been far more elegant than anything he had worn before. He barely recognized himself. The armorers had told him that chainmail was much better for protection than plate armor, but now seeing Aisic in his plate, it didn't appear that way. Aisic looked much more intimidating in his broad-shouldered armor. He wore it like he was born in it, and it suited him well.

Wearing chainmail allowed Nathan to keep his hood, however. Anonymity, he found, was much better protection against enemies than any armor they could provide for him.

Nathan paused and took a pensive breath as they arrived at the door to the war chamber. There was a lot he had to say, and he knew he couldn't look weak—not in front of these men.

"Are you ready for this?" Aisic asked.

Nathan nodded. "Yes, I personally summoned these commanders and generals for the sake of this meeting. My mother said they're sure to listen to my requests."

Aisic smirked, and Nathan could see he wasn't so sure of

this.

They walked into the green-draped war chamber where they were met by five other men and the queen around a long table. Each of them were commanders and lords, and, although a few of them were fond of him, others weren't as convinced of his claim to rule as of yet. His mother was smiling at him, but he had requested that she not intervene.

I have to make my own mistakes and learn to be a good king through them.

Despite this fact, he could still see her pursing her lips and wringing her hands to prevent herself from speaking up at his arrival.

One of the five lords of Avatasc was missing from the room, but Nathan decided not to wait for him. He walked toward the massive table with a map spread out along it.

He had never seen such an expansive and detailed map in all his life, each of the peaks and valleys in the hills painted with remarkable detail. He outlined with his eyes the paths they had walked to get to Avatasc several weeks ago.

It's hard to believe that so much time has passed already.

"Greetings, Your Majesty," said one of the lords, a brownnose if he had ever seen one.

Nathan nodded back.

The others took the first's lead and sought his attention. "Sire," they all said.

Aisic shot fierce looks at any who did not greet him. Nathan raised a hand. His finger drew along the southern border of the Solvena Plains from the marshes toward the forest.

"They have taken everything past here, from Kydia to Garland, and believe me when I tell you, they're coming our way. Remember, this army is not just conquering but ransacking; they are burning everything they can get their hands on. But the real problem is this: they have Melkai marching with them. I must stress how dire this situation is getting. In some regions, there are more Melkai than there are callers to summon them."

"How is that possible?" one of the lords asked.

"The barrier to the Melkairen has weakened enough to let them through. Soon it will crumble entirely. In order to stop this, we will need to complete the Kairen Key, and to get the key we will need to cross the Avatasc-Terratheist border." Nathan scanned their expressions. If anything, the fear from his words should undermine their skepticism and bypass their questions. "Our own forces have gone as far as the Avatasc border to defend it, but I believe soon an offensive will be necessary or otherwise we will be lost. We must cross that line."

"How do we know they're coming here?"

"How do we know they have Melkai?"

"How do we know?" they all asked at once.

Nathan was already prepared for their counterarguments. He drew a knife out of his belt.

"Because . . ." He cut one third of the map away with his blade. "According to our messengers, Avatasc is the last place in the lands that isn't currently on fire. I think that you land barons know that fire kills crops, and this one, my lords, is spreading."

Nathan had seen sketches from the messengers—the burning forests, the sacked villages, the armies of men and Melkai—and he wanted them to be as afraid of the threat as he was. It worked. Their expressions changed, their faces falling. The fear achieved its intended effect on all but two of the nobles: Lord Ronund and Lord Wilkow.

"Preposterous! Scandalous! Outrageous!" Lord Ronund shouted, jowls wobbling.

Nathan knew there would be one, he even knew which one. In fact, he had planned on it. His mother had warned him of Lord Ronund.

"These . . . fear tactics will not work on me. I have served this council for ten—"

"And gotten fat off it," one of the only slender nobles, Lord Wilkow, said to a murmur of laughter.

This was why, in secret, Nathan had bribed some of his soldiers.

"Tell me, Lord Ronund, do you compel respect and trust in your men?" he asked.

Lord Ronund went red in the face. "I don't see how this is any of your business—but yes, I trust them implicitly."

Nathan smiled and gestured to the map, having purposely placed it down so one corner faced him. "Do you recognize this signature, my lord?"

Lord Ronund looked down and his red cheeks went pale.

"As you will see, *my* lord, it was your commander that made these reports and drew up this map, and did a quite good job of it, if I do say so."

The other nobles laughed at this, and fury filled Lord Ronund's glare. "You will not have any of my men!"

Nathan shrugged. "Nor do I need them. They've already risked their lives enough and will be handsomely rewarded for it . . . by you . . . if you want to keep their respect, that is."

"You haven't heard the last of this!" Ronund stormed out of the war room.

Nathan glanced at Aisic and shrugged. "I don't know what he's so upset about. I just pardoned him from the war. I thought that's what he wanted."

Aisic inclined his head. "Some people will always find something to be upset about, even when they get what they want."

"Very well, you can have our men, soldiers to fight back against this horde," another fatter noble, one who Nathan was told owned fruit farms, spoke.

His name was Lord Conner, and he seemed to speak for the rest of them, as the others nodded along with his words—even Lord Wilkow.

Both Nathan and Aisic smiled at this, entertained by the idea. "We don't need warriors. We are not going to sacrifice more men for this fire. What we need are escorts."

"Escorts?" one of the bearded old men asked, his voice hoarse.

Aisic spoke this time, using his low baritone and size to get the message through. "You will only use what men you can to keep the Avatasc border steady, but we don't want this war to continue or escalate. We want to dissolve it. For that, we will need to make a peace treaty, but so far none of our offers have been heeded or replied to, only more fighting and more fire. What we need is a way to be certain that this treaty will get through to the king. Therefore, we are going ourselves. The reason we have asked for you to come here today is to request for your escorts and your promise that what we have done for this country will not be reversed during our absence."

They all nodded. With the irrigation system in place, their produce had grown twofold and they learned that what benefited the many also benefited the few, unlike what the last king had claimed.

"But sire," one of the younger lords called and the others shot looks at him. "Should a king really be sent to the front line to be a simple messenger? What will this do to the hierarchy, to the soldier's morale?"

Nathan looked over his shoulder to say one more thing before leaving. "If anything, sometimes the king must go to the front line to win the morale of his men."

He turned back and walked out, confident they would obey him. Fear would likely keep them on the right path he had started off for them until they both returned.

Coming out of the war chamber, Nathan and Aisic made their way through the long castle corridors.

"I think we got through to them," Aisic said solemnly, "but I'm not sure about the fat one."

Nathan shook his head with a laugh. They were all fat really, except for Lord Wilkow. They spotted each other's grins and moved into the throne room where Nathan casually spun and fell back onto his throne.

The room had been cleaned out after their battle. It took a while to clear away the rubble, the snake carcass, and then to convince Aisic in his dragon form not to eat the Snake King's corpse. Nathan was sure the poison of his corrupted pale body would have stirred up something unsettling in his stomach.

Aisic paced back and forth on the green carpet. "So? When are we planning to go on this little life-risking journey you have in mind?"

"Tonight," Nathan said, caught up in his own thoughts.

"Why tonight?" asked Aisic, voice harsh with impatience.

"I want to leave under the cover of darkness." Nathan exhaled sharply. "I don't want my people to think I'm abandoning them."

"Alright, I'm going to go check up on the battalion to see if our defenses are ready in case we're a bit premature on our predictions."

Aisic left the hall.

Nathan hoped Aisic didn't think it was cowardice that kept from leaving right away; he wasn't afraid of battle. He had to rid himself of such fear during his fight with Kissick, proven by Taiba revealing his true form.

As he met with his mother and those who had been disenfranchised by Kissick, the shadows stretched through the great hall, and his head continued to ache from his need to move.

Taking off his glove, he summoned Taiba to keep him company. Nathan was glad he was no longer trying to sit on his shoulder as he did as a lizard.

"You feel it too, don't you, boy?"

Taiba barked in reply then spun in place before lying down on the green carpet. He placed his muzzle on his folded legs and waited loyally next to the throne on the newly lowered dais. The platform had been taken down after Serraba had destroyed the top half of it. Nathan preferred it, allowing him to see his constituents up close instead of looming over them.

The dawn rays shone through the open door as he waited for the coming evening. Two silhouettes appeared in the corridor, striding toward the throne room. They were warriors . . . no, more than that . . . they were Senadonians. Warriors judging by their body structure and the way they held themselves; Senadonians because of the three slit tattoos under their left eyes, a signature of their race. The focus in their eyes was the only aspect about them that didn't look exhausted.

Seemingly when they needed them the most, two men from the legendary warrior race had finally returned to Avatasc.

Then Nathan's heart stopped as the older one shouted, "New Senadon has fallen!"

CHAPTER 19

THE SENADONIANS

A long time ago, the Senadonians were considered the greatest warriors in the Ramannon army. They fought side by side with the other races of the lands, and on the battlefield, they shared no equal. They were bred to be warriors, to be fast and strong and ambidextrous so they could wield two weapons at the same time.

However, they had a secret. For hidden behind their glory they were protecting something from the rest of the lands: the remaining Kairens. They would go on to rule the lands in place of Ramannon's empire. At the time, however, the Kairens were hunted for fear of their powers.

When this secret became known, the tables were turned for the first time, and Senadon became an enemy of the land. They were attacked on all sides by the Ramannon army, and after Ramannon's downfall, they made a long journey over the Jile Mountains to the other side of the world to found New Senadon. Due to their bloodline mixing with the Kairens whilst hiding them, a few descendent were even able to summon Melkai.

Master Morrow had taught Nathan all of this in his history lessons. Now two Senadonians had come before him, and Nathan couldn't help but grin excitedly.

"Get some water!" Nathan demanded.

A few guards left to retrieve jugs of water.

He led the Senadonians into the large dining chamber where they could sit and rest. He looked them up and down, shaking his head in disbelief. They were very different, one young and one old. The older one was past his middle age, the younger one closer to Nathan's age, and they both looked road-weary. The water arrived and they slaked their thirst. Not a single word had passed their lips since their first proclamation, as though waiting for someone older to show up.

"You've returned," Nathan started, raising his hands to wave away the obvious nature of his statement. "But under what cause? I can see from your state alone that your circumstances may be as desperate as our own, but . . ."

The old one changed his expression from a grim frown to a smirk. From what Nathan had read, Senadonians didn't commonly let people see their emotions, so this shift in expression surprised him.

"As desperate as yours?" the older one intoned.

"Yeah, okay. Sorry, but you do not know desperation yet!" the younger one finished, sounding suddenly hostile. "*You* haven't been forced to abandon your home yet."

"Why?"

The younger one continued, still panting. "Over the mountains . . ." He waved in the direction of them. "New Senadon is gone!"

"The last of us have taken refuge in the Old Senadon fort." The older one held him back with a hand, his rough face stern. "But let's not be informal. My name is Tarros Kahin, and he's Durian Tolbit. Yours is?"

"I'm King Nathaniel, King Nathaniel Armalon."

"*King* Armalon?" Durian asked, eyes widened skeptically. "You?"

"That's correct."

Aisic rushed into the dining hall, exhaling sharply when he saw the Senadonians.

Nathan raised a hand in his direction. "This is my protector, Aisic."

"Who are they?" Aisic asked.

"I think it would be better if we explained fully what happened." Tarros looked to his younger companion. "We were attacked by Terratheist forces, thousands of men. We didn't stand a chance."

Durian handed Nathan a tattered brown journal, already opened to its last page. "This is a journal from one of our war scribes. It might help you get a better idea of what we're dealing with here."

Nathan looked down at the parchment. Despite the writer's odd mix of rough handwriting and flowery prose, he could still make out what it said:

Splinters are appearing on the main gate. The barricade is loosening. Several soldiers are trying to brace it. Our archers are raining down arrows and picking off the enemy, but the Terratheist soldiers are stubborn and almost unlimited in number. The castle walls are high, but they are streaming off the ladders like cockroaches, drawing their swords and then drawing our blood. Our elite battalion is making major dents in their forces, but we still need reinforcements.

Someone behind me calls for Advanced Summoner Tarros. By the sudden intense pounding at the gate, it is clear that no human is working the battering ram. It's a Melkai. Behind us, the water in the fountain ripples with each strike made on the gate. People are backing off from it now. A cloaked caller has arrived.

The gate smashes open, both sides of the door hitting the fountain on either side of Tarros. A chimera with a lion's head enters. It charges through but stops before Tarros. Drawing everyone's attention, including the Melkai's, the caller raises his open hand.

Tarros plants it on the stone floor. The pact item he is using is a necklace. A circle of blue flames appears, and his giant wolf leaps from the circle, from the Melkairen, and lands on the chimera. The wolf is biting at its neck, and they collide with the stone walls.

Soldiers are now flooding through the open passage. Tarros is now working with the soldiers to slay the first encroachment.

I scale the walls to assess our enemy. Behind them are hundreds of soldiers, just waiting for the order to attack, and as each minute goes by, they claw into the castle through the opening. There are too many of them to hold out.

The caller's hood has been torn off. I was wrong. It was not the Advanced Summoner but his apprentice. The soldiers are asking where Tarros is, but Durian only points to the walls.

Tarros is standing there, sword facing the sky. From it, a flame appears and grows above him, wings forming as it flies into the dawn sky. It circles the entire castle, a line of flame raging from it toward the enemy below: A phoenix. It continues to fly above the armies spread over the land, turning the very earth black with its flame.

Not a scream escapes from the burning soldiers. The army is not willing to give up, and the battle is raging on. Just glimpsing the amount of the soldiers out of that gate, I can tell ours is a futile effort. Other Melkai are breaking through the outer walls. We aren't getting out of this place alive.

While Nathan had been reading, Taiba had put his head in his lap and began to whine, clearly concerned with the mounting horror in his expression. Nathan had known that New Senadon had been attacked, but the reports hadn't said how outnumbered they had been.

"We were taken over by midday," Durian said. "We barely had enough time to let the others escape before we all fled into the mountains. The assault was from Terratheist, and we plan to confront the king, but we will need your help."

"I see . . ." Nathan looked up from the journal, having just reread a passage referring to the Senadonians' Melkai. "So, both of you are callers then?"

They nodded, and Durian said, "Picked that up, did you?"

"What a combination. Senadonians, callers *and* warriors . . . the best of both worlds." He turned his attention to Tarros. "But I don't understand. Surely, you were prepared for an invasion."

"It didn't matter. We could have had several fortified walls with moats a dozen yards deep surrounding the city and it wouldn't have mattered. There were far too many of

185

them."

"B-but you're Senadonians."

Durian smirked. "I see our reputation precedes us, Master."

Tarros nodded. "And has been blown out of proportion by our absence. Listen, we are here to follow the teachings of our predecessors. They wrote that the quickest way to defeat an enemy is to strike their heart. That is our aim."

Destiny seemed to pull at the corners of Nathan's lips.

"Why are you smiling?" Durian demanded, sounding suddenly agitated. "You don't think we can do it?"

"I have received no news from Terratheist since this war began. Indeed, I having been waiting for a reason to travel there to see what in the Melkairen has happened for myself." Nathan gestured at the two of them. "I was just thinking your timing couldn't have been better, as we ride for Terratheist tonight."

Durian's eyes shot to Tarros, and the old Senadonian nodded.

Tarros flashed a grin. "Fortune smiles upon us."

"On us both," Nathan agreed. "You two are better than any soldiers we have here; you will be my escorts to Terratheist. We are going to be some damn aggressive messengers." He punched the table in his determination and turned to see Aisic was also grinning. "The sun is setting, when will you two be ready to head out?"

They looked at each other and nodded. "Whenever you are."

"Good. Let's go now then!"

He got out of his chair and made his way to his chambers with Taiba following him. As he entered the wide suite with its four-poster bed, he returned his Melkai to the glove and gazed down at it. His sister's glove was smooth against his hand. Lifting his travel pack, he rubbed his hands together. Touching the glove felt like he was touching Taiba's fur wrapped around his whole hand. Finally ready for his journey, he swiftly made his way back through the corridors toward the courtyard.

It appeared word of his leaving had already been received.

Ignoring the passing nobles trying to get his attention, he came to the large doors of the Avatasc Castle and strode out onto the balcony. Waiting for him outside was Aisic and the two Senadonians, Tarros and Durian. They did not complain, not batting an eye at the fact that they would not get a night's rest before they had to set off again. From the journal, he knew that their revenge for what had been done to New Senadon was much more important to them.

"I'm going to be traveling by air," Nathan said. "Do you think you can keep up?"

The younger Senadonian, Durian, removed a necklace and placed his hand on the ground. As the journal had detailed, a blue circle of light formed at his feet, the jewel which was his pact item glowing in his hand. A massive wolf jumped through the circle and onto the courtyard tiles.

The large, fiery-looking, blue wolf snarled at them, but then calmed as he saw Durian. It was an impressive beast, Nathan had to admit, but if it didn't appear to be on fire, it would have just been a big wolf. It raised a paw, the metacarpal pads at their bottoms looking like actual flames, and both Durian and Tarros jumped up onto the Melkai's back.

"Blazer is the fastest land Melkai I've ever come across,"

Durian bragged as his silent master sat behind, not saying a word about his own Melkai. "But I'd be interested to see how your Melkai can travel by air."

Nathan stepped away from Aisic and raised his glove. "Well, this is the pact item for my Melkai, but Taiba can't fly. As for how I'm going to be traveling by air, well, I think Aisic can answer that question for you."

Durian looked skeptically at Aisic. The sword on Aisic's back straightened. The wings which pointed out from its cross guard spread out and wrapped around him, the blade of the sword stretching out into the tail as the scabbard came over him as his dragon scales. His body grew and stretched as his Melkai form was revealed.

Tarros breathed out heavily, and Durian's eyes widened. Their mouths dropped, stunned into silence by his metamorphosis.

"That's how I'll be traveling." Nathan grabbed hold of Aisic's armor-plated skin and used it as a ladder to climb up onto his back. "You might need a head start."

Durian smirked. He bent down and patted Blazer's back. The wolf huffed a fiery breath, and like its namesake, it blazed a trail of blue fire down the stairs and through the middle of the city. The line of flame clearly showed its path out into the fields.

Nathan grinned and yelled, "Alright, Aisic, let's go!"

Aisic's massive wings flapped down. Flowers from the garden were caught up in the wind and blew around them as they took off into the air and then soared over the city.

Their journey back to Terratheist had begun.

CHAPTER 20

LAINE'S LESSON

Laine was impressed with the Summoners' Pit and could see why King Michael had designated this space for her to meet the apprentice callers. Statues of great Melkai rested on the high walls, the stone was slashed and charred, and the pit itself could have fit most second-circle Melkai with room to spare. She wished such a place existed within the Avatasc Castle. It would have lowered the risk of training with Terachiro by a significant margin.

Since the war with Avatasc began, many callers and Advanced Summoners had left the castle to join the battle on the border, leaving her to deal with the dregs that were held back to protect the castle. As Michael had claimed, there was much she could teach them, but she hadn't predicted the type of people she would be teaching.

So, these are the cutthroat nobility Nathan was telling me about. I better set strong rules right from the beginning.

The sixteen apprentices who had shown up for her

instructions were the type of sniveling noblemen's children she had dealt with in the past. They were the same entitled, frilly laced, petticoated toffs as the sons of Wilkow and Ronund, who, along with several other potential suitors, her stepfather had forced her to socialize with in the hope one could be molded by him to become a potential heir.

Dragon's breath, but I'm glad he never warmed to any of them.

She could tell by the air of disinterest that they exuded with their pursed lips and raised slanted eyebrows that she was going to have to put them in their place right from the beginning. Nothing a little magic couldn't achieve.

"Where is Master Morrow?" one of them, wearing a white wig, whined. "Isn't he supposed to be here to guide a caller as young as you?"

The others standing around the pit sneered and chortled. Laine sighed and raised her hand. The murmurs and laughter cut off as the brats noticed it starting to glow blue.

The one who had commented on her age decided to give her one more poke. "What's that? Is your hand cold, dear? Well, I know of a warm place you can put it."

Laine spun, slashing a statue that resembled a terrifying harpy. The blue blade of her spell cut right through it from hip to shoulder, and the top half of the statue landed inside the walls with a crunch.

Silence proceeded, and she turned back to the apprentices. "I see I have your attention."

"That statue was hundreds of years old!" one of them cried out.

"And yet I'm sure your young heads will fall just as easily."

Some of them paled.

"Now, we are going to play a little game. When I say go, those of you who have summoned a first-circle will run and touch the left wall, those who have summoned a second-circle will run and touch the right wall, and those of you who have never summoned anything during your time under your previous master, stay where you are."

A few swallowed and some nodded, but as soon as she said, "Go," they broke into three separate groups. She kept her eyes on those who did not move. They were mostly young, but several of them were older than her.

She narrowed her eyes at them. "Everyone below the age of fifteen will return to your previous master. You are clearly not experienced enough to be in my class." She jerked her head back toward the gate. "Go now."

They scrambled away.

"What about us?" asked one of the fops who remained where he was. "What do we do?"

Laine's jaw clenched. "I don't care what you do, you aren't callers."

"That's preposterous!" the brat with the wig shouted. "We have Kairen blood in our veins just as you do, and our fathers paid for us to be given lessons—"

"Not by me." Although she tried not to let her expression show her agitation, she let her hand glow with the same blue light. "There are two types of people when it comes to summoning Melkai, those who can and those who can't. I don't have time to waste on those who can't." She pointed to the gate with one glowing finger. "Now leave!"

There were groans, leers, and even a "My father will hear of this," as they removed themselves from the pit, and hopefully from the pool of prospective callers.

She returned her attention to those remaining. As suspected, the majority of those who had only summoned a first-circle were on the younger side, no doubt having been guided through the process by their previous master.

Her gaze shifted to the second-circle group. "Now, right siders, make a line up the pit and show me your Melkai one-by-one. I won't have two Melkai getting into a fight."

There were a few nods, and after Laine clicked her fingers and pointed to the edge of the pit, they scrambled to line up. What followed was a demonstration in Melkai summoning ranging from somewhat impressive to mediocre. The apprentices from the left side stared in amazement at their upper classmen's creatures.

As she would be commanding them in battle, Laine's main concern was where she would place them and how she could use their different advantages.

As a redhead girl summoned a giant wasp looking creature, Laine knew from her experience with Terachiro that the girl would need to be on the towers for recon. Another who summoned a large honey badger-like creature with many legs would be better on the front line. The most impressive Melkai was a beautiful green wyvern summoned from the emerald of a blond apprentice. The boy's second-circle Melkai could have even given Terachiro a decent fight.

Top of the class.

"Good, I see you're not all completely worthless." She kept her frown solidly fixed in place. "Those of you who have ground-based Melkai leave and take two apprentices from the left side of the wall. You can choose who you'll teach but you must take at least two. You will be helping them make pacts with second-circle Melkai of their own. Those of you who succeed in aiding the less experienced novices to make a new pact, I will teach the spell I demonstrated at the start of my lesson."

"Yes, master!" the three she referenced called and moved to where the first-circle group to pick out their apprentices.

Laine would've been lying if she said hearing them say this didn't send a tingle down her spine.

"And then there were three." She turned her focus on the remaining three callers standing before the pit: her flyers. "The reason I have left you three for last is that you will be the most useful callers in this upcoming battle."

The redhead raised her hand. "Why is that, master?"

Laine let her expression slip, a grin escaping. "Terratheist has large walls for a reason: to make sure the Melkai who escape the Melkairen can't enter the city. Of course, some slip inside and the Advanced Summoners handle those, but the real threat is those that can go over the walls."

The blond young man who had summoned the Wyvern nodded. "So, we're going to be protecting the walls."

"That's right. You'll be overseeing the battlement's defenses personally. Once some of the others have summoned second-circle Melkai, they will be put under you, but from now on you will be under me. Understand?"

"Yes, master," they called.

She sighed, the novelty of the title already wearing off. "What are your names?"

"Tuttle," a large young man, who had summoned a giant falcon, said.

"Blake," said the blond with the wyvern.

"Reshal," said the redhead with the wasp.

Laine nodded. "The three of you will learn to work as a

193

team. If any flying Melkai are seen heading toward the castle, you three will need to take it out. Is that understood?"

"Understood!" they said together.

"Good." Laine grabbed the collar of her hood to summon Terachiro. "Then let's practice formations."

CHAPTER 21

WAR OF THE MELKAI

The screams of men and the clash of blades filled the Solvena plains. On Aisic's scaled back, Nathan saw for the first time the war that was taking place, given an unhindered view of the carnage.

"Dragon's breath, they're everywhere . . ."

"This is nothing, not compared to what will be if the barrier isn't fixed," Aisic spoke up in his mind.

Nathan gazed at the unfolding carnage, at the scope of death and destruction that spread out on the fields beneath them. Thousands of soldiers and Melkai filled the grassland, firing and charging at one another in the desperate and bloody struggle of the conflict. The intense havoc of the true war had come to fruition.

Melkai of all shapes and sizes speckled the battlefield, their feet thumping the earth. A giant tortoise with thick leathery skin walked steadily through the battlefield, crushing armored soldiers under its great bulk. This impenetrable fortress also sported Terratheist archers in the crevasses between the thick scutes of its shell.

This is insane. This is all insane.

He looked up. The moon was nearly completely red, all but a pale crescent on its edge.

The barrier has weakened so much.

They flew over a stretch of wasteland. A sandworm erupted from the ground below them, its massive maw encircled with several rows of teeth. It writhed across the ground with another identical head at its opposing end. It slithered toward the grassland where archers tried to kill it before it could reach them. As the worm was pierced by arrows, its oozing green blood hissed out and melted the ground where it fell, preventing any of the soldiers from getting close to it.

Nathan gasped, the consequences of neglecting the mission the king had given to him now starkly apparent.

It doesn't make sense. Why would the king send such a force my way? So many Melkai . . . when he knows that I'm here trying to save the lands from this very thing. Some of the Melkai aren't even controlled by callers. Did he think I failed?

A tree appeared to lumber across the plains below, until Nathan saw that it was mounted upon the skeleton of a giant feline, the roots encircling its bones, binding them together like muscles.

Further down the valley, a Melkai with one giant, black eyeball surrounded by long tentacles emerged from the ground. Its long limbs swept the soldiers, enemies and allies alike, from their feet and then devoured them in its many mouths.

The armored scales shifted beneath Nathan, and Aisic glided down, still trying not to get too close to any of the Melkai. Some were even huge enough that they would've been able to knock them out of the sky.

We can't get too close to these things, but the sun's coming down and we have to find a place to land for the night.

Aisic glided down to the side of the battlefield, out of the way of the army's advance toward Avatasc. There, Nathan located a stretch of grass mostly free of Melkai. It wasn't very far away from the fighting, but neither had their campsites been for the previous two nights.

"We need to land!" he yelled over the howl of the wind and pointed to the ground. "Down there, on the border of the forest!"

A chimera Melkai made up of the body of a gorilla, the head of a horned bull, and the tail of a snake stared up at them, dragging an enormous club-like tree behind it. Seeing them descend toward the clearing, it broke from the distant horde and rushed toward where they made to land. Before they could meet, a streak of blue fire sped its way through the field, cutting off the Melkai before it could swing its club.

Durian looks to be making good distance. That wolf of his really is fast.

The chimera swung its club through the surrounding soldiers and charged through. There were rows of spikes on its back which continued down to its reptilian tail.

Blazer ran in to block its path. On the wolf's back, Durian evaded the swing of its club as the blue flame quickly arced around it, trapping it inside a prison of flame before continuing on its run.

The thump of the chimera's burning body hitting the earth made Nathan's shoulders relax, despite the putrid smell of cooking Melkai. The Senadonians could easily take care of themselves in this battle.

A stray arrow whisked past them from one of the armored turtles and Aisic banked to avoid the arrows from the archer's longbows. It was getting darker and it would be hard for Aisic's dragon eyes to see the arrows coming at them in the twilight.

He arced toward where Nathan had pointed, and Nathan held tight as they glided down from the sky. At a closer look, the area was speckled with smaller Melkai and enemy soldiers. Aisic sprayed down a runway of flame, turning the grass beneath them black. They landed with a thump and Nathan jumped down off Aisic's back.

A dozen soldiers and a large scorpion Melkai turned toward them. The soldiers were wearing full Terratheist armor and marched with a lifeless rhythm. However, Nathan's attention was on the Melkai. As the scorpion raised its tail, he saw its face and torso were at its tip, looking like a man with snipping pincers for arms. Nathan grinned wide.

That's more like it! Hah! Give me more weird ones like this!

Nathan removed one glove and threw it at the scorpion-like he was challenging it to a duel. Instead, the fingers extended into limbs as Taiba morphed into reality before him. The large dog ran toward the massive scorpion as Aisic breathed flame at the approaching soldiers. They burned up in their armor, yet no screams could be heard from them.

Taiba lunged at the scorpion as its pincers flew at him. He was too fast for them and swiftly ran up onto the thing's back, snapping at its tail. Taiba's teeth reached but missed the

Melkai's human throat, and he was knocked aside onto the blackened grass. The Melkai reared up over him and Nathan watched as his companion backed away, snarling.

The thing rose up over Taiba, ready to strike.

"Taiba, get up, run!" Nathan called.

Suddenly there was an explosion away from Aisic's fire. Nathan turned as a giant red bird flew from it. Its massive wings appeared to suck up the fire around them it came down on the scorpion. Following it was Blazer, Durian's Melkaiic wolf, and with a quick sprint, it caught up with Tarros's phoenix and together they drove the scorpion into the ground in a sprawl of pincers, teeth, and feathers of flame.

The scorpion was in pieces in a matter of seconds, and like with the flame around them, the phoenix had vanished, a sword falling to the grass. Tarros and Durian casually walked out of the fire, faces solemn as though the situation was commonplace for them. Tarros sighed and picked up his sword.

I guess it's convenient that Senadonians are dual-wielders.

"Yeah, I know," Tarros said. "Not the best object for pact item." He raised the sword to see if there was any dirt on the blade before returning it to its scabbard. "Let's just say I was young and panicked when making the pact. Anyway, let's set up camp. Durian, have Blazer do a circle around the area so no one can get in."

Durian raised an arm to signal his wolf to do a lap of the area. As it did, it left a blue flame in its wake. Durian's claim about Blazer being the fastest land-based Melkai wasn't an empty boast, it really was a powerful Melkai, much more powerful than Taiba. Recovered from his run-in with the scorpion, Taiba ran to Nathan's side, panting. Nathan put a hand on its head and ran his hand through the thick fur. Taiba formed back into the glove.

It shouldn't matter that I don't have a powerful Melkai when the one I do have doesn't even need a pact item to be loyal to me. That alone should be enough.

They began to set up camp and Nathan went into the forest to collect firewood. Durian accompanied him, talking circles around him about what had happened, even though he had been there and seen it all.

"You should have seen Blazer's retreat from the Terratheist forces. The lines he made through their number was so clean he could have written my name among their ranks."

The forest was filled with Melkai, but Durian kept Blazer out to guard them. After what they had seen the wolf do to the scorpion, he doubted that any Melkai would be able to challenge it.

Nathan stuck out his bottom lip. "Yeah, well, I fought a snake the size of a house with nothing but a knife and small lizard by my side."

Durian's eyes grew wide. "Is that how you killed the Snake King's Melkai?"

Nathan smiled. "You knew of Serraba?"

"I heard rumors. Always thought they were just that though, hearsay."

Nathan shook his head. "Nothing about that man and his Melkai was hearsay; he was as nasty a tyrant as they said."

"And is it true that Serraba was big enough to swallow a castle?"

Nathan scoffed. "What? No! I mean, it was big but not that big."

"Pity." Durian shook his head and returned his attention to picking up more wood. "But it . . . it was the sheer number of soldiers that got us in the siege."

Nathan frowned as he walked ahead. "I don't remember Terratheist's army being *that* big."

Durian caught up with him. "You should have seen the amount of them! If it wasn't for Blazer, Tarros and I wouldn't have had a chance!"

"Yes, yes, Blazer is an impressive Melkai, I won't deny it."

"That's not what I'm getting at. Your majesty, most of the soldiers we were fighting . . . well, it was like they were already dead. They just wouldn't give up."

Already dead? The soldiers that burned up in Aisic's flames didn't even scream. It's like they're zombies or have no mouths to cry through.

"Tarros told me not to say anything until we knew for sure," Durian continued. "There was so much already you would have to believe on face value that he warned me to leave my speculations out of it."

Nathan nodded. "It is quite a claim, but I'm glad you told me."

They left the dark forest to discover it had become night. On the edge of the plane, Aisic and Tarros were removing bodies from the battlefield. As they came to a dip in the field, Aisic returned to his human form and they stood in silence.

As the two met with him and Tarros, Durian used the blue flame from Blazer's tail to light a fire which roared higher and bathed the dip in the field in blue light. They all came around it and hunkered down.

Nathan sat back and stretched his arms above his head.

He was grudgingly relieved that Blazer's ability allowed them to set up a camp and relax after how long they had been traveling through the war zone. From the way the others sat down, even the Senadonians appeared to relax. During the other breaks they had taken over the last two days, they had still been sitting on their heels as though ready to jump back into the fight any second, but now they sprawled out, confident enough in their ability to detect an ambush.

"Why didn't you just use your dragon breath to light it?" Durian asked Aisic, his tone sharp with suspicion.

"The same reason Tarros didn't summon his phoenix for it." Aisic shrugged. "Less time-consuming."

"Forgive my apprentice," Tarros said. "We're not used to seeing a man who has used his own body as a pact item. We didn't know it was possible."

Aisic grinned. "It's not something I would recommend."

Nathan frowned, the idea only now coming to him. "Wait, I just thought you were a Melkai who could transform into a human. Your body is a pact item?"

"It's a long story. I am indeed human . . . and of the Arion race."

Tarros nodded. "You've been behind the barrier, haven't you? You've been to the Melkairen. It's the only explanation. Your body and spirit got combined with a dragon when you were there. That's why you can harness it and transform at will."

Aisic nodded but said nothing more.

Durian shook his head. "But how? No human being, heck, no physical object can enter the Melkairen without losing its form. It's not possible!"

Tarros shook his head. "It doesn't apply to him, Durian.

He's an Arion."

"What do you mean?"

Aisic shrugged. "I can separate myself from my physical body. I did this when I unintentionally trapped myself behind the barrier long ago."

Tarros suddenly broke into laughter. "So, you've been locked in Melkairen for the past five hundred years, eh, Scion of Akai? Or would you prefer me to call you by your real name, Isaac?"

Aisic raised a brow at him. "So, you know me."

Durian's eyes widened, and he gaped at Aisic. Nathan's mouth moved, but he couldn't form the words to express his shock. The Scion of Akai. All this time he had been traveling with a hero of legend, someone who had saved the lands from a tyrant, someone who people still told stories about to this day, a hero who could turn into a dragon and was ready to protect him with his life. Being a king was one thing, but being a hero of legend who had lived over five hundred years was another entirely.

"Know you?" Tarros scoffed and raised his palms. "The tale of the Scion of Akai has been passed down from generation to generation in my family."

"A tale that has no ending," Durian muttered.

Nathan recalled what Aisic told him while walking through the forest. Ramannon was eventually defeated by Cullen Armalon, but only after much sacrifice and the disappearance of their hero . . . the Scion of Akai.

Tarros sat up again. "I'm a descendant of Tarren of Old Senadon. I'm sure you recognize the name, too."

Aisic nodded. "I do. Tarren was a good friend of mine."

He looked up at the stars and breathed out heavily, the

blue light of Blazer's flame dancing along his face.

Nathan raised a hand. "Wait a second, your name is *Isaac*? Why did you say your name was Aisic? And how did you get trapped in the Melkairen?"

Aisic looked down and shook his head. "Aisic is how we pronounced it, but Isaac was a more common name to the rest of the world, and after I became known, that's what they called me, apparently. As for how it happened . . . well, it's a long story."

He returned his gaze to the stars.

Nathan made his tone serious. "Tell us everything."

Aisic raised his eyebrows in amusement. "*Everything*, huh?"

All three of them stared at him until he gave way.

"You *are* the king now, but we might need some sleep for tomorrow, so I'll give you the short version." He gestured at the two callers. "As the two of you should know, the end of Ramannon's reign began when he chose Senadon to be his next target. For years they had been protecting the remaining Kairens, knowing that only they could save the land if the Melkai were to return. Now that I think about it, it only makes sense that a few Senadonian-Kairen couplings would lead to descendants who could create pacts."

Durian rolled his wrist. "We know, we know! Tell us about how you were trapped inside the Melkairen."

"After our first battle with Ramannon's legions, Tarren and I advanced on Terratheist with a weapon the Kairens bestowed upon me . . ."

CHAPTER 22

THE SCION OF AKAI

450 Years Ago

Aisic strode across the Solvena Plains, wiping tears from his eyes.

His path was set. It had been since Amberley's death. Aisic wasn't angry at Tarren for not protecting her as he'd asked. He wasn't even angry at the executioner who had killed her. The system had made her death inevitable, the one put in place by Emperor Ramannon.

Everyone in the lands shared his pain as their turn came. The slow destruction of their race, the killing of their friends and family—they justified it with their will to survive in the present. He wasn't going to allow this to go on any longer.

A wind blew up beside him, and he noticed Tarren walking at his own pace on the grass next to him. He had been so caught up in the news of his loss that he hadn't even noticed the Senadonian until he appeared. Tarren gave him a quick smirk.

"I didn't ask you to come with me," Aisic muttered.

Tarren shrugged. "We're in this together, and besides, I think I'll be able to help."

Aisic nodded. Ahead, the Terratheist Castle was rising above the horizon. Even in the dim light of the stars, he could already see the tips of the towers. The castle grew bigger as they walked through the fields that surrounded the city. When they reached the top of the hills, night was becoming morning, and they saw what was in the distance behind them. Less than a mile off, the united Akai and Senadonian forces were marching across the fields. At their head, Cullen Armalon, the leader of Akai, and the general who led the Senadonian forces rode their great war horses.

Their final battle was waiting for them just over the hills.

Tarren jerked his head at them. "Back up. You think we'll need it?"

Aisic didn't reply, only started down into the valley. The hills horseshoed the valley, so once they descended one arm of the horseshoe—the one the Talis Lake rested atop—there was still yet another to climb. The Menophilly Hills surrounded Terratheist, the seat of Ramannon's empire, its slope leading up to its main gates. The walls attached to the gate spread high up into the hills with the city stretching even higher into the mountains. The valley would be where the final conflict would take place, but their focus would be on getting into the city itself.

They approached the gate. Dark clouds filled the sky, arising from the snowy peaks of the mountains behind. A feeling of vertigo came over Aisic as he looked up at the huge dark gates in front of him.

"How do *you* plan on getting in?" Aisic asked.

Tarren pushed him forward playfully. "Just blow the gates already."

Aisic let out the smallest of smiles, stepped forward, but then stopped. He looked over his shoulder at Tarren, attempting to reinforce the importance behind his words with a glare.

"Once I've done this, it will be up to you to protect me from the guards until I can recover."

Tarren shrugged. "Sure, leave it to me."

Aisic raised his hand toward where the gates split. No army had breached these gates, but now it was time to test the full capabilities of his Arion powers.

There was a sudden groan in the door as his skin prickled. He steadied himself. With an exploding crack, the doors were gone in a burst of dust that ripped up the ground around them. He breathed out heavily and placed his hands on his knees.

"Are you alright?" Tarren asked.

Aisic nodded but was unable to catch his breath enough to speak. Without a word, he rose and walked through the cloud of dust.

Armed guards ran through the dust to attack anything that came into view.

"Your turn," he rasped.

Tarren moved in front of him. He drew out his two short swords, spinning them up into his grip. Dashing up to the first approaching soldiers, he took one out with a quick swing of his blades. As quickly as the first had fallen, he appeared in front of the next, slashing at his neck, and then the next in the same fashion, his body blurring from soldier to soldier. Shocked by his speed, Aisic hurried through into the city streets, the soldiers that approached falling one by one.

The tall buildings stretched up around them, but none were as big as the tower that they were approaching. They climbed the sloping streets, and guards continued to come for them. Tarren didn't just take down the running soldiers. With blinding speed, he rushed forward and cut down the archers eyeing them up from a distance. With Tarren annihilating any obstacle that crossed his path, Aisic didn't need to stop once.

"Your speed . . . this power," Aisic said, "it's akin to an Arion's nearing death."

Tarren was suddenly walking beside him again. "Amberley gave it to me during her passing so I could help you stop Ramannon."

"So, the powers can be passed onto others . . ." Aisic bared his teeth in anguish. "She gave you her life so she could help me . . . even in death."

Tarren nodded. Amberley was still alive inside of him. She and Aisic were together once more. Tarren blurred off again to cut down another soldier.

They came to a plateau on the hill, a round flat opening between the buildings which appeared to be the city center. Waiting for them there was a large legion of the Ramannon army. They covered half the open ground leading toward the castle for a good hundred yards, shield and sword in hand, as still as statues.

Aisic growled, "I can't be held up by this any longer!"

"You won't." Tarren moved forward.

Aisic looked to him in confusion.

"I can hold them here until the army arrives."

"Tarren, are you . . ." Aisic nodded. "Alright, then." He then ran off down one of the side streets.

Aisic moved through the shadowed back alleys of the city until he came to the keep that leaned tall and ominous against the Jile Mountains. He paused to admire the height of its tower and then braced himself to go inside. Entering via the unguarded main doors, he moved through the long hallway toward the throne room. Then he exhaled heavily and blew the doors clean off their hinges. His vision narrowed, but he shook his head and ran in through the dust that had risen up from the impact. The throne room was large, well-draped, and carpeted, but completely empty of people. Or so it appeared until Aisic noticed a set of robes drifting to one side of the tall dais.

Standing there, facing away from him, was the tyrant emperor: Emperor Ramannon.

Despite Ramannon losing his body, he clearly hadn't lost his sense of the monarchy's style. Aisic walked inside, looking up at the portraits on the high walls. He could tell by their faces that they were King Armalon the First's descendants. What he couldn't understand was why Ramannon would keep them up even after he had ascended the family throne. Aisic stared up at them, suspicious that one of them could have portrayed Ramannon himself before he lost his body.

He stopped as he reached the center of the room. Ramannon was looking at the portrait at the back of the hall. The portrait was of an old man, older than any he had seen before, with a long white beard and wild white hair.

"Armalon the First," Aisic murmured.

"My father . . ." a dark voice replied. "Ah, welcome."

As Ramannon whirled about, Aisic laid eyes on that which was the cause of everything. Ramannon had no body. The only thing that revealed his presence was the robe that he animated. Within the hood of the cloak were two glowing red orbs, as though the focus of his power was concentrated there. Aisic bared his teeth. For Tarren, for Amberley, and everyone else, now was the time to end it.

On him were two swords, the longsword the king had given him, had trained him with, and the sword the Kairens had presented him, waiting to be summoned. He drew the longsword and raised it in a dueling stance, but the entity that was Ramannon did not attack him. He simply floated in front of him, walking on legs of air.

Aisic frowned, his eyes focused but keeping his sword at the ready, even though he had a suspicion that such a weapon could do the tyrant no harm. There was no flesh to cut, no bones to break or organs to pierce, only cloth and energy. Nevertheless, he thought that it may show his hostility. He sensed no fear in the presence before him.

"Who are you?" the deep voice asked.

"My name is Aisic. I am the last Arion and the Scion of Akai!" he exclaimed as the cloaked figure swayed weightlessly around him. "I'm here to kill you."

A peal of sudden laughter echoed around the room. "Yes, yes, of course you are. Tell me, boy, are you aware of why the Arions have power?"

Aisic turned as the cloaked figure floated around him.

The voice continued, "It's because the Arions are the only race of men that have a spirit."

Aisic frowned in agitation. "What are you talking about?"

"A spirit is when the energy of the body is anchored to a

single spot, usually located within the heart or the brain," the dark voice continued to rattle around the room, as though coming from the room itself. "It is this energy that is released during the Arion's death that gives them their extraordinary power; concentrated energy channeled through the body."

"What of it?" Aisic spat, following Ramannon's every movement.

"There has been only one other species in the lands that has possessed this attribute. It was wiped from the lands before even my conception, or so it was thought."

"What are you talking about? There were no races wiped out before *you* came along!" Aisic shouted.

"Wrong!" The sudden hiss shook the walls. "You have forgotten about one particular race that vanished from the face of the lands before even the Armalon reign began, those who hold a common ancestry with the Arion. I'm talking, of course, of the Melkai."

Aisic's eyebrows pushed together. "The Arions . . ."

The hood of Ramannon's cloak came down in agreement. "We are Melkai, you and I. The last that were not sealed away," he snarled. "We are, and always will be the bane of man because of this."

Aisic whispered, "It can't be . . . Is that why you decided to destroy us?" He bared his teeth in disgust.

Ramannon continued to float around Aisic.

"The reason we can use our powers before death was not because we were special, not at all." Ramannon flew around him faster as his voice echoed through the room. "Like with everything, it came down to our blood. You see, we are both born from the same kind of accident: the coupling between a Kairen and an Arion. A human and a Melkai."

Aisic's eyes grew wide. The queen had told him Kairens weren't as powerful as the Arions, but unlike the Arions, they could use their powers before death. It only made sense that a child born of those bloodlines would have such abilities.

"That is why the Arions had to die! Imagine it, a race of Melkai with the appearance of men paired with an incredible power they could use at will." His hood came in to face him before he drifted back toward the edge of the room, back toward the portrait of Armalon the First. "That's why both the Kairens and the Arions had to be eliminated. That power, in the end, would only lead to war. They were inherently evil."

"You kill thousands, wiping out entire races of people, and you think the Arions as a people were evil?"

"How could they not be? After all, they created me."

"They also created me!"

"And how are you any different? You've killed hundreds yourself, and in this battle *you* have instigated, hundreds more will die. Do you really think you will be satisfied when I'm gone? You're just as cursed by your power as I am by mine."

"I'm nothing like you!"

"You're the offspring of a Kairen and an Arion. You're exactly like me. The only way we differ is that I was fated to rule and you were fated to die. I succeeded, where you continuously fail to accept your fate. However, succeed or fail, others dying as a consequence will always be the result."

Aisic gritted his teeth. "*You* did that!"

Ramannon stopped in his path and turned away. "And now you and I are the only Melkai left unsealed . . ."

Now that everything was clear for him, Aisic had no

reason to hesitate. "Not for long!"

His hand shot out, but before he could cause a shockwave, he was ripped off his feet and sent flying back against the throne room doors by an even more powerful force. He collided against them with a crack and fell to the floor on his hands and knees, panting in shock.

"You cannot kill me, boy. How can you possibly kill something that cannot die?" Ramannon asked, sounding amused by his efforts.

Aisic coughed dryly. "Let's find out."

He put a hand on the rug beneath him and struggled up onto his feet, his posture slouching. Still, he managed to show the slightest hint of a smile. "I don't have to kill you to defeat you."

He flicked his arms across his body. From the tips of his fingers, a line of light appeared from out of thin air, creating what the Kairens called a seam. Just as Cullen Armalon had instructed him to do, he thrust his fist through the line of light. The glow stretched out from his hand and he pulled out the Kairen Sword—a weapon created by and passed down the Armalon family line—its crystal blade glistening above him.

Ramannon's voice rumbled, "That sword!" sounding suddenly fearful.

Aisic raised the crystal weapon high. "This is a Sword of Sealing. It has the power to lock away anything that does not have a physical presence here in the world. Being without a body, you do not age, but your immortality comes at a great price, and with this weapon, I'll show you why!"

Aisic ran in and swung the blade down on Ramannon. The animated robe swerved to one side and then the other, evading the strikes, but with that, Aisic spun, raising his hand up to release yet another shockwave. His power, however, was then met with Ramannon's own as the two forces pushed against one another.

"What use is a sword if I cannot be cut by it?" Ramannon taunted, but Aisic continued to push forward, baring his teeth in the struggle.

As his shockwave ceased, he was once again flung back onto the carpet by Ramannon's power. As fast as his legs would permit him, he rolled up onto his feet. He rubbed the pain from his neck which had snapped back from the sudden impact. Not only that, but his head was beginning to swim from using his own ability.

The differences between their powers all of a sudden became apparent to him. Where Aisic's body had to recover after each impact, Ramannon didn't have a body, and so could use his power again immediately after.

Looking for another point of attack, Aisic peered into Ramannon's glowing eyes. But no; he had no eyes just as he had no body. Then what Ramannon had told him suddenly made sense. The orbs that moved about within the robe were the concentration of energy he referred to as his so-called *spirit*.

"I keep telling you, it's futile," Ramannon called out. "However, if that won't stop you, I'll just finish you myself!"

Before Aisic could even register his words, he was up and running at him once again. He felt his skin prickle, sensing an upcoming pulse rushing toward him. He readied his own shockwave and launched the energy of it through the sword. Ramannon somehow annulled the shockwave. Aisic raised the sword, and with all his might, thrust it toward the cloaked figure's core.

The third pulse from Ramannon blocked the blade.

Aisic ground his teeth and pushed with all his will against it so it would not knock him back, but as he had expected, Ramannon's power became a torrent. Aisic's feet slipped on the floor, his arm muscles screaming, his fingers tight on the hilt, trying with all his might to thrust with the Kairen Sword. The flaming torches around the hall went out from the rush of wind, leaving the room in darkness.

Gritting his teeth until his jaw hurt, Aisic's rage flared like electricity around him. He pushed the Kairen Sword toward the red cores within the cloaked form, but it was a futile effort. Even as the point of the sword drew nearer to them, the two red orbs parted to the cloak's shoulders. "You put up a valiant effort, even more so than your people's last champion, but I'm afraid you are too much of a risk to keep alive."

As though Ramannon's words had triggered a memory within the weapon, the Kairen Sword appeared to glow and sudden darkness came over Aisic's mind.

His eyes opened to see that he was standing atop a stage of stone. People surrounded him, people he thought he knew although he had never met. Their teary-eyed faces expressed an importance for this moment he couldn't grasp.

His body then moved of its own volition. Clutching the shimmering hilt of the Kairen Sword, he crouched low and jumped, launching himself high into the air as impacts of force lifted him into the night.

Is this . . . a memory from the last person who wielded this weapon?

He scanned the star-speckled sky, and Ramannon's robed

form hovered down in front of him. Raising his blade, Aisic could feel the magic of the Kairens flow through him.

This was the battle that determined the fate of his people.

Aisic watched through the eyes of the Arion warrior as he slashed at Ramannon, following him from one corner of the sky to another. Ramannon evaded each attack, then pointed one sleeve of his robe toward him, and the warrior fell back from an invisible blow. Aisic plummeted, the entire world spinning before he hit the base of a waterfall with a deafening splash.

This fight had sentenced every Arion to death. And his defeat would sentence every Kairen and Senadonian to die along with them.

No, I won't let it!

Aisic awakened with a renewed fury as his skin prickled in warning, sensing Ramannon's final attack. "No!"

There was a crash behind him as the large doors to the throne room were flung open. Dual swords spun through the air, hitting very near to where the two concentrations of light had been. The hood was flung from the empty apparition, pinning it to the back wall. Then Aisic watched as the orbs formed before him, the two lights coming to a single sphere to avoid the blades.

"Aisic, finish it!" Tarren called.

Aisic shut his eyes and screamed, using the last of his will to release a final impact and the last of his strength to push the blade into the sphere. With that final effort, it pierced through the rush of energy and a beam of light flooded the room.

However, he had pushed his power too far. Piece by piece, his body began to vaporize into the air as the force of his energy pushed against what was left of Ramannon's, the orb of light exploding, their willpower alone seeming to draw everything into the core of the room where the Kairen Sword hovered upright, acting as a gateway.

A shockwave of force ripped through the great halls, pushing Tarren off his feet. A groaning sound filled the tower, sounding like it was about to cave in on them. The last thing Aisic saw before he vanished entirely was the Kairen Sword breaking, the blade snapping cleanly in two.

Having been caught up in Aisic's tale, Nathan breathed out heavily as his friend paused. The two Senadonians looked at each other, brows raised.

Aisic gazed down at the campfire, concluding his story with, "When I finally returned, I found a world where Ramannon no longer ruled and I could no longer use my powers. It probably has something to do with sharing my body with a Melkai."

Tarros nodded. "Tarren's account stated that soon after you entered the castle, the throne room collapsed and you were never seen again. He never shared with anyone what happened to you." He inclined his head in Aisic's direction. "Everyone assumed you were dead."

"It was the Kairen Sword, wasn't it?" Nathan asked.

Aisic nodded. "Ramannon could change into his spirit form at will and possess objects. The only way I could defeat him was to lock him in the Melkairen, and that's exactly what the Kairen Sword did. Given that they were both created by the Kairens, I assume it had similar magical properties to the keys you and your sister possess and that they were forged after the sword was broken. In order to overpower him, I had to sacrifice my own body. The Kairen Sword broke in two and—"

"And your spirit got sucked in with his." Durian crossed his arms.

"That's right."

Nathan's brow furrowed and he looked up at the reddening moon. "But if you managed to get through the weakened barrier . . ."

Tarros and Durian's eyes widened, and Tarros whispered, "Oh . . . no."

Aisic nodded again. "That's right. There's a good chance that if I escaped the Melkairen, Ramannon did as well."

CHAPTER 23

THE BATTLEMENTS

High up on the castle's outer wall, Laine looked down solemnly. A mass of opposing soldiers began to form on the outskirts of the Kydian Wood. She knew they weren't Avatasc soldiers, but their numbers were impressive nonetheless, a far greater force than Garland and Kydia could have mustered alone.

A battalion of Senadonian refugees might have joined forces with them, but even had that been the case, it wouldn't matter. Terratheist had the greatest army in the land, bar none. How King Michael could muster men out of what seemed thin air was a miracle to her and one that guaranteed victory.

Even if a few rebels did break through their defenses, Laine had ordered her callers to attack anyone who breached the walls. After raising them all to the contrived rank of *Battle Summoner* under her and allowing them free rein to use their abilities, she had won their loyalty over their previous master. Now, even an enemy caller would have difficulty gaining ground inside the city.

Still, she knew what would come of this.

Laine bit her lower lip, apprehensive about being a part of rekindling the border war between Avatasc and Terratheist. Those who she was fighting against were from her home kingdom where her mother still lived. Although she was doing this for her sake as well, she couldn't help but wonder what her mother would say if she could look upon her now.

Laine had taken a high position in a foreign country that she could use to reform her home, just like her mother had told her needed to be done. However, now that more Melkai were slipping into their world, and with Nathan nowhere to be found, any control over the situation felt like it was slipping through her fingers. Even if she did go after him, she had no idea if she would find him before it was too late . . . if it wasn't already too late.

If I get what I want in the end, does it really matter how I achieve it?

Hundreds of men charged the thousands of armored soldiers outside the great walls and were rebuffed, many wounded or killed from the exchange.

So long as they don't enter the city, Kendra and the rest of the civilians will be safe.

Further fighting would only end in slaughter, and she pitied them, as she knew this wouldn't be the end of it. She grabbed the collar of her robe and was tempted to summon Terachiro. However, in the split second before she went to throw it, she pulled her hand away. Something deep down told her she was going to need her Melkai close by if anything went wrong.

"I'm sorry," she said to her cloak. "You're going to have to be patient."

She could almost hear the screams of the men in the battle below her. Their army charged hopelessly, desperately into the wall of armor and steel, fighting tooth and nail to reclaim ground.

This is necessary. King Kissick must be defeated, and for that, King Michael must triumph.

The rebels had no chance, and after this, the last battle for Avatasc would be at hand. There was a cry of horror below her, and her eyes drifted to the sky. For just a moment, she could have sworn she had seen a dragon flying toward the city.

It can't be the same one I fought, can it?

The familiar form drew nearer. Shots were loosed from the castle walls. The dragon banked sharply and began to circumvent the castle, either to avoid the battle entirely or make a rear assault. The castle and city chapel were nearer to the back of the city highland, so if an attack was its intention, its flight path revealed the high intelligence of the creature.

Even on horseback, Laine wouldn't have been able to make it to the other side of the city to warn Reshal, who was guarding the inner walls.

On the tower platform below, her second-in-command stood ready.

"Blake!" she shouted. "Send out your wyvern as a signal to warn the others. That dragon is headed their way. Send it to Tuttle first, Reshal will need backup."

"Yes, master." Blake pulled out an emerald he'd no doubt received from his wealthy parents and threw it into the air.

The emerald glowed bright green and transformed into

the two-legged wyvern. Although the wyvern was impressive, Laine wasn't confident it could hold its ground against a dragon.

"To Tuttle, go!" Blake cried.

The wyvern took off to circle the castle walls in search of Tuttle and his giant falcon. Laine grinned, glad she had back up against the creature this time.

There was a sudden clanking of armor behind her, and she peered over her shoulder. One of the king's guards waited.

"What do you want?" she asked.

"The king requests your presence."

Her lips curled inward. "Dragon's breath, now?" It would take her near an hour to reach him, placate his majesty's nerves, and return to the wall. "What does he want?"

"He did not say. He only asks you to come immediately."

"Where is he?"

"The chapel."

Jaw clenched in agitation, she shouted, "Tell him I will be there shortly."

The soldier bowed and walked off.

Laine gripped her hood, fully aware her team would not be as effective without her and Terachiro. Nevertheless, she had to go to the king.

"Blake," Laine called. "I'm putting you in charge of the walls while I'm away."

Blake's eyes grew wide with clear panic. "A-are you sure that's wise, Master? D-do you think the others will follow my orders?"

"They'll have to." Laine exhaled. "If the others fall, pull back, and guard the castle. Understand?"

Blake nodded and bolted off. Laine had a feeling he

wouldn't make it to the other side of the castle in time either. She could only hope that Reshal and Tuttle could handle the dragon on their own until he reached them.

Gritting her teeth at the king's audacity to pull her out of the battle at its most crucial moment, she descended the fortified stairwell and made her way to the castle.

What could King Michael possibly want now?

CHAPTER 24

INVASION

The high towers of the Terratheist fortress came into view. The sun was setting and the clouds above them were dark and swelling, but not as dark as the land below them, which was churning with warring soldiers.

All along the Menophilly Hills, they pushed back and stabbed at the rebelling forces on their battlefront, a failing last-ditch effort from villages that lived in proximity to the city. The place had definitely changed from how Nathan remembered it.

"This battle . . ." Aisic spoke in Nathan's mind as he looked down over the Valley of the Two Kings. *"It's just like it was back then."*

He flapped his wings and banked sideways as a volley of arrows flew their way from the archers on the castle crenellations. They passed over the giant city walls, dodging arrows and watching as the soldiers marched through the streets. There were hundreds of them.

With a sudden explosion, Tarros's phoenix torched the gate, and Durian rode through on the great wolf's back. He knocked the soldiers down in their path as they swiftly approached the city square.

"Fly over the city!" Nathan called.

Aisic soared down toward a long barricade that walled off the outer courtyard to the castle. Several cloaked figures came into view, standing on the rise of the barricade. A giant bird Melkai flew toward them as several quadruped first-circles appeared around the barricade. Aisic flapped his wings to avoid what looked like a giant falcon before breathing out his fire upon it. It burned up in his flame and fell to the city below. Banking, Aisic looped around, but was caught by a few arrows as they pinged off his armored skin.

Nathan ducked behind his back as one whisked past him. "Land now! This is where we make our stand!"

An insect-like Melkai flew at them, but Aisic swooped down under it, its wings fluttering like a fly's as a large stinger from its tail stabbed barely inches away from Nathan's head. Aisic swooped low and unleashed a gout of flame, finishing it quicker than the first. On the battlements, archers burst out from the bushes and pulled back their bowstrings.

They had to land somewhere. The gray skies appeared to be ablaze with stars so close that they could actually hit you. They weren't stars but flame-tipped arrows shot skyward by the longbows of the Terratheist archers. They stood alongside cloaked callers, undoubtedly Master Morrow's students, each one summoning a Melkai from a glowing pact item.

Aisic swooped down as another volley of arrows rushed toward them, but he used his own flame to destroy them. They flared up into nothing as Aisic's massive body burst from the flame and landed, his giant tail swatting the soldiers away. Nathan slid down it, landing and confronting those attacking.

"Stop!" He took off his chain mail hood. "It's me, Nathan!"

The archers pulled back and fired another volley. They were too close, and Aisic didn't have enough time to blow them away. However, an electrical charge passed through the air, and they quickly dropped to the ground.

One of the cloaked figures emerged out from the group and stood in front of them, blocking their path. Seeing the tall, frail figure under his robe, Nathan already knew who he was.

The old man pulled back his hood and turned to the other callers. "Stop this! He's one of our own!"

The younger callers shouted out to their Melkai, and the fighting paused for a moment.

Aisic returned to his human form and sheathed his sword. "Nathan, who's that?"

Nathan grinned. "He's my teacher, Master Morrow." But then he asked, "Morrow, why is the king doing this? Avatasc is under new rule now; there is no threat anymore!"

For a brief moment, Morrow's eyes dropped to the ground, his brow furrowed. "Dragon's Breath! That confirms my suspicions. The king passed on several weeks back. Michael has succeeded him."

Nathan halted when he heard the name of his old friend again.

Morrow told him of the events that had taken place during his absence. Michael was now King of Terratheist and keeping to his own counsel, and Laine had taken Morrow's place as the leader of the court callers.

His mouth opened in shock, unable to form words. He had been best friends with Michael, who had treated him like a younger brother from the moment they first met, for most of his life. Michael hadn't been like the other stuck-up, young nobles. He had been jovial with everyone, even going so far as to treat his father, the king, as a friend. Yet now he was acting like the world itself had turned against him.

"This doesn't make any sense."

Michael couldn't have changed that much—could he?

He looked up again to see a soldier pulling back his longbow and taking aim at Morrow's back. "Look out!"

Morrow turned and swiftly raised his hands, opening a seam to the Melkairen as the fired arrows flew into it. "These soldiers seem to believe talking to you is committing an act of treason. I thought something fishy was going on. This war has been far too quiet."

Suddenly, several Melkai, each of the first and second circles, growled behind the archers, ready to attack Master Morrow as well.

Teeth bared, Nathan scanned the faces of the callers. Once he recognized them, he was completely unsurprised by how they were acting. He had shared many lectures on pact making and Melkai control with them and learned that most of them were only trying to become callers because they were pressured into it by their noble parents. Expectations were high for nobles to have at least one Advanced Summoner in their family, and if the father failed to become one, they were sure that the son would. All it would've taken for the student to turn on their teacher, their kingdom, or even their parents, was the promise of getting power of their own, if

227

just to break away from those expectations.

Having grown up as an orphan, Nathan could understand but couldn't relate.

Morrow flashed a look back at Nathan. "You knew Michael better than any of us. Go to him. See if you can talk some sense into him."

"What about you?"

The old man smiled. "I'm not so rusty that I can't handle these novices by myself. Now go!"

If someone were to tell Nathan that Morrow had been brought up on the street or during a time of war, it would not have surprised him.

He nodded to his master and got a smiling nod in return. Morrow still trusted him to do what needed to be done.

"Okay!" Nathan said, but as he went to move on, he remembered Tarros and Durian. "Oh, and if you see two Senadonians come by on a wolf, they are on our side. Just say you are with King Nathaniel Armalon, and they'll know."

Master Morrow laughed. "Finally worked it out, huh? I always knew you had it in you to find out for yourself."

"Really?" Nathan shouted. "I'm surprised you managed to keep that a secret for so long."

"Believe me, Nathan, it nearly killed me."

"Well, don't die for my sake just because I know now, all right?"

"Yes, well . . ." He turned back to the other callers. "Advanced Summoners don't die so easily. Senadon and Armalon though . . . now those are two names I haven't heard in the same sentence for a long time."

Nathan shook his head. Morrow hadn't just known about his lineage, but the history of their connection to the

Akai uprising.

With Aisic following him, Nathan ran down the barricade and into the courtyard. The buildings were cracked and crumbled. The fountain in the courtyard had stopped flowing, the gardens were pulled out, the flowers dead, but the biggest change was the darkness from the clouds that hovered overhead. Nathan felt like he was searching a ruin rather than the most beloved city in the land, not just with the drab look of the place, but also with how all the colors from the garden to the curtains had been removed.

He searched the castle balconies. He barely recognized the place. For nearly a decade, Terratheist had been his home, a place he loved to explore even when he was forbidden to do so. However, now the foreboding felt much grimmer, like poking his head into an off-limits room would now have him fighting a bloodthirsty Melkai rather than being given a tongue-in-cheek telling off.

"I don't understand why Michael's doing this," Nathan said as Aisic caught up with him. "It's out of character for him, almost like . . ."

"He's become someone else."

"Yeah . . ."

"Then I suggest we prepare ourselves for the worst."

They approached the stairs that led up to the castle's gated tower, and Nathan stopped. Despite the chaos going on all around, unlike every other building around them, the chapel was lit with candles. As children, he and Michael had used it as a meeting place. Waiting on the butt-bruising pews before planning to sneak into the castle gallery sprung to mind. If it hadn't been for Michael's prompting, he never would have known his mother's face.

Turning from their original path, he dashed toward the large, steeple-topped tower.

Aisic spun and caught up with him. "Nathan, where are you going?"

Nathan didn't stop. "He's in there. I know he is. He wants to meet."

They ran down the wide pathway and arrived at the chapel doors. He hesitated a moment. Something told him Michael was in there, but that same feeling was telling him not to go inside. He ignored it and shoved the doors open. They swung wide and he slowly stepped in.

He was right. Standing at the back of the chapel was the prince . . . no, the King of Terratheist, but not as Nathan remembered him.

He squinted in the candlelight. It was Michael, but like the city, he was barely recognizable. From his pallid complexion, whatever had infected the castle appeared to have also infected him. In fact, further studying his friend's baleful expression made Nathan start to believe that he wasn't infected, but rather that he was the infection.

As he saw them, he smiled, but it wasn't the smile that Nathan remembered. It was more crooked, and his narrowed eyes topped off the sinister look. A sudden pulse of air blew out the flames along the walls and caused the doors to creak shut behind them. The reddened moonlight outside bounced off the plates of his armored shoulders.

"Michael . . ." Nathan said, advancing cautiously. "What's going on? Why did you start this war?"

Michael's head dipped, his face becoming bathed in shadow. "You still don't understand, even now?"

Aisic stepped in front of Nathan like he was expecting

Michael to attack him, but Nathan raised a hand. "What are you talking about?"

Red glowing eyes flashed from the shadows. "Tell me, child; did you bring the key?" Michael raised a grasping hand. "*Give it to me.*"

Nathan knew he had seen those red eyes somewhere before, but it wasn't until he saw it alongside the palm-up, grasping gesture that he realized where he had seen it.

"You're . . . not Michael, are you?" he asked.

Those red eyes were exactly the same as the first Melkai he and Michael had come across when their journey had begun.

"Who . . . who are you?"

The thing wearing his friend's body asked, "Who am I?"

Aisic stepped forward, drawing his sword, but not yet attacking. Nathan understood why Aisic would need to be ready. He knew this wasn't Michael anymore. But he had to hear it from his own lips before a fight broke out.

"Like your friend here, I have been locked in the Melkairen for the past five hundred years." The Melkai inside of Michael glared in irritation. "But I suppose you want a name."

"Ramannon," Aisic growled.

Nathan took a step back, looking from Michael to Aisic and back.

Using Michael's face, Ramannon smiled. "*King* Ramannon."

CHAPTER 25

THE GATE

From up on the battlements, the fight had appeared organized and under control, but down amongst the people and the chaos, the battle painted a completely different picture. Where before she had a good idea of where everything was, now she felt as lost as any citizen looking for shelter.

Although the summoning had come from the king himself, she was disgruntled to have to cross from the city's outer walls to the castle, which was no leisurely stroll. The castle and neighboring chapel rested at the top of the highland the city surrounded. She would have to climb the hill until finally reaching the inner wall, separating the commoners from the castle, and then ascend the many stairs through the arch of the keep's walls to finally reach the castle courtyard where she could veer left to the tall church.

As she rushed through the cobbled streets, she was forced off her path as a battalion of armored soldiers marched down it toward the gate. In her panic, she noticed women and the elderly fleeing from the gate. This usually meant one thing; a breach.

After what she had seen from up on the wall, this change in the battle didn't make any sense. However, when she saw a plume of fire erupt behind her, it suddenly dawned on her that a Melkai had joined their enemy's ranks.

She took a side street, panting as she dashed through a crowd of people cowering under a stone veranda. Although she wanted to warn them that it wasn't the safest place to hide with Melkai possibly charging through any second, she knew she wouldn't be able to get them to move in time, and by then she would be caught in the thick of it herself.

Gritting her teeth, she pulled her cloak from around her shoulders and tossed it into the air. With a flash, Terachiro landed before her, causing several of the huddled peasants to scream in fear.

"Take to the air!" she shouted to be heard. "Find me the empty passages to the castle! I'll follow you!"

With a sharp huff, Terachiro flapped its wings and took off, darting through the sky in the direction of roads that were less crowded. Like a regular bat, Terachiro was able to use sound to see things that were not visible to the eye. Seeing it circle a distant area, Laine rushed down an alley and found a smaller side street that wasn't so packed. She dashed down it, her heart racing in her chest as she looked up to see Terachiro circling another area of the city.

Following Terachiro's directions, Laine eventually found a way leading up to the castle's inner walls. She had left the redhead, Reshal, in charge of this area, and she hoped the girl had managed to keep the battlements unmolested by the enemy. As she made it to the gatehouse and shouted up for them to open the gates for her, the voice that returned was Reshal's.

In a trembling voice, the redhead called, "Please . . . wait, Master! I'll—" then was cut off by the rattling of the drawbridge being lowered.

Laine ran in and was met by the girl. The rings around the girl's eyes from her rubbing them were redder than her hair, and Laine could tell she had been crying.

"What happened?" Laine demanded. "Did you manage to hold the inner wall?"

Reshal shook her head. "Izzy . . . my Melkai . . . and Tuttle's too. The dragon killed both of them!"

Laine winced. She had known her fliers were inexperienced but thought having two of them standing sentinel on the inner wall would make up for that. It appeared that, when fighting a dragon, the number of Melkai you commanded didn't matter.

"I ordered Blake to send back up. Did his wyvern . . ." She stopped as she saw that Reshal looked like she was about to faint. The girl was clearly catatonic from losing her Melkai in the battle. Laine ran in and slapped her. "Get a hold of yourself!"

Instead of snapping the girl out of her sorrow, tears just welled in Reshal's eyes and she bawled. She raised a shaking hand to her cheek and fled back into the gatehouse battlements. Laine hoped the weak girl would at least lift the gate back up when she made it inside.

She groaned, realizing she couldn't trust her with that in her current state, and if the enemy had Melkai, they could be arriving at any moment. "Dragon's breath!"

She followed Reshal inside only to see her cowering

next to the steps with her knees pulled up to her chest. The girl was a lost cause. Laine would have to do it herself. She climbed the stone steps as a sudden impact rocked the walls and she was forced to stable herself.

"What was . . ." She shook her head, realizing it wouldn't matter if she didn't make it to the gatehouse's wheel, and continued on.

She reached the top and found the wheel that would raise the drawbridge. From the size of the thing, she wouldn't be able to spin it by herself. Then, in the shadows, she noticed a large young man peering out of the slit window. It was Tuttle.

"What are you doing?" Laine asked.

Tuttle spun, his face pale, but then calmed at seeing her. "M-Master, my Garuda! Morrow, he . . ."

Laine realized he was talking about his bird Melkai and figured it had suffered a similar fate to Reshal's. "Yeah, okay, just help me with this wheel, will you?"

He nodded, and they both grabbed the levers to drop the drawbridge. Laine assumed he had been the one to open it before, for his strong arms made quick work of the task.

"What now?" he asked.

"Head to the castle and rally any callers you can find."

Tuttle nodded, hands shaking. "And what about you?"

Laine's lips pulled inward. "I have to go find the king."

She fled back down the stairs, heading to the chapel to receive her orders from King Michael, though at this stage she didn't know what to expect other than to prepare for a siege of the inner wall and wait for reinforcements to arrive.

As she ran up the stairs to the castle courtyard, circumventing the castle's main entrance in favor of taking the exterior path to the chapel, she gasped as an explosion filled the air above her. She peered up and saw an old man using some kind of dome of magic—glowing a similar blue to her own blade spell—to block the arrows of several archers as armored men with halberds closed in on him.

He was using abilities Laine had never seen before, and, as he was the enemy, she was not eager to catch his attention. She stayed close to the wall where he wouldn't be able to see her.

There was a bright flash above, and soldiers came flying down from the walls. Despite one of them landing with a clatter very close to where she was running, she didn't hear a single scream. In fact, it looked like the armor had saved him for he proceeded to silently rise and march his way back to the wall.

She was almost past the fight. However, she then spotted Terachiro landing on the wall near where the old wizard was fighting. She couldn't have her companion, mixed up with such a dangerous caller.

"Terachiro, to me!" she shouted.

Her large bat glided down to meet her, settling around her shoulder as her pact item. She waited a moment, worried the old man would send a Melkai after them, but he was too busy with the soldiers to notice her below.

Laine bared her teeth and continued her way to the chapel. Whatever the king had to tell her, she hoped it was good news for their defenses, because things were not looking good outside the walls.

She had just made to the wide path surround the large building when she noticed someone rushing through the chapel's front doors.

CHAPTER 26

ADVERSARY

Only now did Michael's hostility after defeating the second-circle Melkai make sense. Ramannon, the tyrant king who had ruled five hundred years ago, whom Aisic had locked in the Melkairen, had returned and was controlling his body.

"I didn't want to admit it." Aisic bowed his head and growled, "But I couldn't fool myself! Of course you were the reason for this war! Who else could cause so much chaos and misery so quickly?!"

Ramannon sneered. "It may have taken me five hundred years, but I finally found a way to escape."

"Then why didn't you kill me and take the key when you were in Michael's body that day?" Nathan cried out, grasping at straws.

"It took a while to take control of his body completely, but the weaker the barrier became, the more my influence over him grew." Ramannon peered out the window at the red moon. "In the forest, when the moon was a crescent full, I had enough power to come forward and take over completely." He spun and held out a gauntleted hand. "You are going to give me the key . . . or should your death come first?"

"That's the thing about war . . ." Nathan reached for his glove. "Death isn't picky. You possessed my friend, you killed the man who raised me, and now you're trying to kill everyone else?" His hands shook with fury. "No, not while I'm here."

Aisic shouted, "No, get out of here, now!" Without waiting for a reply, Aisic charged forward into an attack.

Ramannon smirked and drew out his own broadsword, striking away Aisic's first attack, his armor gleaming from the light of the red moon as he spun and struck back.

Aisic locked blades with him, attempting to pin Ramannon's sword with his own, but Ramannon's strength was far greater than Aisic in his human form. Ramannon grinned, aware of his advantage, so much so that he didn't struggle when he pushed forward, making Aisic stagger backward.

Aisic cried, "Go. Run!"

Nathan hesitated, gripping the seams of his glove. "No, I can help. It's two Melkai against one!"

With a scream, Aisic forced Ramannon back and looked like he was about to explain, but before he could get any words in, Ramannon raised a hand out in front of him.

"Two against one, you say?" He shook his head. "The Melkai behind the barrier are in league with me now."

Although close to being so, the moon was not yet completely red. There was still a little time left.

"The barrier has not given way. Without that, you have no Melkai here to control!" Nathan called.

Ramannon's grin remained. "I may not yet be able to control the Melkai that have a physical presence here, but remember that I once ruled this kingdom. I know what is buried below this chapel." He looked down, his eyes burning a bright red. "And the very spirits of the Melkai that can come from the Melkairen can possess them just as I have possessed this body here!"

There was a sudden rumble, and Nathan finally realized why the soldiers Aisic had burned up hadn't screamed, not to mention the sheer size of the army. Ramannon's soldiers were the army of the dead, and now the dead buried below the chapel were digging, climbing, and reaching toward the surface.

Nathan felt a terror pull inside him. His possessed friend's smile widened, and with a splintered crack, a bony arm penetrated through the floorboards. It was a thing of nightmares. Nathan stumbled back in horror. Aisic ran forward and cut the arm off with his blade.

More arms began breaking through.

Nathan was freezing again, hands trembling in fear. He told himself he would never do that again, but Melkai possessed corpses was on another level of horror. It was ridiculous.

Nathan's hands stopped trembling. Ridiculous circumstances demanded ridiculous actions. He stamped down on the nearest hand rising from the floorboard, snapping it off at the wrist. However, for every arm he shattered with his boots, two more would start breaking through.

This isn't getting us anywhere!

Ramannon laughed in glee. "Now, now, don't be so hasty. Some of these could be your old relatives after all. Don't you believe in respecting your elders?"

More cracks and groans arose from the splintering wood, and with it, the Melkai-possessed dead, tattered, and decomposed, rose all around them. Aisic tried to cut them down as they rose up, but the sheer number of them revealed how pointless his struggle was.

Ramannon laughed harder, and before long, they were encircled by the dead, back to back. The corpses halted.

"Living in the Melkairen taught me one important thing," Ramannon said. "It's the humans of this world, those who have no spirits, who are the true monsters."

Aisic slowly rose from his fighting stance and slid his sword back into his scabbard. Before he began his transformation, he spoke.

"Nathaniel Armalon, heed my words and obey this last wish of mine." His head was high and proud. "I want you to run from here and finally allow me to repay my debt to your ancestor in full by killing this Melkai."

"No, I can't! You'll—"

"I didn't choose to be your protector because you saved me by the river that day! Your ancestor, Cullen Armalon, took me in as a child and taught me everything I knew, but I was never able to repay him. When I escaped the Melkairen, I thought my chance gone forever, but then sensed his Kairen magic from you. After your sister attacked me, I figured it was you who would need my help the most. When your mother revealed you to be Cullen's heir, I knew it was fated to be so. I was glad to be able to fight beside you, but no more.

"This is my dying wish, Nathaniel. For the sake of your ancestors, go!"

I . . . no! This was not about freezing or running away. This was more than Nathan; this was a wish that had come from over five hundred years ago. *To repay his debt, to even his score with Ramannon, I must grant him this wish.*

"Don't lose!" Nathan cried. "That's an order from your king!"

Aisic ground his sharpened teeth to show his intent, and with a quick exhale, the wings from the hilt of his sword stretched out. The blade of his sword became his tail which swept out at the walking skeletons behind him, clearing a path for Nathan to the door.

With the harsh fury of his dragon's voice, he shouted, *"Run!"*

Nathan didn't hesitate. He ran to the door in the sheer shock of his guardian's voice.

With a sudden pulse, Aisic's body grew into its dragon form, smashing the bones of the living dead around him, crushing them underfoot.

Nathan saw this in his one glance back. He spun and burst through the chapel door. Hearing the sound of the battle waging between Ramannon and Aisic inside, he shut it and ran.

He heard footsteps running toward him and paused. A person stood on the wide footpath in front of him. The shock paralyzed him as he came face to face with the one person he never considered meeting in a situation like this.

Not only was she the one he had been sent to find since the beginning of his journey, but also someone he had met before. Someone who was unknowingly one of Avatasc's rightful heirs. Laine Armalon, his sister, stood before him.

CHAPTER 27

SISTER

The world felt like it was spinning around him. Nathan stared at Laine as she glared back. From her narrowed eyes, he couldn't tell if her expression portrayed suspicion or confusion. There was too much to explain everything all at once, and he knew it. But he had to try and get everything out before she made up her mind.

"Nathan?" she asked.

At least she's not calling me boy anymore.

Although taken aback by her appearance, he was honestly glad to see her, not just because he knew she was his sister now, but because he could finally complete his quest to unite the Kairen Key. And if the moon was anything to go by, they had left their reunion to the very last minute.

His heart dropped as her puzzled expression became cold, warning him that even if he walked on eggshells during their conversation, she still might not listen to him.

"I was told you were imprisoned by Kissick; did you

escape or have you . . ." Her eyes widened as she saw what he was wearing under his chain mail: a doublet of green and gold. "You work for him now, don't you?"

Nathan raised his hands, noticing the glove, her glove, still on his right hand. "Wait! Please let me talk before you jump to any conclusions. I've learned a lot that you need to know!"

She stepped back, her hand slowly rising to the collar of her cloak, the one that turned into that massive savage bat. He had to explain what was going on as carefully as he could, but first, he had to get her attention.

"Laine . . . you're . . . my sister!"

She hesitated. "What?"

"I'm Nathaniel Armalon. I met our mother while in Avatasc. She recognized me and showed me our family tree." He breathed in deeply, and before she could interrupt, he continued, "Kissick was our uncle. He wanted the throne and our father knew this. He also knew that killing him wouldn't be enough to usurp the throne but that Kissick would have to make sure there were no legitimate male heirs. For that reason, I was sent here to live before our father was murdered."

"What do you mean Kissick *was* our uncle?" she asked, her chest quickly rising and falling.

"I killed him myself; the Snake King was crushed beneath the weight of his own Melkai." He shook his head. "But please, let me finish before the world ends."

Laine's mouth dropped, but she continued to listen, though he was unsure how much of what he was saying she would actually believe.

"Unlike Kissick, our father was friends with the King of

Terratheist; the two kingdoms had been friends ever since the War of the Two Kings until Kissick took over. It was the Terratheist king who our father sent me to stay with when we were both children. You must have thought I looked familiar. Well, it's because we're twins!"

Laine shook her head, as though trying to reject this claim. "But why are you here now? If you're now the king then you should be in Avatasc, unless you were sent by Kissick and you're lying to me!"

Ramannon must have planted these suspicions in her.

She sighed and caught his eyes. "Why did you even go to Avatasc in the first place? Can you at least tell me that without lying?"

That's right, I lied about our journey. That's why she doesn't trust me.

"How can I believe anything you tell me?" she asked.

She could use this lie to undo his whole argument, but he had to try. He looked down and took off the Kairen Key necklace from his collar to reveal it to her. It was out on his sleeve now, or his collar at least, everything that was important about his quest.

"Here's how!" he shouted, lifting it high. "Now, you show me yours."

Startled by this, she slowly pulled out her own key. It was exactly the same as his, the crystal sparkling in the red moonlight. Silence filled the air, and they looked at each other's keys. He knew that, to both of them, this signaled the end and success of their quests.

Laine's eyes became hawkish. "I need your key."

Nathan nodded. "We both need each other's; we both know that, but do you know why?"

Laine stalked forward. "This will be what creates the power shift I spoke to you about. With it, I will be Queen of Avatasc and make my country better, once I give that key to King Michael."

Nathan shook his head and returned the key around his neck.

"You don't understand what's going on yet. Look!" He pointed to the red moon. "That means that the barrier to the Melkairen is weakening. You know what that means as much as anyone. The only thing that can stop this weakening is to combine these keys! After that you can have them, I don't care, but first we need to reinforce the barrier!"

"What, so you can bring it back to Kissick? I don't think so!" She reached up to her cloak, removed it from around her shoulders and threw it at him.

"I'm telling you he's dead!"

The bat transformed before him. Negotiations had broken down. He ground his teeth, removed his glove, and threw it. Taiba flew from it toward the massive bat.

The sharp talons of the bat stretched out, but before Taiba could be caught, he used his impressive speed to turn sharply. As Terachiro was forced to land, Taiba jumped onto its back, sinking his teeth into its furry skin.

Laine ran toward Nathan with one hand out to grab the key. As he leaned back, he noticed a bright blue glow behind her back like some kind of blade. As she brought it around, he caught her wrist and fell backward as she slashed over his head with a magical blade. He landed hard on the cobblestones, but he managed to kick his sister over him and then roll back on top of her, pinning her glowing hand to her chest.

Nathan growled as he struggled to restrain her. They were running out of time, and she was too stubborn to listen to him. It was his fault too, he knew. He had wasted so much time in Avatasc while he let the true threat creep up on him. Now, like forgetting to study for an exam and cramming as much study in as possible, he had rushed what should have been a drawn-out conversation.

Terachiro spun and flapped its wings, trying to get into the air. Taiba flew from its back, landing in a hard roll on the tiles before coming to his feet again. Both the dog's and bat's fangs were bared in a snarl, but sensing their masters were in danger, they both turned toward them.

Nathan used his weight to make sure she could not strike him with her spell again. However, leaning over her made his necklace fall from his collar. Seeing her necklace, he knew he just needed to rip it from her neck and it would be over, the threat of the Melkairen annulled. However, as he snatched at it, Laine reached up and grabbed his own necklace and with a sharp kick managed to push him off her as they both stood again, holding each other's keys. They both gasped as a paralysis pulled them in like a vortex.

There was no doubt now, they could both feel it pulsing between their fingers. There was magic within the Kairen Keys, a lot of it. As the power of the crystal keys had sucked in and sealed away the spirits of the Melkai, it had also drawn in their memories while they had worn them.

Nathan saw all of Laine's memories in the blink of an eye, just as he was sure she was seeing his. However, he knew his own memories, and they were nowhere near as cruel as hers. He saw every verbal slight and dismissal from their uncle, every scornful glare and harsh remark, as well as her memory of watching Kissick treat their mother even more coldly. He watched as their mother became distant and bitter, saw her hopeless frustration under her new husband.

He watched as the years went past and Laine was punished for expressing any emotion. How, when she let one sneer for the king slip out, the king had forbidden her from talking to her mother. Although she had snuck out to see her often, her mother refused to see her. Her giving up had hurt Laine more than anything.

In a strange way, he wished he had seen this before the king had died. It would have made defeating him in their fight a lot more cathartic. It also made Laine's intentions clearer. She had been trying to return glory to Avatasc, to free their mother from Kissick's grasp, and most importantly, prove to herself that she wasn't the weak girl that he made her out to be. She had been no one, nothing but the power to create pacts and summon Melkai.

The liar was on top of her, stopping her from using her spell to finish him. No matter how much she struggled, she couldn't free her pinned hand to slash at him. She hated it. She hated him. Despite being the same age, Nathan still had more weight and physical strength than her. Just another man in a long line of men who thought that strength made them better than her.

She knew otherwise. Strength didn't matter, and nothing made this clearer than when a powerful magical artifact fell right before her eyes as they wrestled. Dangling in front of her face, Nathan's key looked nearly symmetrical to her own. She just needed to grab it from him and the power would be hers, but with him pinning her, there was no way she could reach it.

Suddenly one of Nathan's hands let go of hers, freeing the one not glowing with her blade. She didn't have time to ask herself why. She snatched at the key, bucked under him, and just as he grasped something with his free hand, she kicked him off her and scrambled to her feet. However, even as she stood, she felt like she was falling.

A scene played before her eyes. It was windy, and she was standing beside someone massive . . .

No, I know this place. I've been here before. This is a memory!

In the first memory the necklace showed her, Laine could see the fields outside Avatasc. From her place hiding behind the skirts of her mother, she could see herself as a little girl.

This confused her. If this was her memory, how could she see herself?

Her vision was brought forward, her hand passed from her father to another large man. The man gripped her wrist tightly and pulled her across the field.

It wasn't until the man in her memory said, "Come, Nathan. We have a long journey ahead of us," that she realized what she was seeing.

He said . . . Nathan?

She knew then that she was feeling the same fear and sorrow Nathan had felt back then. She looked back to see herself, the emotion of being taken away reflected in her own young expression. They were two halves of a person: twins.

If these are his memories, then why am I in them? Why didn't I remember this? Why didn't he? Did the keys take these memories from us?

The scenes continued: flashes of memories of his lessons

with Master Morrow, every bit of emotion and information, struggle and failure. She witnessed the summoning of his first Melkai, the horror of nearly being killed by the second-circle that came partially through into his room.

Next, she was playing with the prince who was now the king. Michael seemed such a different person to the one who was commanding her now. Through Nathan's eyes, they explored the castle and were brought before the previous king and scolded. Year upon year of accumulated experiences were flung at her in little bits and pieces, revealing large chunks of Nathan's life.

The next series of memories showed Nathan's journey to Avatasc, how they met Aisic at the lake, losing Michael in the forest, until finally, she saw herself again. She had grown up, and when they saw each other, she could hardly recognize herself from the innocent girl she had been in the previous memory. The change was frightening.

Her suspicion of men had blinded her, even to the point that she failed to see how much they resembled one another. Yet their meeting in the forest had been their first true reunion in ten years and the first time since their separation that she had let her emotional walls down and allowed herself to act normal around someone.

He was so naive, without a malicious bone in his body. His life hadn't hardened him as it had me.

Despite wanting to stay in this time, Nathan's memories continued to flow into her. She watched as he and Aisic arrived in Avatasc, snuck into the castle, and ran into her mother. Every word of their conversation with the queen made her want to cry out . . . every explanation of Nathan's lineage, revealing him as the heir, that they were siblings.

They all felt as shocking to him as it was for her now.

He wasn't lying, but then, did he really . . . ?

Next came his desperate battle against Kissick. Although not her own memories, she experienced defeating the king as though it was her who had done it. She felt immense satisfaction seeing Serraba, the giant snake Melkai Kissick had been so proud of, crush him on his own throne.

It was this feeling of justice enacted upon such a foul man that finally allowed her to awaken to the truth of these visions, and the truth revealed why she thought Nathan had reminded her of an old friend. Nathan was her twin and what he'd said was true.

However, the memories didn't end there. She was brought to the war and Nathan rebuilding and reuniting Avatasc, traveling with the Senadonians, and finally uncovering the truth about King Michael—or as he had been since she had met him—King Ramannon.

And if it's all true, that means . . .

The images and emotions ended, and they were pulled back to reality, breathing heavily. Nathan's jaw was slack, and tears flowed down his cheek. He had just experienced his sister's darkest moments and was unable to deny that she had done the same with his.

"I've been helping Ramonnon," Laine cried. "I . . . Dragon's breath . . . what was that? Those memories were yours!"

Still speechless, Nathan nodded.

"It doesn't make sense!" Laine shouted, clearly still shaken from what she had learned. "If this is the real power of these keys, why does King Michael want . . ."

Nathan tried to catch his breath. "That's what . . . I was trying to tell you . . . these keys." He shook his head to correct himself and pointed to both of their hands. "*This key* is literally the key to the Melkairen. It was created by our ancestors . . . the Kairens, way before any of this started. The barrier must weaken every five hundred years or so, and the keys need to be used to lock the Melkai away again. That's why the moon is red!"

Laine's eyes widened, and she looked up at the moon in horror.

"Mich . . . no, Ramannon wants the barrier to fall so the Melkai will be freed. He must have made a pact with them when he was inside the Melkairen!"

Nathan stopped as Laine's eyes drifted back to him. He could see the understanding and the horror that came with it, and he sighed in relief. She was finally listening to him. She was beginning to understand not only what their quests were for, but also the dire situation they were in now that the moon was nearly . . .

A shiver went down Nathan's spine, and his eyes shot back to the moon. There was no pearly silver left on it; the moon was completely red.

Oh, crap!

Nathan ran over to Laine in panic and grabbed her by the shoulders. "Laine, quickly. Michael's been possessed by Ramannon. He's trying to stop us from locking the Melkairen. That's why he wants the keys. He wants the Melkai to be set free, don't you see!"

Laine looked stunned for a moment, and he couldn't blame her. From what he had seen of her memories, she had gone from being manipulated by one tyrannical king to being fooled by the lies of another.

Please, trust me!

She nodded. "What do we need to do?"

Nathan held up his key, his hands shaking. "Connect your key to mine, now!"

She brought her own key up and was about to join it with his when there was a sudden explosion of mortar from the chapel. It rocked the courtyard, and they stepped back to balance themselves.

Aisic's dragon form smashed through the massive stone wall. Flying from the dust, a brick hit Nathan in the shoulder and he fell, his vision going black.

CHAPTER 28

MELKAI OF THE THIRD CIRCLE

When he came back to his senses, the wrenching pain in Nathan's shoulder burned like nothing he had ever felt before. He lay on the hard tiles of the wide chapel pathway, a chapel that there was barely anything left of. As he rose, a searing pain went through his shoulder. It looked dislocated, and the key was missing. He had been holding it in that hand.

Despite the immediacy of his agony, this was the least of his worries. Aisic's dragon form lay unconscious before him. His friend had been defeated. A low roar came from the dusty ruins of what had once been the Terratheist chapel. In the smokescreen, he caught a glimpse of the swoop of a large tail and the glint of a fang. Ramannon no longer possessed Michael's body.

The dust settled onto the giant Melkai's body as it arose

from the bricks and mortar. It resembled the possessed Melkai Ramannon had worn when he had first seen him.

No . . . This one is much larger.

Ramannon now had an extra pair of legs that allowed him to stand upright like a centaur; his front arms had massive clawed hands. He moved slowly from the ruins, raising a head with horns that pointed to the reddened sky. As Ramannon moved down the path, he passed Laine, ignoring her presence. After all, she was just another pawn to him.

Nathan didn't know how he acquired the body, but from Laine's shocked reaction, the fear Ramannon emitted didn't just affect him. Ramannon stalked toward Aisic's unconscious dragon form, looking down on him. With a snapping movement, he kicked it from his path. Aisic's body landed within reach of Nathan. Although he already appeared unconscious, the strike triggered him to transform back into his human form.

Ramannon kicked his sword away so it was lying just out of reach. He then turned toward Nathan, staring down silently at him. Nathan awoke from his horrified trance when he heard the sound of snarling in front of him. Taiba was standing in front him and Aisic, growling at Ramannon as he came forward, looking ready to pounce.

Ramannon ignored his Melkai, as well as Nathan, and turned to walked a few paces to his left. He bent down, and with one hooked claw, picked up something from the debris of fallen rock. It was Laine's half of the Kairen Key that he had dropped. That was all that mattered to him, one half of the object that could be his undoing. With that in his possession, the battle was already over.

"It's time," Ramannon's Melkai voice rumbled. He turned his face to the sky.

Holding his aching arm, Nathan couldn't help but look up also. The moon was fully eclipsed by the glowing red blur that completely changed the color of the sky to crimson. A circle of white light ringed the moon, and jagged lines of the same light spread out from it like the webs that formed on cracking glass. It was the exact same light that appeared when making a seam to the Melkairen.

There was a sudden lunar flare as lines of light escaped through the cracks, the sky itself appearing to shatter. As the glowing, snake-like spirit forms of the Melkai rained over the land, shadows began to emerge everywhere, even in the cities. There was what felt like a pull of gravity for a moment as the bodies of the Melkai formed in their world, and as the flare faded, there was a loud roaring, groaning, screeching sound that covered the plains.

To Nathan's ears, it resembled a horrifying victory cry or a sudden cry of relief from finally being set free. The luminance from the sky darkened to the natural look of night, but another kind of night: a darker night, a more frightening night, where now everyone in the lands of the two kingdoms was no longer safe.

The Melkai had finally been set free.

A low satisfied rumble arose from deep within Ramannon's throat. His red eyes slowly opened, and his lips curled around his fangs. "It is done. I now estimate that every man, woman, and child should be dead in the coming month. The fall of man will be a fast extinction."

"Right now . . . people are dying?" Nathan asked.

"They were dying before the Melkai came to this world.

Now they are just dying a little bit faster, although much more painfully." Ramannon turned to meet Nathan's gaze, slowly raising one clawed arm up to swat him like a bug against the tiles.

Nathan's eyes widened as the shadow of the monster's massive arm loomed over him, the sharp nails of his claw spread. Taiba leapt, but with a yelp, was knocked to one side.

"Do not despair. You will follow the same fate much sooner than the rest of them. Unlike your war, the Melkai will leave no one out."

Nathan's hand snapped into a fist. "You created the war! You released the Melkai!"

"And now I'm going to kill you."

Nathan tried to stand, but his legs buckled. After his arm had been dislocated, he had been staying conscious on nothing but the pain of his wound and his remaining self-preservation. Now he was beginning to feel faint. People were dying because of him. Teeth gritted, he desperately fought his hopeless state of exhaustion.

Ramannon slashed down his hand. He was stopped mid-swing, and Nathan looked up to see Terachiro's own claws holding the strike at bay, straining against the weight of the wrist. As Nathan rolled out of the way, Terachiro released it and rose back into the air. A line of blue light shot between them and one of Ramannon's arms was severed at the shoulder by Laine's blue hand-blade.

It dropped to the ground with a thump and Nathan saw that it was the hand that had held Laine's half of the Kairen Key. Growling, Taiba quickly leapt up onto Ramannon's back and bit into one of his curled horns like a dog with a bone. This forced his head back as Terachiro's massive fangs sunk into his chest.

Ramannon roared in pain and struck at Terachiro to free himself. Taiba swiftly leapt over his swiping claw and landed in front of Nathan, snarling protectively. Terachiro flapped its wings and flew back as Ramannon sunk to his knees on the cobblestones.

Laine came to Nathan's side. "Are you okay?"

"My arm is dislocated."

"Hang on, I'll—"

She was interrupted by Ramannon's deafening roar. He was refusing to stay down, struggling to his feet as blood ran from his open wounds. Laine charged up her cutting spell once again, the blade of her hand glowing violently. However, before she could deliver the final blow, a forming sneer appeared on Ramannon's lips.

"It's over!" she yelled.

Ramannon started laughing in his Melkaiic body, shoulders shaking in sudden jolts. "You pathetic people don't seem to understand. The Melkai are free, they work for me now and not just that, I can move into the body of any Melkai that I wish. And soon, when only Melkai live here, I will become the god of this world . . . No, I already am the god of this world!"

Ramannon's red eyes lit up a bright crimson, and a massive rumble similar to that of an earthquake began to shake the entire city. They widened their stances to stay on their feet, but this was no ordinary tremor. Like something from a nightmare, a colossal being of darkness reached around the mountain's edge and pulled himself over the great back walls of the city. Entire chunks of its structure came away in its grasp.

"I-I don't believe it!" Laine marveled.

Nathan was shocked also; nothing could have prepared him for this. He had never seen one of these beings in all his life. Before the castle, the place he had grown up as a child, was a Melkai that could only be compared to a god.

"It's . . . it's a . . . a Melkai of the third circle!"

"Now . . ." Ramannon's voice returned, but this time not coming from the Melkai he had possessed. "I will show you . . . how much of a god I truly am."

The bright red glow in Ramannon's eyes quickly darkened. Then above them, in the head of the third-circle Melkai leaning over the city, they saw those exact red eyes. Ramannon had possessed the third-circle Melkai.

Much to their disbelief, the immortal emperor, the lord of the Melkai and self-proclaimed god of the new world, was now larger than the tallest tower in the known lands.

A great shadow fell over the Terratheist city, a complete body that eclipsed the sky. Below them, people were screaming and wailing in terror. The third-circle Melkai Ramannon had possessed was colossal, its black shape leaning over the tower, its clawed hands up at either side of the city like massive black walls. Its bat-like wings blocked the clouds above, and its red eyes replaced the light of the red moon that was eclipsed by the behemoth.

Ramannon loomed over the great city, cradling it within his arms, ready and willing to smash it between his claws. His wings spread. If seen from a distance, the entire area would've been completely shadowed by the sphere of darkness that his closing wings created around it, sealing away the city and trapping both Melkai and human inside.

He's trying to prevent us from escaping!

Nathan watched as a line of light streaked toward them. However, as the Senadonians and Master Morrow arrived on the backs of their Melkai, he knew the battle wasn't yet over.

"We have to defeat him now!" Morrow called. "Before the land is taken over completely!"

Beat him . . . a third-circle Melkai . . . but wait a minute—

"No, you can't beat him!" Nathan called, and they all turned to face him. "But if you can stall him for time, I think I know of a way we can win!"

"And how's that?" Durian asked.

Nathan eyed Morrow. "Remember what you told me about Melkai of the third circle?"

Morrow paused for a moment and then smiled. "Ah, indeed I do."

"It's the one weakness all third-circle Melkai share; all you have to do is keep his attention on you for five minutes."

"Very well," Tarros confirmed. "We will stall him for as long you need. Durian, let's go!"

Durian reached out his hand as the blue flame of his wolf, Blazer, ran off in a line of light soon followed by the red flame of Tarros's phoenix. The light of their flames spread across the darkness as they made their way up the path to the tower Ramannon was leaning over.

Master Morrow pulled something from his pocket. He threw it up, and with a flash of light, the pact item became a white griffin. It followed the blue and red paths of the Senadonians' flaming Melkai toward Ramannon.

Laine looked to Terachiro and pointed to where the lights were heading. "Help them!"

With a snort, the massive bat swept itself into the air to follow the other flying Melkai. It caught up with the phoenix, the griffin, and the wolf for one last stand. Nathan grinned seeing Taiba was still by his side. Even when the world was taken over by their own kind, their Melkai still allowed their pacts to hold strong.

He turned to Laine. She looked like she expected him to do the same thing and send Taiba off to fight. But he knew there was no need.

"W-why are you smiling?" Laine asked.

Without even realizing he had been, he beamed at her, and with a swell of determination, said, "This battle is already over, and Taiba will be able to help me find your key."

Chapter 29

The Fall

Ramannon watched from on high as the tiny second-circle Melkai made their final struggle. Their minuscule lights streaked through the darkness toward him. Debris fell from its crenellations as he lifted a giant claw slowly away from the outer wall of the city, ready to swipe the Melkai down from their path.

The phoenix met him first. As it flew up, ready to breathe flame down over his shadowy body, he slashed one claw down at it. His hand hit the bird like a wall and it exploded in a ball of flame. The shockwave hurt, but he felt no need to draw back his hand from the pain. Above him, the phoenix reappeared, swooping backward through the darkness.

He jolted from a sudden pain below. The phoenix had been a diversion for the next Melkai to rush in. A blue wolf had leapt up onto his thigh and was running up his side with incredible speed. Its path left a stinging line of blue fire along his black body, actually damaging him, but not enough.

"*Impressive . . .*" Ramannon bellowed internally to the Melkai. At a simple shift in his body, the wolf lost its balance and stopped in its tracks. He backhanded the tiny creature. "*But don't you see? You are nothing but servants to these people. We are brethren, you and I. Why are we fighting each other? Don't you see? I am one of you! My ancestors, the Arion, they were Melkai born of human flesh. I, like you, have a spirit, and it is those with spirits that will inherit the future of this world!*"

A voice returned, "*Yet you were the one who killed the Arion.*"

"*Indeed. After the end of the War of the Melkai, I thought humans were destined to rule the world. However, spending half a millennium within the Melkairen revealed my error. Now that I have freed our brethren, are you really planning to undo everything we have worked so hard for?*"

Another voice said, "*Each of us would rather fight as servants side by side with our masters than have our free will be ruled over by a god who can possess us whenever he wishes.*"

"*You will never be seen as equals with them.*"

A third, harsher, voice replied, "*Nor will we with you!*"

The girl caller's giant bat flew in with the phoenix, one on each flank, along with what appeared to be a griffin.

"*You will continuously be in the shadow of your masters!*"

"*Masters that we chose!*"

Ramannon spread his huge arms and flapped his massive wings. The force of the wind blew back the flying Melkai. Somehow, the blue wolf had been riding on one of the Melkai's backs and leapt from it onto him. As it landed, burning his shoulder, Ramannon reached up and swatted it off him like an insect.

It plummeted toward the city, but it appeared its caller

had been watching the battle for it transformed back into a necklace before hitting the ground.

"This is a good world," the first voice called again. *"We like it here and we have even grown fond of our masters. And if they use us to protect it, then we will gladly fight alongside them!"*

He couldn't tell where this voice was coming from until he saw another canine Melkai standing and staring up at him. It was the boy's Melkai. Ramannon growled, the rumble of his voice shaking the castle. His feeling of triumph was slowly turning to frustration as they stubbornly refused to bend the knee.

"You're fools!"

Before they had recovered from the impact of his flapping wings, he slashed down his arm taking out the griffin, the phoenix, the bat, and several buildings all in one strike. Dust rose up from the air, and he couldn't tell if he had hit the dog or not.

"Whether you want this or not doesn't matter. The barrier to the Melkairen has been broken, the Melkai are free, and in return for being their savior, I am their ruler. You are traitors to your own kind!" He roared with laughter. *"I can even control the third-circle Melkai as easily as—"*

GET OUT . . .

The red slits of his eyes narrowed of their own volition, and he paused. He went to lift his arm again and realized that he could barely move.

"What is this?"

Behind the Melkai on the courtyard pathway two of their masters stood, his brother's descendants—the Armalon siblings. The boy was crouched low, Aisic already lying unconscious on the cobblestones, welcoming him to squash them like insects.

GET OUT . . .

"*No . . . Not yet! I will set you all free!*" Struggling against the sudden will overcoming him, he managed to lift one arm. "*Now watch as I smear your masters over the rock of their own kingdom!*"

Trembling, his sharp claws stabbed into the earth as he gripped the stone floor of the kingdom, bringing himself slowly over the tower toward them.

GET OUT, NOW!

CHAPTER 30

THE KAIREN SWORD

As soon as the barrier to the Melkairen had broken, Nathan had believed Ramannon to have won the fight. After all, he could move into the body of any Melkai he wanted, so when the world was full of Melkai, defeating him seemed an impossible task. Yet when he grasped for further power by possessing a Melkai of the third circle, Nathan realized the exact opposite was true.

No matter the situation, Ramannon's lust for power was entirely predictable, and because of this, it would inevitably be his undoing.

Nathan breathed out painfully through clenched teeth, his eyes darting around the cobblestones for where Ramannon had left Laine's key-half. Taiba was sniffing around the rubble, trying to pick up her scent.

Laine grabbed hold of him. Despite the pain, despite the

exhaustion, he rose slowly from the cobblestones, confident that the massive hand looming over them wouldn't touch them. Neither Taiba nor the other Melkai could challenge the force behind a third-circle Melkai's attack, but size wasn't the secret to winning this battle.

All they needed was time, time that the other callers and Melkai had already given them by moving the fight towards the back wall of the city, averting Ramannon's attention away from their location, but more importantly, away from the key.

After all, if Ramannon used his Melkai host to destroy the area, they would never find it. But he wasted too much time, and now it was too late.

Laine cringed away from the attack as the shadow covered them. Taiba rushed to his side, and just like he had as a tiny lizard, he was ready to fight something larger than him— even this behemoth. However, as Nathan had predicted, the massive claw stopped right above them. He smirked up at it.

"Hah, you just defeated yourself!" he shouted triumphantly. "It's over!"

Laine was staring up at him, one eyebrow raised in confusion.

"What . . . what is this?" Ramannon's arm shook violently as he struggled to push it down and crush them to no avail. "What have you done to me?"

"I did nothing. *You* took control of a third-circle Melkai." Nathan gripped his upper arm, the pain sharpening his condemnation. "And even if you are just a spirit, every caller knows that a third-circle Melkai is impossible to keep control of because they eventually become self-aware."

"What are you say—"

"I'm saying your time is up!"

Ramannon's giant hand shook violently, and the red began to fade from his eyes. The Melkai regained control and lifted the hand to its face, appearing to no longer recognize it. There was a jolt from the earth as its face quickly descended toward them, the red of Ramannon's spirit burning back to life for an instant longer.

"Who do you think I am? I can go into the body of any Melkai near me!" The massive red eyes shifted suddenly from them to Aisic's unconscious body. "*Any* Melkai."

Nathan inhaled sharply. At this point, their odds of defeating a dragon weren't much better than defeating a third-circle Melkai.

Dragon's breath! If only I could find where he put the key... As soon as the thought hit him, Taiba returned to where he had been sniffing around and barked. Nathan glanced over to him, to where the corpse of the second-circle Melkai lay. *Oh, that's right. He still has it!*

Laine's key had been in Ramannon's grasp when his arm had been severed by her spell. And there, a dozen yards away from him was that arm, the glimmering Kairen Key still hanging from its clawed finger.

His discovery was too little too late as the red glow faded from the third-circle Melkai's eyes and Aisic's own eyes sprung open. He bared his teeth in a grin, but it was a grin that Nathan recognized, Aisic's own.

Was Aisic only pretending to be unconscious?

Aisic jumped to his feet and dashed toward where his sword had fallen. Before Ramannon could take over completely, he dived toward the sword, grabbed it in a roll and came to land on his knees. He then reversed the grip of its hilt, spinning the sword to point the tip of the blade at his torso.

"Aisic, no!" Nathan cried. "You don't have to do this! You're supposed to protect me, remember?"

"Indeed, even at the cost of my own life."

Even if it meant stopping Ramannon, Nathan didn't want him to die too.

"No, that's not fair!"

Aisic turned at Nathan's call, their eyes connecting in the desperation of the moment. "I do have to do this, Nathan. This is the reason I came back. I swore I would finish what I started. I will not let him kill anyone else and will gladly give up my life to do so!"

"Y-you want this?"

Nathan stared into Aisic's eyes. The irises were turning bloodred. Fighting against Ramannon's presence in his mind, Aisic's face contorted furiously.

What if I can use the key to lock him away first? What if he just jumps bodies again? What if I don't make it to the key in time?

Aisic and Ramannon had both been cursed at birth, their mixed bloodlines giving them power that no man should possess. Yet where Ramannon had slaughtered thousands in his need for power, Aisic had become the hero who had brought peace.

And now, to destroy one, I have to sacrifice the other.

It felt like too much of a cost to pay. Yet the consequences, of which the proof was now all around them, revealed the truth of it. Nathan understood now how much it needed to be done, and although Aisic was the only one who could do it, he was giving him the choice. He had to allow his protector, his friend, to kill himself to save the rest of the world and make sure Ramannon never returned.

He hated him for doing it, but it had to be done.

Nathan nodded to his protector. Aisic ground his teeth and swiftly impaled himself on his sword.

He coughed, and blood leaked from the wound. He fell to the hard tiles as Nathan and Laine ran to be at his side.

"You two must . . . seal the Mel . . . kairen!"

As long as the Melkai are in this world, once Aisic dies Ramannon can just transfer his spirit into another. Aisic's body is his pact item now. He must die with Aisic! It's the only way to finish him off for good.

Nathan ran over to where Laine's key-half was hanging from the severed arm. He snatched it up with his good arm and rushed over to Laine, gesturing for her to hand over his necklace with his own half of the key. She did so, and right away, Nathan saw how the keys could be connected.

The spines themselves had small T-shaped slits and protrusions going down them for where they could be slotted into place. As he slid them together, the forks glowed white and stretched up from his hands, the grip of the key doing likewise to become the hilt and handguard of a crystal sword.

"Those things make a sword?" Laine cried out.

Nathan lifted the ancient weapon, gaping in awe. He recognized it from Aisic's descriptions. "It's the Kairen Sword. A weapon our ancestors created to lock away Ramannon *and* the Melkai." They hadn't made the keys to replace his broken blade. The keys *were* his broken blade.

The crystal blade gleamed in the blazing white light. Nathan struggled to keep the sword aloft with his one good arm, but Laine helped him raise the magical artifact toward the red moon. A sudden rift of light shot into the sky. The cracks that had formed after the barrier had broken were now being filled with the many lines of white light that had spread over the land. The Melkai's spirit forms were being drawn back into the Melkairen. Both of the Melkai Ramannon had possessed began to glow white and were sucked up, back into the cracks in the night sky. The darkness of the third circle's wings vanished from overhead as the barrier began to recover.

Light flooded around them, the power of the Kairen Sword drawing everything toward it like they were suddenly at the center of the world. The warm light felt like the living embodiment of everything they had worked toward. The line of light rising from the crystal sword receded as the cracks in the darkness healed over. It vanished in a sudden blinding flash, and all they could do was breathe.

The red moon was replaced with one of pearl white. Not only was the barrier to the Melkairen reinforced, but the Kairen Sword had returned all the released Melkai to the Melkairen.

Their own Melkai had also vanished, only their pact items remaining on the cobblestone tiles of the tower pathway. Nathan was tempted to test if his glove—Laine's glove—still held its pact with Taiba, but right now the deciding conflict was happening at their feet.

Aisic lay dying before them, and although he was shaking in pain, he still had a smile on his face. They crouched next to him.

"The Melkai . . . are sealed? The barrier . . . reinforced?" he asked.

They both nodded. "It is."

His tense body relaxed slightly hearing their tone of relief.

"It's . . . done," he struggled to say, his voice trembling. "The world . . . is yours again. You two . . . are the king and queen . . . of these lands. You must . . . learn from the mistakes of the past . . . to create a better future."

"We will. But Aisic . . ." Nathan shook his head in sorrow. "We could have found another way. So long as he was possessing a Melkai, he would've returned to the Melkairen."

"And let him return when the barrier weakens again? No. There was . . . no other way." Aisic exhaled heavily. "I've managed . . . to contain his spirit. He'll finally die . . . with me. I've lived for five hundred years . . . I've seen the future . . . it couldn't have ended any other way."

Aisic turned to Nathan, his voice quavering as he said his final words: "Keep your head up . . . you're a king now . . . after . . . all."

Aisic's body went limp, and the Scion of Akai, the last Arion, died.

Nathan had heard stories of heroes, people who would sacrifice themselves for the greater good, saving others even at the cost of their own lives. He didn't think they actually existed. Yet he had spent the better part of a month traveling with one, and now that such a hero had died in front of him, all he could feel was sorrow for his lost friend.

It made him feel like there was a downside to heroes which no one ever talked about. Where they died, those who remained were left with sorrow, forced to grieve and move on. There was no sudden end for them, no satisfaction at a job well done, only the responsibility to live up to the sacrifice the hero made.

Nathan took up the responsibility of living up to Aisic's sacrifice eagerly. After all, his story wasn't over yet.

Tears poured down Nathan's cheeks. Through his blurring vision, he saw the same glow from the sky that had surrounded the other Melkai surround Aisic. It grew until it was the shape and size of his dragon form.

The glowing Melkai gracefully flapped its mighty wings and then sailed up into the night sky toward the moon, returning to its spirit form as it returned to the Melkairen. Nathan knew that a little piece of Aisic would forever linger within the dragon's memory.

The world was finally back to normal. The moon looked the way it had before their quests began, as though nothing had changed, but they had learned much about their origins and who they were to each other.

Master Morrow came running back. "Nathan! You're alright?"

Nathan managed to nod, but he couldn't look away from Aisic's body.

"I saw the barrier seal. You did well."

"I couldn't save him."

"You saved the rest of us."

"What about the king?" Laine asked.

Morrow's face tightened. "I doubt he survived the destruction of the chapel. I must go check on my pupils."

Nathan ignored Morrow's departure and made his way to the destroyed chapel to see if they could find Michael's body.

When still standing, the chapel had been massive, and now that it was in ruin, it covered most of the surrounding pathways and bushes. Laine spread out to assist his search. They'd spent several minutes looking through the rubble and mortar when Laine gasped.

"What is it?" Nathan asked.

"It's the king!" she called.

Nathan's eyes widened, and he rushed over to see his old friend lying within the rubble.

"Is he dead?" Laine asked.

Nathan crouched down over him. Michael didn't look like he was breathing. Nathan looked around in panic; he didn't want to lose two friends in one night. He turned back and saw someone walking up the stairs toward them. It appeared that fate was on the king's side as Kendra was the person walking up the pathway.

"Kendra!" Laine called.

Kendra stopped, her mouth dropped, and she ran over. "I was looking for you. Oh no, what happened to Aisic?" she cried.

"He killed himself to take out Ramannon. There's no time to explain, but there might still be a chance to save Michael, so please, if you can help him . . ." Nathan pleaded, knowing Kendra would have heard of King Michael's tyranny from the people. "Please, Kendra."

"You don't have to say anything." Kendra bent over the body of the king. "I follow the healer's code after all."

The plates of Michael's armor were crushed under a layer of cobblestone and brick. Laine helped Nathan lift the bricks off him so Kendra could have a better look. Her hands ran along the armor until she found a buckle and unfastened the breastplate before putting her head on his chest. She pulled back in shock.

"He's alive, but he has a collapsed lung," Kendra said as her hands began to glow the same way they had when she healed Aisic's leg.

"Will he survive? Can you make him better?"

She gave him a dazzling smile. "Not a problem."

Laine looked like she didn't know if she was relieved or not. "Nathan, are you sure we should be doing this?"

Nathan put a hand on her shoulder. "Don't worry. Before he was possessed by Ramannon, Michael was a good man. He was my best friend."

"Right . . . okay." Laine nodded warily.

She had seen his memories of Michael. It made sense why she believed him.

Kendra's expression grew more focused as she went to work on Michael. The green glow of her spell covered Michael's chest.

After no more than five minutes, Michael's eyes sprang open. He gasped air back into his healed lung as consciousness return to him. He breathed heavily, his wide eyes their original blue color. His gaze flashed to where Nathan stood over him.

"Nathan?" he asked, voice risen in panic. "Dragon's breath, what happened?"

Nathan suddenly realized the harsh reality that he was going to have to reveal to him. The words didn't come.

"Please!" Looking around, Michael grabbed Nathan by the collar in his panic.

Nathan gasped in pain as his dislocated arm was jostled. Laine grabbed Michael's wrist in return, teeth bared protectively.

Nathan shook his head at her, their eyes locked, and she

stayed her hand. "It's okay. It's okay."

"How do we know he's himself again?" Laine asked. "He could be—"

"Who on earth are you?" Michael coughed. He turned back to Nathan. "Who's your girlfriend, little buddy?"

Nathan grinned at Laine. "It's him."

Laine's shoulders relaxed, and she sat back.

"Please, Nathan, tell me what happened," Michael pleaded.

Before Nathan could answer him, Kendra was at his side, touching his arm. "That's going to need resetting."

Nathan winced and nodded. "Make it quick."

Her touch, which had been so gentle before, became firm, and with a wrench forward, a pull, and a sudden explosion of pain in his shoulder, he felt his bone being set in place.

"Thank you."

Her touch turned gentle again as she checked him quickly for other injuries. Finding none, she sat back.

It was time for Nathan to explain. He started off by telling Michael of their time in the forest and how, out of the blue, he had tried to attack him.

Michael's eyes continued to widen as he heard everything he had done after his mind had left him. Afterward, Nathan and Laine took turns telling him about their journey until Kendra ended it.

"You skipped the part where he killed the king."

Michael jolted suddenly, his jaw going slack, his eyes filling with tears. "What? I killed my father?" He rose quickly, walked from them as though in a dream, then collapsed into the rubble, weeping in sorrow.

Nathan followed him, thinking of how his mother had

commanded him after the death of Kissick. "Michael, you have to take your father's throne. It's the only way to return things to the way they were before."

"I cannot become king. There is no honor in what I did, even if I was possessed. I cannot live in this place with people knowing how I became who I am. I have to find some other way, any way to redeem myself."

Nathan frowned, unsettled by such aggrievement from someone he had only seen confidence from in the past. They had been best friends, still were in Nathan's eyes, yet that didn't stop Ramannon changing everything for the worse in both of their lives. Not only had Michael ruined what the people of Terratheist thought of him, but his body had been used to kill the king, someone who had been like a father to Nathan, and was an actual father to him. Things would never be the same between them, no matter how much they wanted them to be.

Nathan couldn't imagine the pain he was going through and wished he could have delayed telling him until after he had recovered, like Aisic and Master Morrow had done with him. Maybe there was something in keeping the truth from people until they were ready. After all, if he knew he had been the heir of Avatasc, he never would have become who he was.

Yet something also told him that Michael would never be ready to hear about the war Ramannon had created in his skin. While Michael sobbed, Nathan quickly discussed it with the others. They agreed not to tell him the full story right now.

Yet, despite all of their grief, there was one thing to celebrate. The Second War of the Melkai was finally over.

CHAPTER 31

PEACE

With the Melkai gone and Ramannon dead, the fighting stopped almost immediately. Many of the dead soldiers fell, revealing those who were merely possessed corpses, controlled by Ramannon just as he had controlled the dead beneath the chapel. Those who remained alive, most injured and bloodied, eagerly set off for home in search of their families. Soldiers threw down their weapons, the dawn sunlight making their blades glimmer against the grassland. Again, birds flew through a peaceful sky now empty of flying Melkai. Even the monsters from callers below had left so that only humans remained. The battalions that had been clustered together to stop themselves from being picked off by the Melkai separated, peeling off layer by layer like an onion in order to return home.

The horrific experience of the land being engulfed in Melkai for over an hour was enough to make the blood lust of any soldier run dry, quelling the conflict faster than a grand speech from any reigning monarch. Fighting monsters rather than men had dissipated their need for war. Nathan, Laine, and Kendra watched from the heights of the castle as the battle came to an end, the killing ending much faster than it had begun.

The three of them smiled at each other, turned, and walked to where Aisic's body lay. They looked down at him with sorrow tugging at their hearts. The Scion of Akai was said to be a hero and he had definitely lived up to his reputation, but this time Nathan would make sure the people of Terratheist would remember him.

"He looks so peaceful," Kendra sighed.

Next to him lay the Kairen Sword, the magical weapon that had saved them all. However, as Laine bent down to pick it up, there was a flash of light, and it separated into two key-half necklaces. She picked up both and handed one to Nathan, an heirloom they would both pass down to their descendants until the time came that they would need to be combined once more to seal away the Melkai.

Nathan put his around his neck and only then registered the two Senadon warriors resting nearby, bloodied and battle-weary, along with their Melkai. Durian had a smile on his face, though Tarros had the same solemn look as always. Nathan thought he saw deep shadows in the creases of his old face, but it could have been a trick of the light.

"Hey, Nathan." Durian gestured to his face. "You look like you're holding your head a little higher now. What happened?"

"I guess I was feeling a little inferior to you before, but how can I feel inferior now?" He grinned. "I just sealed away a third-circle Melkai."

"And in a way that would make even an Advanced Summoner envious." Durian grinned back and playfully shoved him. "Don't let it go to your head, Your Majesty."

Nathan asked, "New Senadon was destroyed during the attack, wasn't it?"

They nodded gravely.

Tarros cleared his throat. "Now that the war is over, we must return and rebuild. It will take a long time to reforge what was lost, but us Senadonians are a stubborn lot, and I have faith that, in the end, New Senadon will be greater than ever before."

An idea came to mind. There was something Michael could do to both redeem himself and strengthen Terratheist's cracked relationship with the Senadonians. Nathan walked over to his friend, crouching next to where he sat so he was on eye level with him.

"Michael, you should go with the Senadonians and help rebuild New Senadon. I think they will need your help more than anyone. If you help to rebuild their home, it will also help rebuild our broken ties with them."

It would take a long time for the people to forget what Michael did. Until then, he would be seen as an enemy of the people. He would need a fresh start, one that could only be achieved after a long absence and a triumphant return.

Michael looked up at him, his deep set eyes gaining meaning and determination once more. He frowned and nodded fiercely.

Nathan grinned. "I'll keep the throne safe as your steward until you get back and feel you are up to reclaiming it. Believe it or not, after being King of Avatasc for a while, I've actually gotten the hang of politics."

Michael's eyebrows pulled inward. "Then who will rule Avatasc?"

Nathan turned to Laine, still grinning. "I think I know someone who would make a perfect queen."

Laine's mouth dropped, but he knew this was what she had wanted. She bowed her head wordlessly.

Michael nodded. "Very well, I shall go to New Senadon and rebuild their kingdom with your comrades. However, even after that, I would not deem myself fit to take the crown." Nathan shook his head, but then noticed Michael smiling himself. "On the other hand, I think I would make a good general when I get back."

Nathan put his hand out. "It's a deal," he said as the once-prince grabbed his hand, and he helped him up to his feet.

They made their way back toward the other four, all looking solemn in the silence. Nathan stood before the Senadonians.

"This is Michael, trueborn heir of Terratheist." He gestured to him. "He's a strong worker and an even better leader. I'm sending him with you two as an emissary and to help you rebuild New Senadon."

"The heir?" Tarros looked shocked, but then he nodded. "I see. Very well then."

Durian's eyes lit up, as though this gift of the kingdom's heir was the sign that he was looking for. Not only has the war ended, but Terratheist was finally making up for the near-genocide of their people nearly five hundred years ago.

"No one will attack New Senadon under my rule," Nathan added. "You have my word." He looked at the others. "Together, I think it's possible to create true peace and make it last."

The two Senadonians nodded, and Nathan led them back to the castle to change clothes, clean up, and eat a meal. After sleeping off their wariness, with the sun rising behind them, they made to leave. Without even a goodbye, they left the castle and started their journey back to their own country over the Jile Mountains, Michael following them with new ambition and hope in his life.

Nathan had the feeling that when he saw him again, Michael would be the greatest general Terratheist had ever known.

Nathan put Kendra in charge of aiding the wounded and rounded up callers to hunt down any Melkai that remained. A few days passed, and Nathan and Laine slept in the castle. They went for meals at an inn every evening, the food warming them.

Kendra was glad to catch up with everyone; however, without Aisic, the original group she wanted was incomplete. Despite this, she'd had a very exciting time in Terratheist with each event she had gone through climaxing at the Melkai invasion which, with her healing gifts, made her a hero among the people.

She told her story like she did all her stories, in full detail, and afterward asked for their own. Nathan let Laine tell her side first. As Laine told her version of what happened, he realized he was still staring at Kendra, and she was looking back at him. Laine appeared to pick up on this too.

"Laine, why are you looking at me like that?" Kendra asked, realizing she had been caught.

"No reason really." Laine looked away and took a drink from her mug. "I just thought I could see another future queen somewhere in the room."

They both blushed at this.

"Nathan, you seem to be just as enamored with this city's new hero as everyone else here. Am I wrong?"

Nathan broke his gaze and drank deeply. "Yes—well—I . . ."

"Maybe you two should spend more time together," Laine said. "After all, if you're seen helping people with the savior of the war, you would gain their support as well."

Kendra's eyes lowered to the table. "I'm alright with that if you are, Nathan."

Nathan smiled and nodded, cheeks still slightly flushed. "Alright, ah, it's a date then."

Nathan wrote up a letter giving all his power and kingly rights in Avatasc to Laine with no exceptions to the lords that may oppose her reign before marriage.

He wrote the letter on a scroll, sealed it with his insignia in wax, and gave it to her. She had packed her gear and was preparing to leave.

"Everything you need to know about running the kingdom is in that scroll," he said as he handed it over. "But don't hesitate to ask our mother about some of the details. In all honesty, I'm sure she's been doing the job in my absence."

"Thank you," she said solemnly. "Now that that tyrant has been dethroned, we can bring some civility back to the kingdom. I suppose I should thank you for that."

Nathan shrugged, noticing she was avoiding using

Kissick's name. "It was mostly Aisic and your mother who did it. I just played a part."

She smiled and patted his shoulder. "You're too modest, Nathan."

"Well . . ." Nathan said nervously as the sun rose with his sister's departure.

After seeing her memories, Nathan could tell why she wanted to return home quickly. Now that Kissick was dead, she could finally let her walls down and talk to her mother on equal footing, no longer afraid that she would be punished by him. Nevertheless, it had been less than a week after Laine had found out they were brother and sister, and he was sad to see her go. Even now, as they walked, he could feel himself slowing his pace, knowing that once they reached the edge of the courtyard, they would have to part ways.

They made their way to the cobblestone pathway leading from the castle; the wind was cool, just as they had remembered it being from their shared memory. Unlike when they had left each other as children, this time they were aware of the significance.

She laughed. "Who would have thought when we first met that we would be ruling the lands together, let alone as brother and sister?"

Nathan looked down and smiled. "Yeah . . . when I first left, I didn't think I had any family left. I'm glad I was wrong."

She nodded. "Me too."

Despite the drag of her backpack, she moved in and hugged him. He wrapped his arms around her.

"Say hello to our mother for me." Nathan knocked on his head once, a trait he had picked up from Kendra. "I forgot to before leaving."

Laine nodded and began to set off.

Behind she could, they heard the sound of running footsteps, and despite wanting to leave before she had woken up, Kendra came dashing toward them. She collided with Laine in an embrace, but before she could say anything, she demanded of her, "You better come and visit again soon!"

Laine smiled. "I will, I promise."

Keening at her friend's reluctant departure, Kendra let her go, and they parted ways.

Before she made it to the stairs, Laine turned and called, "I've been meaning to ask, have you tried summoning Taiba again yet?"

Nathan looked down, lips drawn in a grim line. "I was kind of avoiding it in fear that he might not be bonded to the glove anymore."

Laine raised her eyebrows and smiled. "Well then, give it shot."

Nathan reached his gloved hand out and willed his friend to appear. There was a flash of light and suddenly Taiba stood, not trembling, but jumping at his side with tongue wagging. Nathan couldn't help but pat Taiba. He hadn't seen him in weeks. Laine laughed as she strode down the stairs toward the city gates. With the sun at her back, she left Terratheist for Avatasc, Terachiro still within the pact item resting on her shoulders.

If you loved

War of Kings and Monsters,

check out *The Dream State Saga* by Christopher Keene

beginning with *Stuck in the Game!*

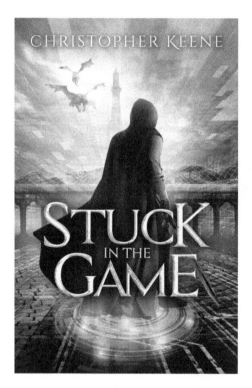

https://www.futurehousepublishing.com/books/stuck-in-the-game/

Connect with Future House Publishing!

http://www.futurehousepublishing.com/

www.facebook.com/FutureHousePublishing

twitter.com/FutureHousePub

www.youtube.com/FutureHousePublishing

www.instagram.com/FutureHousePublishing

ACKNOWLEDGMENTS

A few years back, I wrote two books set in the same fantasy world, 500 years apart, one with monster battles and one without. So, when I pitched both books to my project manager, Emma Hoggan, I wasn't surprised when the book with monster battles was chosen. Funnily, the reason it has monster battles in the first place was because my partner, Hayley, read the first book and said somewhat tongue-in-cheek, "It's alright… needs more monster battles." Needless to say, I acknowledge both of these women and their enjoyment of monster battles for this book getting published.

ABOUT THE AUTHOR

Growing up in the small town of Timaru, New Zealand, Christopher Keene broke the family trend of becoming an accountant by becoming a writer instead. While studying for his Bachelor of Arts in English Literature from the University of Canterbury, he took the school's creative writing course in the hopes of someday seeing his own book on the shelf in his favorite bookstores.

In his spare time, he writes a blog to share his love of the fantasy and science fiction genres in novels, films, comics, games, and anime (fantasyandanime.wordpress.com).